Daisy and the Egg

Jane Simmons

ORCHARD BOOKS

To my Dad

Orchard Books
96 Leonard Street, London EC2A 4XD
Orchard Books Australia
14 Mars Road, Lane Cove, NSW 2066
1 86039 622 4 (hardback)
1 86039 655 0 (paperback)
First published in Great Britain in 1999
This edition published in 2000
© Jane Simmons 1999
The right of Jane Simmons to be identified as the author and illustrator of this work has been
asserted by her in accordance with the Copyright, Designs and Patents Act, 1988.
A CIP catalogue record for this book is available from the British Library.
3 5 7 9 10 8 6 4 2 (hardback)
5 7 9 10 8 6 4 (paperback)
Printed in Singapore

"How many eggs now?" asked Daisy.
"Four," Auntie Buttercup said proudly,
"my three and Mamma's green one."
"Your Auntie's sitting on an egg for me,"
said Mamma Duck.
"Can I sit on one too?" asked Daisy excitedly.

It wasn't easy.

Every day Mamma Duck
sent Daisy with some food
for Auntie Buttercup.

Daisy listened as the chicks
tapped softly inside their shells.
"You'll have a brother or sister
soon," said Auntie Buttercup.
Daisy was so excited.

When they saw Auntie Buttercup the
next day, she was flapping her wings.
"They're hatching! They're hatching!"
she called.

One duckling had cracked
the shell. Daisy watched her
first cousin struggle out.

"Yuk! It's all wet!" said Daisy.
"Shhh!" scolded Mamma Duck.
Then two more eggs hatched.

While Mamma Duck and Auntie Buttercup talked about names, Daisy waited for Mamma's egg. She thought she heard something . . . but nothing happened.

They all listened . . . but there
was no sound from the egg.

That night Mamma Duck sat on her
egg but the next day it still hadn't hatched.
"Some eggs don't. Come and play with
your cousins, Daisy," said Mamma Duck.
But Daisy wanted to stay with Mamma's egg.

Daisy made a hole in the feathers, rolled the egg in and sat on top. "Come on, Daisy!" called Mamma Duck. But Daisy wouldn't move.

It was getting dark and Daisy
was cold and tired.

Mamma Duck came back.
"We'll sit together until
morning," she said kindly.
"Yes," said Daisy. . .

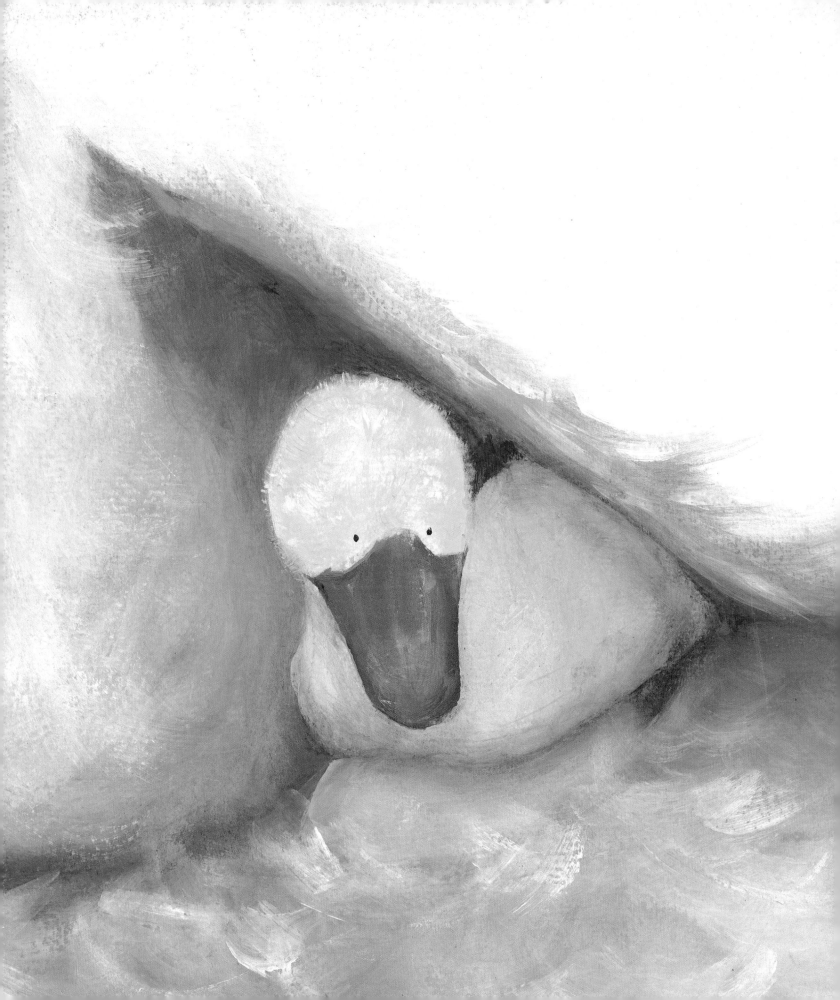

Pip! Pip! Pip! Daisy
woke up. It was the egg!

Her new brother struggled out
of his shell and went "Pip! Pip!"
"Coo!" said Daisy.
"Pip!" he went again.
"Pip!" said Daisy.
"Hello, Pip," said Mamma Duck.

And they all watched
the sun rise on Little Pip's
hatching day.

Contents

How to use this book

This textbook contains all three units for the Cambridge National Child Development Level 1/2. These are:

- Unit R018: Health and well-being for child development
- Unit R019: Understand the equipment and nutritional needs of children from birth to five years

- Unit R020 Understand the development of a child from birth to five years.

Each unit is then divided into learning outcomes. All of the assessment criteria for each learning outcome are covered in the book.

Key features of the book

Unit R018 Health and well-being for child development

About this unit
There are 60 GLH (guided learning hours) in this unit. This unit is about understanding the important roles and responsibilities that come with

- understand antenatal care and preparation for birth
- understand postnatal checks, postnatal provision and conditions for development

Learning Outcome 1

Understand reproduction and the roles and responsibilities of parenthood

Assessment criteria
In this learning outcome you will cover:
- The wide range of factors that affect the decision to have children.
- Pre-conception health.
- Roles and responsibilities of parenthood.
- Recognise and evaluate methods of contraception, their efficiency and reliability.
- The structure and function of male and female reproductive systems.

The book is organised by the units in the qualification. There are three units in the book. Each unit is broken down into the learning outcomes from the specification. Each unit opener will help you to understand what is covered in the unit, the list of learning outcomes covered, and what you will be assessed on, fully matched to the requirements of the specification.

The learning outcomes are clearly stated, along with the list of assessment criteria so you know exactly what is covered.

2.2 Key factors to consider when choosing equipment for children from one to five years

The key factors to consider when choosing equipment for children from one to five years include:

Assessment criteria are clearly listed and fully mapped to the specification.

Getting started

Thought storm all of the responsibilities you can think of that are part of the role of being parents to children aged from birth to five years. In pairs, compare and discuss your lists. If your partner has a suggestion you have overlooked, add it to your own list for future reference.

Short activity or discussion to introduce you to the topic.

? Did you know?

All three and four year olds in England are entitled to 570 hours of free early education or childcare a year. This is often taken as 15 hours each week for 38 weeks of the year. Some two-year olds are also eligible.

Learn useful facts and statistics related to the topic. These are correct at the time of writing.

Key term

Transition stage this links the end of the first stage of labour and the beginning of the second stage of labour.

Understand important terms.

Activity

1   Visit this NHS weblink and read more about SIDS: www.nhs.uk/Conditions/ Sudden-infant-death-syndrome/Pages/ Introduction.aspx.

A short task to help you understand an idea or assessment criteria. This includes group, and research tasks. Look out for headings as these activities specifically link to the assessment criteria.

✔ Good practice

Planning play activities well helps promote each area of development thoroughly. It also allows you to ensure that you provide activities that are well organised, safe and relevant for the children you look after. Happily, this will also increase the activities' fun factor.

Useful advice, dos and don'ts for when you are working with children.

Stretch activity

Produce a plan for an activity that promotes your chosen developmental area.

Decide which developmental area you would like to focus on. Choose from:

Take your understanding and knowledge of a topic a step further with these stretch activities designed to test you, and provide you with a more in-depth understanding of the topic.

Case study

Imogen and her partner Caleb have a four-year-old child named Aiysha. Providing food for Aiysha has not been straightforward, because she has been diagnosed with Type 1 diabetes.

See how concepts are applied in settings and learn about real life scenarios.

Test your knowledge

1 Explain the ways in which immunity can be acquired.
2 What are the common signs of illness?

Test your knowledge and understanding with this end of unit task.

Question practice

Question

a Postnatal checks are carried out on newborn babies. Explain the five reflexes medical professionals will normally expect to see.

This feature appears in Unit R018 where you will be assessed via an exam. This feature includes practice questions, mark schemes, additional guidance, and example answers to help you prepare for the exam.

Grading explanation

Learning Outcome 1: Know the dietary needs of individuals in each life stage

Marking criteria for LO1 part A

Mark band 1	Mark band 2	Mark band 3
Demonstrates basic knowledge of the different life stages (young people, adults and older people) with limited reference to the function of each nutrient.	Demonstrates sound knowledge of the different life stages (young people, adults and older people) with detailed reference to the function of each nutrient.	Demonstrates thorough knowledge of the different life stages (young people, adults and older people) with comprehensive reference to the function of each nutrient.

What you need to do

- make sure your work covers the dietary needs of all three life stages: young people (5-16 years), adults and older people.

Guidance and suggestions on what you will need to cover for the OCR model assignment, a breakdown of what the command words mean, and top tips.

Read about it

Great Ormond Street Hospital. Visit: www.gosh.nhs.uk/children/staying-hospital

Meningitis Now. Visit: www.meningitisnow.org/meningitis-explained/signs-and-symptoms/meningitis-babies-and-children-under-five/

Includes references to books, websites and other various sources for further reading and research.

Acknowledgements

From the author

Thank you to everyone at Hodder. Love and thanks to Nick for his endless support.

Picture credits

Every effort has been made to trace and acknowledge ownership of copyright. The publishers will be glad to make suitable arrangements with any copyright holders whom it has not been possible to contact. The authors and publishers would like to thank the following for permission to reproduce copyright material.

P.1 © Jules Selmes/Hodder Education; p.4 © Andrew Callaghan/Hodder Education; p.8 © Jules Selmes/Hodder Education; pp.20, 23 © kzenon – 123RF; p.31 © Rafael Ben-Ari – 123RF; p.38 © Tomorrow's Child UK Ltd; p.40 © Jules Selmes/Hodder Education; p.41 © Andrew Callaghan/Hodder Education; p.50 © all_about_people/Shutterstock; p.52 © Jules Selmes/Hodder Education; p.54 left © Jules Selmes/Hodder Education, right © spotmatikphoto – Fotolia; p.62 © Jules Selmes/Hodder Education; p.64 © Andrew Callaghan/Hodder Education; p. 65 bottom © British Standards Institute; p. 66 top © BHTA, right © John Gustafsson - S McTeir, bottom © European Commission p.69 © Jules Selmes/Hodder Education; p.70 © Brebca – Fotolia; pp.72, 74 © Andrew Callaghan/Hodder Education; p.76 © Andy Dean – Fotolia; pp.82, 85 © Jules Selmes/Hodder Education; p.86 © ACORN 1/Alamy Stock Photo; p.87 left © Africa Studio – Shutterstock, right © Keerati Thanitthitianant – 123RF; pp.88, 90, 93, 94 © Jules Selmes/Hodder Education; p. 91 bottom © British Standards Institute; p.98 © krugloff – Shutterstock; p.99 left © indigolotos – Shutterstock, right © Billion Photos – Shutterstock; p.100 both © Stockbyte/Getty Images/Child's Play SD113; p.101 left © Wilawan Khasawong – 123RF, right © Jules Selmes/Hodder Education; pp.103, 114 © Andrew Callaghan/Hodder Education; p.116 © Desislava Vasileva; p.120 top © Hodder Education; p.123 © Jules Selmes/Hodder Education; p.126 © pressmaster – Fotolia; p.128 top TBC, bottom © Dmitry Kalinovsky – 123RF; p.129 top © Africa Studio – Fotolia, bottom © S McTeir/Hodder Education; pp.131, 133 © Jules Selmes/Hodder Education; p.136 © Andrew Callaghan/Hodder Education; pp.137 both, 140, 142, 147, 152, 153 © Jules Selmes/Hodder Education; p.155 © Andrew Callaghan/Hodder Education; p.157 © Jules Selmes/Hodder Education; p.158 © Andrew Callaghan/Hodder Education; p.159 © Getty Images/Thinkstock/Daniel Hurst; p.166 © Jules Selmes/Hodder Education; pp.175, 176, 178 © Jules Selmes/Hodder Education.

Unit R018

Health and well-being for child development

About this unit

There are 60 GLH (guided learning hours) in this unit. This unit is about understanding the important roles and responsibilities that come with parenthood – from reproduction and pregnancy – through to preparation for birth. You will also learn about postnatal care following the birth, and how to create the right conditions in which a baby can develop and thrive. The focus then moves to keeping a baby safe and well. You will learn about childhood illnesses and how to prevent them, as well as safe practices to prevent harm, accidents and injuries.

Learning outcomes

By the end of this unit you will:

- understand reproduction and the roles and responsibilities of parenthood

- understand antenatal care and preparation for birth
- understand postnatal checks, postnatal provision and conditions for development
- understand how to recognise, manage and prevent childhood illnesses
- know about child safety.

How will I be assessed?

This unit will be assessed through a 1 hour and 15 minute externally assessed examination.

Learning outcome 1

Understand reproduction and the roles and responsibilities of parenthood

About this Learning outcome

Before deciding to have children, a couple will want to be sure that they are ready for the long-lasting responsibilities that come with parenthood. To do this, they need a realistic understanding of a parent's role.

To ensure that they do not conceive before they are ready, and to know what to expect when they do try to conceive, couples need a good understanding of reproduction and contraception.

Assessment criteria

In this learning outcome you will cover:

1.1 The wide range of factors that affect the decision to have children.

1.2 Pre-conception health.

1.3 Roles and responsibilities of parenthood.

1.4 Recognise and evaluate methods of contraception, their efficiency and reliability.

1.5 The structure and function of male and female reproductive systems.

Getting started

Thought storm all of the responsibilities you can think of that are part of the role of being parents to children aged from birth to five years. In pairs, compare and discuss your lists. If your partner has a suggestion you have overlooked, add it to your own list for future reference.

1.1 The wide range of factors that affect the decision to have children

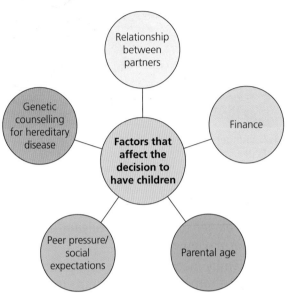

Figure 1.1: Factors that affect the decision to have children. Why do you think each of these is important to prospective parents?

Relationship between partners

The relationship between partners is a very important consideration when making the decision to have children. Couples who decide to start a family will generally have been together long enough to form a happy, stable, caring and secure relationship. This will be based on love and trust, and the couple will share their lives. They will be committed to one another, and will share respect, loyalty and priorities.

It is important that each partner trusts in the other's ability to make the major life changes necessary to become a reliable and responsible parent. The partners will also need to feel confident that they can cope with the demands of being a parent, because while having a child is wonderful in many ways, caring for a child can be exhausting, overwhelming and challenging at times. This is especially so when the baby is young and the parents are likely to be both inexperienced and very tired.

Couples also need to be able to talk through any problems together, share their feelings honestly

in a respectful and caring way and support one another in times of difficulty. They need to think carefully about whether each partner wants to start a family, because all children need to feel wanted and loved. If one partner does not particularly want children but is prepared to have a child for the sake of the relationship or to make their partner happy, they might feel resentful in the future. This could lead to the breakdown of the family unit.

Finance

Raising a child is expensive. In 2016, the Centre for Economics and Business Research and insurer LV found that the average cost of raising a child to the age of 21 (the end of university education) in the UK was £231,843. This means that households typically spend around 38 per cent of their combined net incomes on raising a child. According to building society Nationwide, the average UK home cost £196,829 in 2016, therefore raising a child is much more expensive than buying a house.

The most expensive years are between the ages of one and four, when parents spend an average of £63,224 on their child. Research shows that the average cost is currently rising – in the 12 months prior to the time of writing, it increased by £2,500. Over the preceding five years, the average cost of bringing up a child increased by £13,000.

Education is the most expensive aspect, costing an average of £74,430 up to the age of 21. This does not include private school fees, but does include school uniforms, lunches, trips and equipment, as well as university costs. Feeding children well also costs a significant amount of money – around £19,004 up to the age of 21.

Parents will approach finances differently, and there is no right or wrong way. In most families, one or both parents will work to earn the money needed to live. Part time work can range from a few hours to several days each week. While stay-at-home fathers are on the rise, figures show that it is still most common for the mother to work part time and to care for the children part time. Working parents are currently likely to spend around £70,466 on childcare and babysitting costs throughout a child's life. The most expensive childcare years are when the child is under two.

Did you know?

? Did you know?

All three and four year olds in England are entitled to 570 hours of free early education or childcare a year. This is often taken as 15 hours each week for 38 weeks of the year. Some two-year olds are also eligible.

Parental age

The age of the couple can affect the likelihood of conception, and how they experience parenthood. Parental age can also increase the chances of a baby being born with certain conditions.

Age of the mother

As a woman ages, her ability to conceive begins to decline, as does the quality of her eggs. This decline becomes more rapid after the age of 35. When she stops having a reproductive cycle (known as menopause), she will no longer be able to get pregnant. In recent years, figures have shown more mothers are waiting to have their first child until between the ages of 35 and 45. This might be because they have settled down/got married later in life than used to be case, or because they have waited until they are financially secure. They might have been building a career, gaining qualifications and/or training for work. Recently, some fertility experts have been warning women to start their families by the age of 30 to give themselves the best chance of getting pregnant.

Age of the father

Men produce sperm all their adult life, including into old age. As long as they are physically capable of sexual intercourse, men can father children.

Age-related advantages and disadvantages

There are advantages and disadvantages to be being a younger parent and an older parent.

Younger parents:

- may be healthier and fitter, with more energy and a longer life expectancy
- may recover from pregnancy and birth faster (mother only)

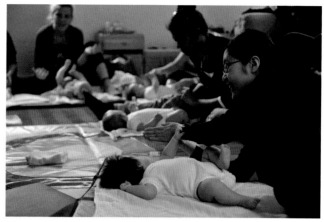

Figure 1.2: Younger mothers may recover from pregnancy and birth faster.

- are less likely to have a child with Down's syndrome (this is less likely under the age of 35)
- may find it easier to return to studying/having a career after having a family
- will have family members such as parents who are younger themselves and perhaps more able to help out, for example with babysitting
- are less likely to be financially secure and to have a home that is stable – if they are prevented from having a career that pays well, this could affect their finances on an ongoing basis
- may not yet feel ready for, or confident about, the responsibilities of parenthood
- may not yet be in a secure relationship
- may resent needing to give up a large part of their social life.

Older parents:

- are more likely to be financially secure
- are more likely to be mature, relaxed and confident about parenthood; they may enjoy parenthood more
- have increased life experience, which can increase their ability to handle challenges
- are more likely to have established a career, completed training/qualifications and perhaps travelled before starting a family
- may recover from pregnancy and birth more slowly (mother only)
- are more likely to have a child with Down's syndrome (this is more likely over the age of 35)
- are likely to have less energy.

Did you know?

The National Health Service (NHS) reports that around one-third of couples in which the woman is over 35 have fertility problems. This rises to two-thirds when the woman is over 40.

Peer pressure/social expectations

Parents can feel pressured by peers to have a baby. This can occur when several members of a friendship group have babies, leaving someone yet to have a child feeling excluded. There also tends to be a social expectation for a couple to start a family, from friends and family. People can sometimes be surprised by a couple who do not want children. However, what is right for the couple should always be the most important consideration.

Genetic counselling for hereditary diseases

Genetic disorders are inherited. Some can only be passed on by the mother, and some only by the father. They are most commonly passed on through either the egg or the sperm. Genetic disorders include:

- Down's syndrome
- cystic fibrosis
- sickle cell anaemia
- muscular dystrophy.

Parents at risk of having a child with a genetic disorder will be offered genetic counselling (genetic tests). Examples of when tests might be offered include the following:

- if parents already have a child who has a genetic disorder or congenital defect such as club foot
- if there is family history of birth defects, genetic disorders or some forms of cancer
- if there have been repeated miscarriages or problems getting pregnant
- if there is a blood relationship between the partners (for example cousins)
- if a parent's ethnic background is one in which genetic disorders are more likely.

There is more information about genetic tests in Learning outcome 2.

1.2 Pre-conception health

When a couple decide that they want a baby, they should consider their pre-conception health, because this can have a significant impact on the health of the baby they conceive. In some circumstances, this can affect a baby throughout its whole life.

It is best to address any health concerns before starting to try for a baby. This might require a change of lifestyle, but it will help to give the baby the healthiest start possible. This is because in the first trimester (the first 12 weeks of pregnancy), the liver, lungs, heart and brain are forming, and by the end of this period they will be working. A mother might be pregnant for several weeks before she finds out, so even if there are good intentions to address health concerns – such as giving up smoking once she knows she is pregnant – the damage might already have been done. It can also take time for the effects of a lifestyle change to have an impact.

Areas for consideration include:

- diet
- exercise
- healthy weight
- smoking/alcohol/recreational drugs
- up-to-date immunisations.

Diet

A healthy diet is extremely important for the mother, both before and during pregnancy. The baby will be completely reliant on its mother for all of the nutrients it needs to grow and develop. The Food Standards Agency (FSA) guidelines for a healthy diet should be followed. These include:

- at least five portions of fruit and vegetables per day
- foods that provide protein and iron, such as chicken, meat, fish, eggs and pulses
- starchy foods, including potatoes, bread, rice and pasta
- fish at least twice a week
- dairy foods in moderation, including milk, cheese and yoghurt
- only consuming sweet/processed foods in moderation.

Exercise

Being fit and healthy before conception will help a woman to cope with the strain her body will be under during pregnancy and birth. Regular exercise is also important to maintain ongoing fitness during pregnancy, and most forms of exercise can carry on safely, as long as the mother feels comfortable and does not become overtired. Popular choices include walking, swimming and cycling. In many local areas, groups of expectant mothers get together to enjoy gentle exercise and companionship.

Healthy weight

Being of a healthy weight helps to safeguard both the mother and the baby. Being overweight or obese:

- can affect ovulation, which can in turn affect fertility and make it harder to conceive
- can interfere with the monitoring of the baby's growth and development
- can lead to health issues in pregnancy such as high blood pressure, pre-eclampsia or diabetes (even if the mother has not previously had diabetes)
- can increase the likelihood of needing a caesarean.

Meanwhile, being underweight can affect periods and ovulation, which can in turn affect fertility and make it harder to conceive.

Dangers of smoking/alcohol/ recreational drugs

Very serious damage can be caused to an unborn child by smoking (including passive smoking), drinking alcohol and using recreational drugs in pregnancy. It is extremely important to protect a foetus from these factors throughout its development in the womb.

Did you know?

Strict weight-loss diets should not be embarked on without the supervision of a general practitioner (GP) or medical professional. It takes time to address weight issues and achieve a healthy weight.

Smoking

Smoking (in men and women) can make conception more difficult. A women's fertility can be affected, and men who smoke may have a lower sperm count than non-smokers. They may also produce a higher proportion of abnormal sperm.

Once she is pregnant, the chemicals from smoke inhaled by a mother will pass from her lungs into her bloodstream, then to the unborn child via the placenta. The poisonous gas carbon monoxide will replace oxygen in the blood, affecting the baby's growth, while nicotine actually makes the baby's heart beat faster. There is also a risk of premature birth, miscarriage, stillbirth and foetal abnormalities. Damage to the placenta can affect the nutrients received, and low birth weight is common among smokers. Babies may also go on to experience learning difficulties and poor growth. If a child grows up in a home with smokers, the likelihood of them dying from Sudden Infant Death Syndrome (SIDS) is doubled. They are also more at risk of asthma and chest infections, and according to some research, some forms of cancer.

Alcohol

Lower sperm counts are evident in men who consume a lot of alcohol. There has been much debate over how much alcohol it is safe for a mother to drink during pregnancy. However, it is clear that the more a woman drinks, the higher the risk to her baby. The Chief Medical Officers (CMO) for the UK recommend that if a woman is pregnant, or planning to become pregnant, the safest approach is not to drink alcohol at all.

A mother regularly drinking or binge drinking (drinking a lot of alcohol in a short space of time) is very dangerous for the unborn child, because the alcohol enters the mother's bloodstream and is then passed on to the baby via the placenta. A baby's liver will not mature until the later stages of pregnancy, and too much exposure to alcohol can seriously affect its development. Drinking alcohol, particularly in the first three months of pregnancy, also increases the risk of premature birth and low birth weight. After the first three months of pregnancy, the effects of alcohol include learning difficulties and behavioural problems.

Drinking heavily throughout pregnancy can cause your baby to develop a serious condition called foetal alcohol syndrome (FAS). Children with FAS have poor growth, facial abnormalities and learning and behavioural problems.

Recreational drugs

Recreational drug use in pregnancy can seriously affect an unborn baby's growth and development as the amount of oxygen reaching the baby can be reduced. There may also be problems with the placenta, which can cause severe bleeding that can be life threatening for mother and baby. If certain drugs have been taken regularly, the baby may suffer withdrawal after birth and will need to be treated in hospital.

Up-to-date immunisations

Keeping immunisations up to date will contribute to keeping a woman healthy both before and during pregnancy, which in turn benefits the baby. Pregnant women can also help protect their unborn baby from getting whooping cough in their first weeks of life by having the whooping cough vaccine. The annual flu vaccine is also made available from October each year in advance of the winter flu season, because pregnant women are at greater risk of complications from flu.

1.3 Roles and responsibilities of parenthood

Meeting primary needs

Providing for a child's primary needs (the basic needs necessary for survival) is a crucial part of a parent's roles and responsibilities, as shown on the table below. Can you think of any additional ways in which parents can meet a child's primary needs?

In addition, it is within a parent's roles and responsibilities to provide:

- love and nurture – all children need and deserve to be loved and brought up in a supportive, nurturing environment. A child who does not receive love and nurture may fail to thrive. They may also be unhappy and experience social and emotional difficulties both at home and in the wider world –

Primary need	Parental roles/responsibilities
Food	Children must be provided with food and water – their very survival depends on it and it is one of their most basic needs. Parents must supply food that is sufficient and that contains the right nutrients for a baby/child at each stage of their development (see page 115). Children also need to be provided with regular mealtimes and snacks if they are to thrive and have the energy they need to learn, grow, develop and play. It is a big undertaking to be responsible for food and drink, because there are a lot of guidelines to consider, and healthy food must be shopped for (sufficient money is required for this), prepared and cooked. The responsibility to provide food is there every single day, for many years.
Clothing	A parent must provide sufficient clothing throughout childhood. Children grow out of clothes rapidly, especially when they are young, so this is a considerable expense. Children also need parents to ensure that they have clothing for all weathers. Parents must also see to the laundering and ironing of clothes, which can add considerably to a parent's workload.
Shelter	Parents must provide somewhere safe for children to live. The home in which a child grows up has a huge impact on their childhood. For example, a child who lives in damp conditions may develop asthma and/or frequent chest infections. It is important to a child's wellbeing that they feel sufficiently settled, safe and secure in their home. Paying rent or a mortgage is a big ongoing expense for most families, and typically takes up a significant chunk of the parental income.
Warmth	Children need their parents to provide them with warmth. Heating a home is a significant expense, and parents will need to plan to pay for this. If heating breaks down, it can cost a lot of money to get it fixed. Parents also need to provide sufficient clothing and bedding to keep their child warm.
Rest/sleep	Sufficient rest and sleep is crucial to a child's wellbeing, learning, growth and development. Ensuring children get enough rest and sleep is therefore a very important parental responsibility. New parents can underestimate how much they might need to reduce their own social life to ensure that their child gets enough good-quality rest and sleep. It is unrealistic to expect to provide sufficient rest and sleep if a child has to accompany a parent as they go about their life as before.

Table 1.1: Roles and responsibilities of parenthood.

when interacting with their peers at playgroup, for example. A lack of love and nurture in the early years can continue to impact on a child as they grow up, and the effects may even continue to be felt into adulthood. Some adults who lacked a loving and nurturing role model in their own childhood can find it more challenging to adjust to the role of being parent themselves, and may need additional support at this time in their lives.

- **socialisation, customs and values including patterns of behaviour, social interaction and role models** – as they grow up, children need to come to understand socially acceptable behaviour. They need to be supported in learning how to experience and manage their feelings, and parents have a responsibility to guide children in this area. An important part of the

parental role is to be an appropriate role model – this means demonstrating how to behave by example. Parents will also want to give their child an understanding of their family's customs and values. Customs and values may be influenced by a family's religion or ethical beliefs. For example, these may include what and how a family celebrates, whether and how a family prays, what and how a family eats and the activities in which a family participates. The customs and values of a family are very personal, and they tend to influence a child's sense of identity.

Together, these things enable a child to successfully interact socially. Parents need to plan opportunities for their child to socialise with their peers to ensure that they are confident around others, and to be able to make friends and enjoy social times.

Case study

Imogen and her partner Caleb have a four-year-old child named Aiysha. Providing food for Aiysha has not been straightforward, because she has been diagnosed with Type 1 diabetes. Eating a healthy, balanced diet is a very important part of managing Aiysha's diabetes, and her doctor has told them that they should think of this as part of their daughter's ongoing treatment. As a result, Imogen and Caleb plan meals very carefully.

Question:

1 How do you think this information impacts on the role and responsibilities of Aiysha's parents with regard to providing for her primary care needs?

Figure 1.3: Parents must provide for a child's primary care needs.

1.4 To recognise and evaluate methods of contraception, their efficiency and reliability

There are many factors to consider for any couple when it comes to choosing an appropriate method of contraception, from a range of options, that will suit their preferences and needs.

Barrier methods

The term **barrier method** means that a device is used to prevent semen (containing sperm) from passing through the cervix and coming into contact with the egg, thereby preventing conception. Barrier prevention methods are:

- male and female condoms
- diaphragm or cap.

Male and female condoms

A male condom is a sheath made from latex. (Polyurethane condoms are also available for those with a latex sensitivity or allergy.) It is put onto the erect penis before it comes into contact with the vagina, which does mean interrupting sex in order to put one on. A condom is 98 per cent effective if used correctly, and it also helps to protect against many sexually transmitted infections (STIs). If used incorrectly, however, a condom can come off or split open, making it ineffective. Condoms are widely available from chemists, supermarkets, pubs, clubs and garages. They are also provided free by family planning clinics. They must be discarded after one use. An advantage of condoms is that they allow the man to take responsibility for contraception.

A female condom is a sheath made from polyurethane. It is put inside the vagina before it comes into contact with the penis, again meaning that sex is interrupted in order to put one in. It is 95 per cent effective if used correctly, and it also helps to protect against many STIs. A disadvantage is that it is possible for the condom to be pushed too far into the vagina. Female condoms are widely available in chemists and supermarkets, but they are more expensive than male condoms. They are often free from family planning clinics.

Diaphragm or cap

This is a dome-shaped piece of latex or silicone that covers the cervix. It is inserted into the vagina before sex, and must be used alongside spermicidal gel or cream, which will kill sperm. It can be inserted a few hours in advance, so it need not interrupt the enjoyment of sex. It is reusable, so must be removed and washed after intercourse. It is 92 per cent effective if used correctly, and helps to protect against some STIs. Women can have difficulty learning how to use diaphragms and caps, and they can cause cystitis.

Contraceptive pill

The contraceptive pill is a **hormonal method** of contraception, and comes in two forms:

- combined pill
- progestogen-only pill (sometimes referred to as the 'mini pill').

Combined pill

The combined pill is a tablet containing hormones (oestrogen and progestogen) that prevent ovulation, therefore reducing the likelihood of sperm reaching an egg and of the egg becoming implanted in the womb lining. The woman takes the pill for 21 days, then has a break for 7 days, in which time she will have a period. She then resumes taking the pill for another 21 days, and so on. The pill needs to be taken regularly at the same time of day. It is 99 per cent effective if used correctly, but a woman can still become pregnant if she forgets to take it, vomits after taking it or has severe diarrhoea. While it can

🔑 Key terms

Barrier method: a method of contraception in which a device or preparation prevents sperm from reaching an egg.

Hormonal method: a method of contraception in which hormones prevent eggs from being released from the ovaries, thicken cervical mucus to prevent sperm from entering the uterus, and thin the lining of the uterus to prevent implantation.

help women with heavy/painful periods and may help to protect against cancer of the womb, ovaries and colon, it can also cause side effects such as weight gain, headaches, mood swings or depression, raised blood pressure and, uncommonly, blood clots. Using this method does not interrupt sex.

Progestogen-only pill

This pill contains the progestogen hormone only. It is taken every day, and this needs to be done within a specified three-hour period. It works by causing the mucus in the cervix to thicken so that sperm cannot come into contact with an egg. It thins the womb lining too, stopping a fertilised egg from becoming implanted. (Some women actually stop ovulating altogether when taking this pill.) It is 99 per cent effective if used correctly, but a woman can still become pregnant if she forgets to take it, vomits after taking it, has severe diarrhoea or takes certain medication. Women who cannot take oestrogen may be able to take this pill. Side effects can include spot-prone skin and tender breasts, and periods may be irregular. Using this method does not interrupt sex.

Intrauterine device/system

An intrauterine device or system (IUD or IUS) is a small, t-shaped plastic device that is inserted into the uterus by a doctor or nurse. It releases the progestogen hormone into the womb, which thickens the mucus in the cervix, preventing sperm from reaching an egg. It also thins the womb lining so that a fertilised egg is less likely to be implanted. (Some women actually stop ovulating altogether.) It is 99 per cent effective if used correctly for five years or three years, depending on the type, therefore the couple do not need to think about contraception every day or whenever they have sex. It may make periods lighter, shorter or stop altogether, so it can help women who have heavy periods or painful periods. It can also be used by women who cannot take the combined pill. Possible side effects include mood swings, skin problems, breast tenderness and getting an infection after it is inserted. Insertion can also be uncomfortable. It does not protect against STIs.

Did you know?

There is also a copper IUD, which is also 99 per cent effective. The copper, rather than a hormone, stops the sperm moving through the womb towards the egg. In the first six months of use, spotting and light bleeding between periods, and heavier or prolonged bleeding and pain are common.

Contraceptive injection

A woman receives an injection every few weeks – the most common type is given every 12 weeks. This might be a suitable choice for women who find it difficult to take a tablet at the same time each day. It works by causing the mucus in the cervix to thicken so that sperm cannot come into contact with an egg. It thins the womb lining too, stopping a fertilised egg from becoming implanted. (Some women actually stop ovulating altogether.) It is 99 per cent effective if used correctly, and can protect against some cancers and infections. Side effects can include headaches, tender breasts, weight gain and mood swings, and there may be irregular periods. After stopping the injections, it can take up to a year to get fertility levels to back to normal, so this is not a good choice for those planning to start a family in the near future. Using this method does not interrupt sex.

Contraceptive patch

This is worn on the skin and it introduces hormones to the body (oestrogen and progestogen). It works by causing the mucus in the cervix to thicken so that sperm cannot come into contact with an egg. It also thins the womb lining, stopping a fertilised egg from becoming implanted. It is 99 per cent effective if used correctly, and may protect against some cancers and infections. It is still effective if the woman vomits or has severe diarrhoea (unlike the pill). Side effects can include headaches and raised blood pressure, and uncommonly, blood clots. The patch must be changed each week for three weeks, then there is a week off. Using this method does not interrupt sex.

Contraceptive implant

A health professional will insert this small flexible tube into the skin of a woman's upper arm. It releases the progestogen hormone into the body to stop the ovaries from releasing an egg, and thickens the mucus in the cervix, preventing sperm from reaching an egg. It also makes the womb less likely to accept a fertilised egg. It is 99 per cent effective if used correctly for three years, after which time it is removed, therefore the couple do not need to think about contraception every day or whenever they have sex. Some medicines may make it ineffective, however. Possible side effects include swelling, tenderness or bruising after it is inserted, and periods may change to become lighter, or heavier and longer. It does not protect against STIs.

Natural family planning

In this method, a woman records the symptoms in her body (by taking her temperature and monitoring bodily secretions, for example, perhaps using apps to help her track observations) that indicate when she is fertile and able to conceive – a period of around eight days in each month. On other days, she will be able to have sex without conceiving. On the fertile days, a condom can be used if the couple wish to have sex, or they can abstain (not have sex). This means that the method is compatible with all cultures and faiths (because some do not permit the use of contraception). It is up to 98 per cent effective if used correctly, but it can take time to learn to identify the fertile days and it does not offer protection against STIs. There are no side effects or costs.

In another natural contraceptive measure, the man withdraws his penis from the vagina before

Activity

Recognise and evaluate methods of contraception, their efficiency and reliability.

Imagine that you have been asked to make a poster that informs young adults of the important factors to consider when choosing a method of contraception (for example effectiveness, protection against STIs).

- Decide what factors the poster will incorporate.
- Decide what information will be given about each factor.
- Design the poster.

he ejaculates semen into it. However, semen can be released before ejaculation, so this is an unreliable contraceptive measure. It can also be frustrating for both partners.

Emergency contraceptive pill

This is designed to prevent pregnancy after a woman has had unprotected sex, or if she thinks that the method of conception used has failed – a condom may have split, for instance. The sooner it is taken the better, but it must be taken within 72 hours of unprotected sex. If taken within 24 hours, it is up to 98 per cent effective. The effectiveness decreases over time – after 72 hours it is just 52 per cent effective. It can be bought from a pharmacy (by those aged 16 and over) and it is also free of charge from some GP surgeries, family planning and sexual health clinics, NHS walk-in centres and hospitals.

1.5 The structure and function of male and female reproductive systems

To understand how reproduction happens, you first need to understand the structure and function of the male and female reproductive systems.

Female reproductive system

This includes:

- ovaries
- fallopian tubes
- uterus/lining of the uterus
- cervix
- vagina
- the menstrual cycle.

Ovaries

A woman's two ovaries control the production of the hormones oestrogen and progesterone, which govern the development of the female body and the menstrual cycle. Within the ovaries are undeveloped egg cells called ova (one cell is called an ovum).

Fallopian tubes

These tubes connect the ovaries to the uterus, and are lined by minute hairs called cilia. Each month, one of the ovaries releases an egg into a tube, and the hairs help the egg to reach the uterus by wafting it along the tube.

Uterus/lining of the uterus

The uterus (also called the womb) is the hollow, pear-shaped muscular bag where an unborn child grows and develops. The lining of the uterus is soft, and it is here that an egg will become implanted.

Cervix

This is a very strong ring of muscles between the uterus and vagina, and it is usually closed. It keeps the baby securely in place in the womb throughout pregnancy. The cervix dilates (opens) during labour to allow the baby to be born.

Vagina

This muscular tube leads downwards, connecting the cervix to the outside of the body. It is here that the man's penis enters the body during sex. Folds of skin called labia meet at the entrance of the vagina, forming the vulva. The urethra, through which urine passes, opens into the vulva but is separate from the vagina.

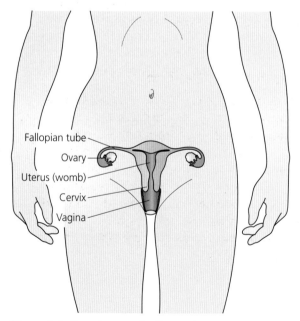

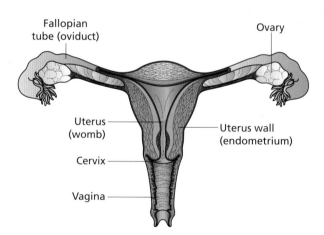

Figure 1.4: Female reproductive system.

The menstrual cycle

This is the cycle in which women have their periods and are fertile (can conceive a baby). Girls begin their periods when they become sexually mature (the average age for periods starting is 12) and they continue until menopause (the average age for this is 51). Women experience periods differently, but menstruation (a period) generally lasts 3 to 7 days and an average of 5 days. This is the start of the menstrual cycle, when blood flows from the uterus and leaves the body via the vagina. A new egg then develops in one of the ovaries. About 14 days after the first day of menstruation, the egg is released from the ovary and travels along the fallopian tube to the uterus. The lining of the uterus will be thickened and ready should an egg be fertilised by sperm. If this occurs, the baby will start to grow. If it does not occur by the end of the cycle, the blood, uterus lining and egg are flushed out via another period and the cycle begins again.

Male reproductive system

This includes:

- testes
- sperm duct system/epididymis
- urethra
- penis
- vas deferens.

Testes

The scrotum is a bag of skin that contains two testes. These make millions of sperm – the male sex cells. They also produce hormones including testosterone, which governs the development of the male body.

Sperm duct system/epididymis

The sperm duct system consists of the epididymis, which contains the sperm, and the vas deferens, which are the sperm ducts (tubes) that sperm pass through. Glands produce nutrient-rich fluid – called semen – which mixes with the sperm and carries it.

Urethra

This tube inside the penis carries both urine and semen, but not both at the same time. A ring of muscle controls this.

Penis

The penis consists of the shaft (the main part that goes inside the vagina) and the glans (the tip), which has a small opening. Through this opening, sperm and urine leave the body (separately) via the urethra.

Vas deferens

This is a muscular tube that extends upwards from the testicles, transferring sperm that contains semen to the urethra.

How reproduction takes place

Reproduction happens at a point in the menstrual cycle, which ends with conception if a baby is to be born, or else with the woman's body flushing out an unfertilised egg.

Ovulation

This occurs when an egg is released from one of the ovaries and travels along the fallopian tube, around day 14 of the menstrual cycle. A jelly-like coating ensures that it does not stick to the sides of the tubes, and is moved along by the cilia.

Conception/fertilisation

This occurs when a sperm penetrates an egg following ejaculation of sperm from the penis into the vagina. On passing through the cervix and uterus, the sperm meets the egg in the fallopian tubes and loses its tail, which is no longer needed. The egg and sperm then fuse as one cell. The fertilised egg continues along the fallopian tubes. Between four and five days later, there is a mass of around 16 cells. This forms a ball of tissue (the blastocyst).

Implantation

After around another seven days, the fertilised egg arrives in the uterus and implants itself in the enriched lining. Once it is attached firmly, conception has been achieved and the egg is called an embryo. Its outer cells link with the mother's blood supply, forming the baby's support system – the umbilical cord, amnion and placenta (via which it will receive nutrients from the mother).

Development of the embryo

The development of the embryo is shown on the following diagram. Study this carefully.

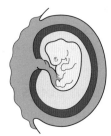

Embryo 6–7 weeks

Figure 1.5: Development of the embryo.

Development of the foetus

The development of the foetus is shown on the following diagram. Study this carefully.

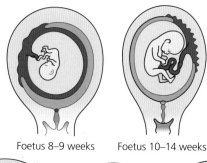
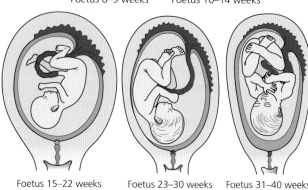

Foetus 8–9 weeks   Foetus 10–14 weeks

Foetus 15–22 weeks   Foetus 23–30 weeks   Foetus 31–40 weeks

Figure 1.6: Development of the foetus.

Activity

- At what age do you think the foetus looks human, and is fully formed in miniature?
- At what age do you think the foetus can be felt by the pregnant mother?
- At what age do you think the baby could realistically be expected to survive if born early? (This is known as the age at which a baby is 'legally viable'.)

Multiple pregnancies

A multiple pregnancy is when more than one baby grows in the uterus. Identical twins are the result of one fertilised egg dividing into two cells. Non-identical twins are the result of two separate eggs being released and fertilised by two different sperm.

The signs and symptoms of pregnancy

There are some common signs and symptoms of pregnancy, but not all women will have all of the symptoms. Women also experience signs and symptoms at different rates, therefore some are further along in the pregnancy than others when they find out that they are pregnant.

Missed period

The first sign of pregnancy is often a missed period, or a very light period. This is generally the most reliable sign for women who usually have a regular monthly menstrual cycle.

Breast changes

The breasts may feel similar to just before a period, becoming larger and feeling tender. Some women may feel tingling and veins may be more visible. The nipples may appear darker and stand out.

Passing urine frequently

Pregnant women often need to pass urine more frequently. There may also be constipation and an increase of vaginal discharge without any soreness or irritation.

Tiredness

Women may feel tired or exhausted, particularly during the first 12 weeks of pregnancy, due to hormonal changes in the body. These changes can also cause a woman to feel emotional and upset at this time.

Nausea

Feeling sick and nauseous, and/or vomiting when pregnant is often called 'morning sickness', but although it can occur at any time of day. This symptom generally begins around six weeks after a pregnant woman's last period.

 Good practice

Hyperemesis gravidarum (HG) is a serious condition that causes severe vomiting in pregnant women and requires treatment. If a pregnant woman is frequently being sick and cannot keep food or drink down, she should see her GP.

Test your knowledge

1 State three factors that affect the decision to have children.
2 Outline why diet and exercise are important to pre-conception health.
3 Name five primary care needs for which parents are responsible.
4 Outline the choices available for couples seeking to use barrier methods of contraception.
5 Explain the function of a woman's ovaries in reproduction.
6 Explain how identical twins are conceived.
7 Outline five signs and symptoms of pregnancy.

Question practice

Question

Daniel and Melanie have been trying for a baby.

a   State five signs and symptoms of pregnancy that Melanie may notice should she conceive.

Mark scheme and additional guidance

Expected answers	Marks	Additional guidance
Five required, **one** mark each. ● Missed period ● Breast changes ● Passing urine frequently ● Tiredness ● Nausea	5	Five signs and symptoms are stated. One mark is awarded for each correct answer.

Candidate answer

● Missed period

● Breast changes

● Nausea

● Tiredness/exhaustion

● Increase in visits to toilet

Commentary

Question context/content/style:

Five signs and symptoms of pregnancy listed. (Five marks)

Requirements:

● Correctly listed five signs and symptoms of pregnancy.

Marks awarded and rationale: 5/5

● Five correct signs and symptoms of pregnancy have been listed, gaining five marks.

Question

b   As they prepare for the arrival of their new baby, Daniel and Melanie are considering the roles and responsibilities of parenthood. State five primary care needs that they will need to meet.

Expected answers	Marks	Additional guidance
Five required, **one** mark each. ● Food ● Clothing ● Shelter ● Warmth ● Rest/sleep	5	Five primary care needs are stated. One mark is awarded for each correct answer.

Candidate answer

- Food
- Shelter
- Warmth
- Toys and equipment
- Rest and sleep

Commentary

Question context/content/style:

LListed four primary care needs. (Four marks)

Requirements:

- Correctly listed five primary care needs.

Marks awarded and rationale: 4/5

- The fourth answer is incorrect. Toys and equipment are not primary care needs.

Learning outcome 2

Understand antenatal care and preparation for birth

About this Learning outcome

Antenatal care is the care given to a pregnant mother and her unborn baby during pregnancy and ahead of the birth. Some aspects of antenatal care also extend to the father or the mother's partner. This Learning outcome looks at how antenatal care helps to ensure the health and well-being of all involved, and why it is an important part of preparing for both the birth and the child's infancy.

Assessment criteria

In this learning outcome you will cover:

2.1 The roles of the different health professionals supporting the pregnant mother.

2.2 The importance of antenatal and parenting classes.

2.3 Routine checks carried out at an antenatal clinic.

2.4 Specialised diagnostic tests.

2.5 The choices available for delivery.

2.6 The stages of labour and the methods of delivery, including pain relief.

Getting started

Working with a partner, thought storm all of the concerns you think a pregnant mother might have about birth and motherhood. Take into consideration everything you have learnt so far, as well as your own opinion.

2.1 The roles of the different health professionals supporting the pregnant mother

A pregnant mother will be supported by a diverse team of health professionals, as shown on the diagram below.

Figure 2.1: Health professionals who support the pregnant mother. Can you think of any additional professionals who may play a role?

Midwife

Midwives are experts in normal pregnancy and birth (vaginal birth without the need of interventions). They look after a pregnant woman and her baby throughout the phase of antenatal care, during labour and birth, and for up to 28 days after the baby has been born.

The responsibilities of midwives include:

- providing full antenatal care, including parenting classes, clinical examinations and screening
- identifying high-risk pregnancies
- monitoring women and supporting them during labour and the birthing process
- teaching new and expectant mothers how to feed, care for and bathe their babies.

Midwives fall into three categories.

Hospital midwives

These midwives are based in a hospital, a birth centre or midwife-led unit. They also work in antenatal clinics, and on the labour ward and postnatal wards.

Community midwives

These midwives see pregnant women at home or at a specialised clinic. (Clinics may also be found within children's centres and GP surgeries.) They also attend home births, and are responsible for the provision of postnatal care for both home births and hospital births. They will visit new mothers at home after the birth for up to ten days. Midwifery services are increasingly moving from hospitals to the community.

Independent midwives

These midwives work privately, outside of the NHS. They are most likely to work with women intending to have a home birth.

Also, see the section on the importance of antenatal and parenting classes below.

? Did you know?

The word 'midwife' means 'with woman'.

Obstetrician

Midwives take on the antenatal care of mothers considered at low risk, and the supervision of uncomplicated deliveries that will not require medical intervention. More complex cases are taken on by an obstetrician. This can be in response to:

- a pre-existing acute or chronic medical condition in the mother that complicates the pregnancy and/or birth
- a complication with the mother or baby identified during pregnancy that complicates the pregnancy and/or birth
- a baby becoming distressed during labour.

An obstetrician's role includes assisting delivery and performing caesarean sections (see page 29).

General practitioner

The general practitioner (GP) is generally a mother's first port of call following a positive home pregnancy test. The GP will confirm the pregnancy and book the mother into the 'maternity system' so that specific appointments for scans and check-ups are triggered. Some mothers will receive news of their pregnancy from the GP after presenting with signs of pregnancy at the doctor's surgery. The GP's role also includes:

- answering any initial questions the pregnant woman may have
- discussing any specific issues they think may be relevant to the pregnancy, for example a mother's existing medical condition, and making referrals to other professionals as necessary
- treating the mother for any non-pregnancy related medical problems during pregnancy
- responding to emergency concerns relating to the pregnancy – for example, they may be called out to visit a mother experiencing abdominal pain
- potentially being involved in the delivery of babies in GP-led units (see page 26)
- providing postnatal medical care, including giving advice on matters such as contraception following the birth.

Gynaecologist

A gynaecologist is a specialist in the female reproductive organs and the ability to reproduce. Gynaecologists treat fertility conditions and early pregnancy symptoms. Their role includes:

- care of mothers with complicated medical problems
- emergency care for problems in early pregnancy, for example abdominal pain or bleeding
- termination of a pregnancy, including pre-assessment and counselling.

Paediatrician

A paediatrician is a doctor specialising in babies and children. They may be present at the birth if there is a concern about a baby's health. If there is an unexpected concern following the birth, a paediatrician is also likely to be called. A paediatrician may check a healthy baby over before it leaves hospital; however, a midwife trained in this specialised area of care may also undertake this task.

2.2 The importance of antenatal and parenting classes

These classes help with preparation for a safe pregnancy, labour and parenthood. Most mothers will start attending classes once a week, in the daytime or the evening, around weeks 30–32 of pregnancy. Those expecting twins will generally begin in week 24 of pregnancy, as the babies are more likely to be born early.

Classes are generally informal and fun, but there are local differences in provision. For example, some areas may offer mothers two separate classes – one focusing on pregnancy, labour and birth, and another focusing on parenthood and baby care. In some areas,

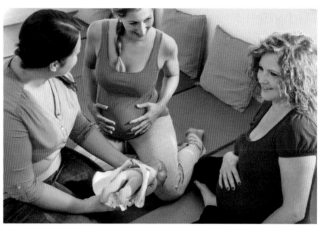

Figure 2.2: Antenatal and parenting classes help a mother to prepare for the birth.

parents may only be offered antenatal classes on the NHS, but may choose to also attend a private parenting class.

Preparing for a safe pregnancy and delivery

Antenatal and parenting classes can help with preparing for a safe pregnancy and delivery by:

- providing advice on staying fit and healthy during pregnancy through safe exercise and a healthy diet
- providing information on the various arrangements for labour and birth; this information will enable a mother to create her own personal birth plan, and to discuss this with professionals
- giving mothers the chance to talk over any concerns; mothers may also be able to meet key professionals who will care for them during labour.

Preparation of both parents for labour and parenthood

Antenatal and parenting classes usually help to prepare both parents for labour and parenthood by covering:

- what happens during labour and birth, so parents know what to expect
- how to cope with labour, including information about different types of pain relief and relaxation methods, including breathing techniques
- information on different types of birth (for example home birth, hospital birth)
- information on different types of birth interventions, such as ventouse or forceps delivery (see page 29)
- caring for a baby (for example feeding, sleeping and bathing)
- the mother's health after the birth.

Role of the father/partner in supporting the mother throughout pregnancy and birth

The father/partner can do much to support the mother throughout pregnancy and birth. During antenatal and parenting classes, they will learn:

- how to help the mother during pregnancy – by providing practical support with tasks if the mother is feeling tired, or being emotionally supportive if the mother is anxious about coping with birth
- how to help the mother during labour and birth – by massaging the back, shoulders or legs, supporting the mother's body, timing the contractions, giving encouragement, offering drinks, snack or ice cubes, sponging the mother down, talking or finding ways to pass the time, helping the mother to find a comfortable position, making sure health professionals are aware of the birthing plan
- learning relaxation and breathing techniques alongside the mother – they can then encourage the mother to use the techniques by participating alongside her during labour and birth.

Did you know?

Antenatal and parenting classes give new parents the chance to make friends with one another. These are often supportive friendships that help parents through the early weeks and months after birth.

For the birth to be an emotionally satisfying experience

Antenatal and parenting classes focus on making the birth an emotionally satisfying experience by:

- enabling discussion of emotions and feelings during pregnancy, birth and after the birth, so that parents have realistic expectations
- enabling the creation of a personalised birth plan
- enabling the father/partner to plan how they will participate in the birth and support the mother
- providing refresher classes for those who have already had a baby
- providing information about the sources of support.

Promotion of healthy lifestyle and breastfeeding

Promotion of a healthy lifestyle is a key part of antenatal classes. As well as learning about diet and exercise, parents will learn about the negative impact of smoking, alcohol and recreational drugs during pregnancy and after the birth. (See Learning outcome 1.) They will also learn about the many benefits of breastfeeding. You can read about these on pages 126-7.

Activity

The importance of antenatal and parenting classes

Find out more about private parenting classes by visiting this link: www.parentskool.co.uk.

- Read the information.
- Click the link to explore the 'practical tips and links' section. Read the advice.
- Now use a search engine to research the antenatal and parenting classes available in your local area.

2.3 Routine checks carried out at an antenatal clinic, including scans

At week eight of the pregnancy, a mother will have her first antenatal appointment, usually with a midwife. During the appointment, the midwife will carry out some routine checks (see below). These checks will be repeated on later visits, to monitor the health of mother and baby. The midwife will ask lots of questions to build up a picture of the mother's medical history, and an appointment for the first scan will also be organised.

Weight check

Women are weighed when they are first booked in to record a baseline weight. The weight of the mother can then be tracked and monitored against this throughout the pregnancy. If a woman gains more weight than expected, it could be a sign of a medical condition called pre-eclampsia, and treatment will be necessary. Weight loss could indicate that the baby has stopped growing, and can also be a sign of illness in the mother.

? Did you know?

Women are expected to gain 10–12.5 kg during a normal, healthy pregnancy.

Blood tests

Blood tests are taken when booking in, to check for the following and reveal possible problems:

- Anaemia – this condition can cause tiredness and listlessness, due to a lack of iron. Folic acid and iron tablets may be needed.
- High blood sugar – this will reveal if the mother has diabetes. It is possible for diabetes to develop during the pregnancy and pass afterwards.
- Blood group – this information is required in case a blood transfusion is needed during pregnancy or birth. This can occur if the mother bleeds excessively.
- German measles (rubella) – this will reveal whether the woman is immune to German measles, a very dangerous disease for the developing unborn baby. It can cause brain damage, deafness and blindness.
- Hepatitis B and C – without treatment, these conditions can cause liver disease.
- HIV – this can be passed from mother to baby via the placenta in pregnancy or via breastfeeding after birth.

Blood pressure

A baseline blood pressure (BP) measurement is taken to be used for comparative monitoring throughout the pregnancy. The average healthy BP range for a younger mother (35 or under) is 110/70–120/80. Blood pressure above 140/90 can indicate pre-eclampsia in a mother whose BP is usually within the average range.

Urine test

A urine test can also reveal potential problems during pregnancy. Protein in the urine might be the result of an infection. It can also indicate the onset of a serious condition such as pre-eclampsia further along in the pregnancy. Glucose (sugar) in the urine can indicate diabetes, which will need to be controlled by diet and sometimes also insulin. Ketones might be present if a mother has been vomiting excessively (known as hyperemesis). In this case, hospitalisation is needed, and fluids and glucose might need to be replaced via a drip. Without treatment, a condition called ketosis can occur, which can lead to a coma and even death, so this test is very important.

STIs

Sexually transmitted infections (STIs) can be harmful for an unborn baby. STIs can be pre-existing, or caught during pregnancy. When caught during pregnancy, they can be more serious, and even life-threatening in some cases, for the mother and the baby. STIs including chlamydia, gonorrhea, syphilis, trichomoniasis and bacterial vaginosis (BV) can be treated and cured with antibiotics during pregnancy. STIs caused by viruses, such as genital herpes, hepatitis B and HIV cannot be cured. But these conditions may be treated to reduce the risk of the STI being passed to the baby.

Examination of the uterus

Examination of the uterus is routinely performed throughout a pregnancy, by both doctors and midwives. The doctor or midwife will place a gloved index and middle finger into the vagina up to the cervix. They will assess:

- how soft the cervix is
- whether there is any thinning (effacement) or opening (dilation) of the cervix
- the position of the cervix, whether posterior (facing the tailbone) or anterior (facing the front)
- how far into the pelvis the baby has descended
- which way the baby is facing (presentation).

Baby's heartbeat

The baby's heartbeat will be checked and monitored at each appointment. This confirms that the baby is alive. The midwife will also be listening to hear if the heartbeat is normal. The expected heartbeat of an unborn baby is 110–160 beats per minute.

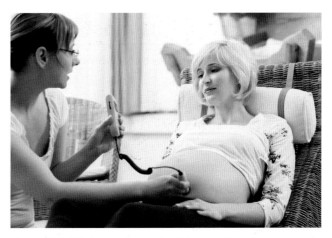

Figure 2.3: A baby's heartbeat will be monitored.

Ultrasound dating scan

Around 8–14 weeks into pregnancy, an ultrasound dating scan is offered to the mother, with a professional called a sonographer. It is usually carried out in a hospital ultrasound department. This scan checks:

- how far along the pregnancy is, enabling the sonographer to work out the baby's due date
- the baby's development
- whether more than one baby is expected
- that the baby is growing in the right place.

Some abnormalities may also be detected, such as neural tube defects (for example spina bifida).

? Did you know?

During an ultrasound scan, the sonographer passes the ultrasound probe backwards and forwards over the skin to build up an image of the baby. Gel is applied to the abdomen (tummy) to form a bond between the probe and the skin for a better result.

2.4 Specialised diagnostic tests

A number of these are offered to women during pregnancy:

- ultrasound anomaly scan/mid-pregnancy scan
- nuchal fold translucency scan
- alpha fetoprotein (AFP) test
- chorionic villus sampling (CVS)
- amniocentesis
- non-invasive prenatal testing (NIPT) blood test.

These tests are described in more detail below.

Ultrasound anomaly scan/ mid-pregnancy scan

This is a more detailed scan, generally carried out between 18 and 21 weeks of pregnancy. It checks for major physical abnormalities in the baby, but cannot find everything that might be wrong. The scan looks at the baby's:

- bones
- heart
- brain
- spinal cord
- face
- kidneys
- abdomen.

The sonographer will look for the following 11 conditions:

- anencephaly
- open spina bifida
- cleft lip
- diaphragmatic hernia
- gastrochisis
- exomphalos
- serious cardiac abnormalities
- bilateral renal agenesis
- lethal skeletal dysplasia
- Edwards' syndrome, or t18
- Patau's syndrome, or t13.

Most babies will be developing normally. But serious problems are identified in a small amount

Good practice

Mothers can choose whether to have scans – not everyone wants to find out if their baby has a problem. If a mother decides against having a scan, her antenatal care will continue as normal in all other respects.

? Did you know?

The NHS offers a two-dimensional black and white image, giving a side view of the baby, at the anomaly/mid-pregnancy scan. This is treasured by many parents.

of cases. Some of the problems identified may mean the baby will need treatment or surgery after birth. In rare cases, no treatment is possible, and the baby will die during pregnancy or soon after birth. If a scan picks up a problem, further tests may be offered.

Nuchal translucency (NT) test

Nuchal translucency refers to a fluid under the skin at the back of the unborn baby's neck. The amount of fluid present can be measured using ultrasound; babies with Down's syndrome often have an increased amount (Snijders et al 1998: 351, 343–6) of this fluid. All mothers are offered a test to look for this at around week 11–13 of pregnancy, to assess whether their baby is likely to have Down's syndrome. Screening can only estimate the level of risk – it cannot determine whether or not the baby definitely has Down's syndrome. Other tests (see below) can accurately diagnose Down's syndrome, but as these carry a small risk of miscarriage, the obstetrician will carry out a screening test first to see whether a diagnostic test should be offered. A blood test may also be carried out alongside the NT test. Not all mothers will choose to have the NT test, and not all mothers who are given a high likelihood of Down's syndrome result will go on to have a diagnostic test. This is the mother's decision.

Alpha fetoprotein (AFP) test

AFP is a substance made in the liver of an unborn baby. An AFP blood test checks the level of AFP in the mother's blood. This can reveal whether a baby might have a condition such as spina bifida or anencephaly.

Chorionic villus sampling (CVS)

This test checks if a baby has a genetic disorder, such as Down's syndrome, through the removal and testing of a small sample of cells from the placenta. The test is only offered if there is a high risk of a baby having a genetic condition – if:

- an earlier antenatal screening test has indicated a problem
- the mother has had a previous pregnancy with these problems
- there is family history of a genetic condition.

CVS is usually carried out between weeks 11 and 14 of pregnancy. Cells are removed from the placenta via:

- transabdominal CVS – a needle is inserted through the mother's abdomen, or
- transcervical CVS – a tube (or small forceps) is inserted through the cervix.

Risks of CVS

The CVS test carries a risk of miscarriage, which occurs in between one and two per cent of women who have CVS. There is also a risk of infection, and for these reasons, not all mothers offered the test will decide to go ahead. There is no cure for the majority of conditions detected via CVS. If a serious disorder is detected, the implications will be fully discussed. The mother may choose to continue with the pregnancy, while gathering information about the condition so she is fully prepared, or she may consider a termination.

Amniocentesis

This procedure also tests for genetic disorders and may be offered as an alternative to the CVS test (and in the same circumstances as the CVS test). It is generally carried out between weeks 15 and 18 of pregnancy, when a small sample of amniotic fluid (the fluid that surrounds the baby in the womb) is removed for testing.

Risks of amniocentesis

The risk of causing miscarriage is slightly reduced with amniocentesis as compared with CVS, but results cannot be given until a later stage of pregnancy, which has implications for the possibility of terminating the pregnancy if a problem is found.

Non-invasive prenatal testing (NIPT) blood test

NIPT is a screening test that assesses the likelihood of having a baby with Down's syndrome, Edwards' syndrome or Patau's syndrome. It can be carried out from week ten of pregnancy, which is earlier than alternative tests. It is also more accurate and does not carry a risk of miscarriage. A blood sample is taken from the mother's arm, and fragments of the baby's DNA within this are analysed for possible chromosomal abnormalities. If the risk of chromosomal abnormality is found to be high, a diagnostic test such as CVS or amniocentesis will be offered.

NHS hospitals do not generally offer NIPT, therefore most parents wanting the test will need to pay to have it done privately. Some choose to have NIPT before deciding to have a diagnostic test that carries a risk of miscarriage, because when a high-risk NIPT result is given, it is likely that the diagnostic test will also be positive. If the NIPT is negative, the parents may decide against a diagnostic test.

2.5 The choices available for delivery

There are several choices available when it comes to the delivery and birth. To make the right choice, a mother needs the right information. The GP will normally be the first to provide information explaining the options. The mother can also talk the options over with her midwife at an early appointment, and with the leader of antenatal and parenting classes. The following diagram shows the choices available. Often, not all of the provision will be available within one local area. For example, some mothers may have a consultant-led unit nearby, while others may have a midwife or GP-led unit.

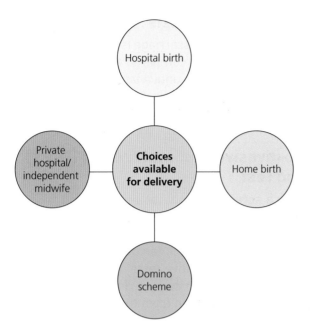

Figure 2.4: The choices available for delivery. Which of these options is available in your area?

Hospital birth

Types of hospital provision vary locally and can include:

- consultant-led units
- midwife or GP-led units
- birthing centres (this environment is generally the most homely).

Delivery rooms in hospitals are becoming increasingly home-like and comfortable, with furniture such as soft chairs and beanbags. These enable mothers to change position, which can help with pain management. Warm baths and showers may also be available (most commonly in birthing centres), and these can also soothe and ease pain during early labour.

Maternity units increasingly offer birthing pools, which as well as comfort and pain relief, also enables a water birth if labour progresses normally. A water birth will need to be arranged ahead of time as part of the birthing plan, because of the limited number of pools available.

Advantages of hospital births include the following:

- Highly trained staff and equipment are available should an emergency arise – this could save a baby's life and is reassuring for parents.

- Some types of pain relief can only be given in hospital.
- Forceps, ventouse and Caesarean section deliveries can only be carried out in hospital (see below).
- Midwives are on hand after the birth to help with concerns and issues such as feeding, and can let a mother rest by taking a baby into the nursery.
- The demands of the mother's home life are left behind.

Home birth

Home birth is an option when the pregnancy is normal and mother and baby are both well. Support is given by a midwife, who attends during labour. If the labour does not progress normally or the mother needs help, the midwife's role is then to arrange a transfer to hospital. Advantages of a home birth include the following:

- The mother is in familiar, relaxing surroundings.
- Labour is not interrupted by travelling to hospital.
- If the new baby has older siblings, they will not need to be separated from the mother as she gives birth, and they can be involved in the labour/birth.
- The mother is more likely to be looked after by a midwife she has seen throughout the pregnancy.
- An intervention such as forceps or ventouse is less likely than when giving birth in hospital.

Other considerations with home birth:

- A transfer to a hospital may be needed if there are complications.
- The NHS report that for women having their second or subsequent baby, a planned home birth is as safe as having a baby in hospital or a midwife-led unit. However, for women having their first baby, home birth slightly increases the risk of a poor outcome for the baby (from 5 in 1,000 for a hospital birth to 9 in 1,000 – almost 1 per cent – for a home birth). Poor outcomes include death of the baby and problems that might affect the baby's quality of life.
- Epidurals (for pain relief) are not given at home.
- A midwife or doctor might advise that a hospital birth is safer for a mother and baby in some circumstances.

Domino scheme

The Domino scheme is operated by some hospitals. It involves community midwives providing antenatal care and then meeting the mother at the hospital for the delivery. In many cases, the midwife is able to assess the mother closely during labour, so the move to hospital will not be made until close to the delivery. If all is well, the mother and baby will be able to leave hospital after six hours. This means that the hospital stay can be shortened.

Private hospital/independent midwife

Some parents pay for a private hospital or independent midwife, rather than accessing free NHS provision. This decision might be made by some parents who can afford it because they feel that the standard of the provision is higher than that of the NHS. A private hospital is also a popular choice for families who are in the public eye. As they are not public buildings, it is easier for their privacy to be protected.

You were introduced to independent midwives on page 19. An independent midwife might not undertake all of the responsibilities of NHS midwives, so mothers may in fact use both services. For example, post birth and with support given soon after, an independent midwife may have fulfilled their role. If advice on feeding is needed after a few weeks, the mother might then contact an NHS midwife for advice.

Activity

The choices available for delivery

Find out more about choices available for delivery by visiting this NHS website: www.nhs.uk/conditions/pregnancy-and-baby/pages/where-can-i-give-birth.aspx.

- Read the information and watch the video clip.
- Now follow these NHS links, reading the advice and watching the video clips about home birth: www.nhs.uk/video/Pages/what-is-a-home-birth-like.aspx, www.nhs.uk/video/Pages/Givingbirthathome.aspx.

2.6 The stages of labour and the methods of delivery, including pain relief

Every labour is different, but all pass through three common stages. These are divided into:

- stage one – labour
- stage two – birth
- stage three – delivery of placenta and membranes.

Read on to learn more.

Stage one – neck of the uterus opens

Signs that labour is beginning include the following:

- Contractions – the uterus muscles start to contract and release. Contractions gradually become stronger and occur increasingly closer together.
- The waters break – the bag of amniotic fluid around the baby bursts, causing anything from a trickle to a gush of liquid from the vagina. It is now time to go to hospital (or chosen birth option) because there is a risk of infection for the baby.
- Show – not all women experience a show, but it can occur when a plug of mucus that has sealed off the uterus during pregnancy comes away from the cervix as it dilates (gets wider). This will be stained with blood, but no blood should be lost.

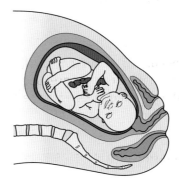

Figure 2.5: The first stage of labour.

As the neck of the uterus continues to open:

- More pain relief is required as the contractions become stronger, more regular and longer lasting. A warm bath can help.
- Mothers are encouraged to actively move around in an upright position.
- The cervix gradually dilates to 8–10 cm wide.
- If the head of the baby is not already engaged in the mother's pelvis, it will move into position.
- As the end of this stage approaches, intense contractions can cause the mother to feel agitated, and to vomit, sweat or shiver. Due to pressure from the baby's head, she may lose bladder and/or bowel control.
- When contractions get even closer together, stronger and more intense, the mother enters the **transition stage** that leads into the second stage of labour.

🔑 Key term

Transition stage this links the end of the first stage of labour and the beginning of the second stage of labour.

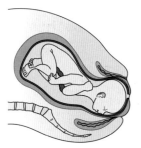

Figure 2.6: Diagram of a baby with the head engaged.

Stage two – the birth of the baby

This stage starts when the cervix becomes fully dilated at 10 cm, and ends when the baby has been born.

- The vagina and the open cervix now form a single passage known as the birth canal. The head of the baby moves into the birth canal.
- The mother begins to push with each contraction, to help move the baby down the birth canal. This can be exhausting, and she will need to rest between contractions.
- When the baby's head can be seen (crowning), it is time to stop pushing so that the head is born gradually and safely. Instead, the mother will pant or blow out, to control her breathing. The head must be born slowly to avoid the mother's skin tearing between the vagina and rectum (the perineum). A cut (an episiotomy) may need to be made if the perineum does not stretch enough.
- The hard work of labour is over once the head has been born, as the body can be turned so that the shoulders are delivered one at a time. This will be followed by the rest of the baby's body, which slides out easily. If the baby needs mucus removing from its airways or to be given oxygen, this can be done as soon as the head is born, before the rest of the body is delivered.

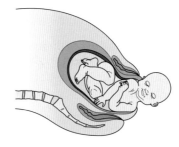

Figure 2.7: The second stage of labour.

- Finally, the umbilical cord will be clamped and cut. The father/partner might cut the cord themselves. The baby is likely to be placed on the mother for skin-to-skin contact. Some blood from the birth and a protective layer of oily vernix (see page 35) are likely to be present on the baby's skin.

Stage three – delivery of placenta and membranes

In the shortest stage of labour which follows the birth:

- contractions begin again and these push the placenta out
- an injection of syntocinon may be given to stimulate contractions and speed up the process. This helps to prevent the loss of blood and is helpful if the mother is exhausted
- if a tear occurred in the perineum or a cut was made, it will sewed up under local anaesthetic.

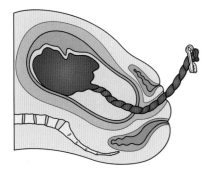

Figure 2.8: The third stage of labour.

Methods of delivery

There are various methods of delivery. Some will be planned in advance, while others become necessary should help be needed during labour. The NHS reports that about one in eight women has an assisted birth, where forceps or a ventouse suction cup are used to help deliver the baby's head. This can be because:

- there are concerns about the baby's heart rate
- the baby is in an awkward position
- the mother is too exhausted.

The procedures are safe but are only used when necessary.

Forceps

Forceps looks similar to tongs – a curved metal instrument that fits around a baby's head. They are carefully positioned, then joined together at the handles. As the mother pushes with a contraction, an obstetrician gently pulls to help deliver the baby. Some forceps are designed to turn the baby to the right position to be born, if this is necessary. Forceps are usually more successful than ventouse (see below), but are more likely to result in vaginal tearing.

Ventouse

A ventouse (vacuum extractor) is a plastic or metal cup that fits firmly on the baby's head and is attached by suction. As the mother pushes with a contraction, an obstetrician gently pulls to help deliver the baby. The process leaves a small swelling on the baby's head, which will disappear quickly. The cup may also leave a temporary bruise. A ventouse is not used with babies born before week 34 of pregnancy because the head is too soft.

> **? Did you know?**
>
> Risks of assisted birth include vaginal tearing or episiotomy, higher chance of having a vaginal tear that involves the muscle or wall of the anus or rectum, higher risk of blood clots, leaking urine, anal incontinence. A catheter is sometimes needed for a short period.

Elective/emergency caesarean section

A caesarean section is an operation to deliver a baby through a cut made in the abdomen and womb. A caesarean may be recommended as an elective (planned) procedure or done in an emergency if a vaginal birth becomes unsafe. Reasons for a caesarean include:

- the baby being in the breech position (feet first)
- a low-lying placenta (placenta praevia)
- pre-eclampsia
- infections such as STIs and untreated HIV
- the baby not getting enough oxygen and nutrients so needs to be delivered immediately
- labour is not progressing
- excessive vaginal bleeding.

Caesareans are a major operation and there are risks, so they are not suitable for every mother.

Did you know?

Around one in every four to five pregnant women in the UK has a caesarean.

Pain relief

It is natural for mothers to be concerned about handling the pain of childbirth, so it is important that they consider the options for pain relief when they make their birth plan.

Gas and air (Entonox)

This mixture of oxygen and nitrous oxide gas does not remove all the pain, but it can help to reduce it. Mothers breathe in the gas and air through a mask or mouthpiece which they hold themselves – this gives them a sense of control. It works within about 20 seconds, so a deep slow breath will be taken as a contraction begins. There may be a light-headed sensation, and some mothers decide to stop using it as they may feel sick, sleepy or unable to concentrate. A painkilling injection can be given alongside if this pain relief is not sufficient.

Pethidine

This opiate-based drug is given by injection. It quickly makes the mother feel relaxed because it causes the muscles to relax. This makes pain more tolerable, but it does not take it away altogether. Used in early labour, it can help the mother to settle and rest. It cannot be used too close to birth because the mother might not be sufficiently alert and it could also cause the baby to become sleepy. This could adversely affect feeding and even breathing. Pethidine can cause some mothers to feel sick or disoriented.

Epidural anaesthetic

This is a local anaesthetic that numbs the nerves that carry the pain impulses from the birth canal to the brain. It can provide total pain relief, but it is not always 100 per cent effective. It is often used when a mother is experiencing a very long or painful labour, or when a mother becomes distressed. An epidural can only be given by an anaesthetist in hospital.

The mother lies on her side or sits curled up. Local anaesthetic is used to numb the back, then a needle is inserted. A tube passes through the needle into the back, near the nerves that carry pain impulses from the uterus. Drugs, usually a mixture of local anaesthetic and opioid, are administered through this tube. It takes about 10 minutes to administer an epidural, and up to another 15 minutes for it to work. It can then be topped up if necessary. An epidural does not usually cause sickness or drowsiness, but the mother's contractions and the baby's heart rate will need to be continuously monitored. Possible side effects include:

- legs feeling heavy
- blood pressure dropping (this is rare)
- prolonged second stage of labour as contractions may not be felt, leading to increased likelihood of assisted delivery
- difficulty passing urine
- a headache (this can be treated)
- a sore back for a day or two afterwards.

TENS

TENS stands for 'transcutaneous electrical nerve stimulation'. A TENS machine is a small device that has leads connected to sticky pads called electrodes. These are attached to the mother's skin. Small electrical impulses are delivered– these give a tingling sensation. They reduce the pain signals going to the spinal cord and brain, relieving pain and relaxing muscles. It is possible that they also stimulate the production of endorphins – the body's 'natural painkillers'. For most people, TENS carries no side effects (there are special pads for people with allergies), but it should not be used:

- if the mother has a pacemaker or another type of electrical or metal implant
- if the mother has epilepsy or a heart problem
- in some cases early in pregnancy.

Water birth

Water can help a mother to relax, and this in turn makes contractions more bearable. The water should be kept at a comfortable temperature, but not above 37.5°C. The mother's temperature will be monitored throughout. This is because a raised maternal temperature increases the oxygen requirement of the baby, which may not be able to meet an increased oxygen need. There is more about water birth on page 26.

Figure 2.9: Waterbirth: water can help a mother to relax.

Breathing and relaxation techniques

See page 21.

Activity

Look back over the thought storm you created in the 'Getting started' activity on page 2. With the knowledge you have now gained, repeat the activity, adding to your previous thought storm.

Now choose three of the concerns. For each of these, explain and discuss what information a mother could be given for reassurance purposes.

Test your knowledge

1 Explain the roles of three different health professionals who will support a pregnant mother.
2 Outline why antenatal and parenting classes are important.
3 What is an ultrasound scan?
4 Outline the purpose of two different diagnostic tests that are offered during pregnancy.
5 Outline the choices available for the delivery.
6 Outline the three stages of labour.
7 What is pethidine?

Question practice

Question

Some methods of baby delivery are shown in the box below.

| Forceps | | Caesarean section | | Ventouse |

Complete the table to match each method of delivery with the brief description given.

Method of delivery	Description
	This method is an operation to deliver a baby through a cut made in the abdomen and womb.
	A plastic or metal cup that fits firmly on the baby's head and is attached by suction. As the mother pushes with a contraction, an obstetrician gently pulls to help deliver the baby.
	A curved metal instrument that looks similar to tongs and fits around a baby's head. They are carefully positioned, then joined together at the handles. As the mother pushes with a contraction, an obstetrician gently pulls to help deliver the baby.

Mark scheme and additional guidance

Expected answers	Marks	Additional guidance
Three required, one **mark** each. The answers should appear in the table in the following order: ● **Caesarean section:** This method is an operation to deliver a baby through a cut made in the abdomen and womb. ● **Ventouse:** A plastic or metal cup that fits firmly on the baby's head and is attached by suction. ... ● **Forceps:** A curved metal instrument that looks similar to tongs and fits around a baby's head. ...	3	One mark is awarded for each correctly matched answer. No other answers are acceptable.

Candidate answer

Method of delivery	Description
Caesarean section	This method is an operation to deliver a baby through a cut made in the abdomen and womb.
Forceps	A plastic or metal cup that fits firmly on the baby's head and is attached by suction. As the mother pushes with a contraction, an obstetrician gently pulls to help deliver the baby.
Ventouse	A curved metal instrument that looks similar to tongs and fits around a baby's head. They are carefully positioned, then joined together at the handles. As the mother pushes with a contraction, an obstetrician gently pulls to help deliver the baby.

Commentary

Question context/content/style:

Match the method of delivery with the brief descriptions given.

Requirements:

- Correct matching of three methods of delivery with their brief descriptions.

Marks awarded and rationale: 1/3

- The first method of delivery has been matched correctly, gaining one mark.
- The second and third methods of delivery have not been matched correctly, so no marks are gained.

Question

b   Anya is pregnant and has received her first blood test at an antenatal clinic. State one condition and a reason for which her blood will be checked.

Expected answers	Marks	Additional guidance
One condition and **one** reason are required.	3	A condition is stated for which Anya's blood will be tested. A reason is also given.
● Anaemia. This condition can cause tiredness and listlessness, due to a lack of iron. Folic acid and iron tablets may be needed.		
● High blood sugar. This will reveal if the mother has diabetes. It is possible for diabetes to develop during the pregnancy and pass afterwards.		
● German measles (rubella). This will reveal whether the woman is immune to German measles, a very dangerous disease for the developing unborn baby. It can cause brain damage, deafness and blindness.		One or two marks: you will only state a condition and give a basic reason. This will lack clarity OR just justification/reasons for which Anya's blood will be checked.
● Hepatitis B and C. Without treatment, these conditions can cause liver disease.		Three marks: you will state one condition and a reason that clearly shows you understand the condition and why her blood will be checked for it.
● HIV. This can be passed from mother to baby via the placenta in pregnancy or via breastfeeding after birth. Specific care practices and treatment will be needed.		Please note: Only a three mark answer is shown in the first column.

Candidate answer

The blood test will check for HIV. This is an important check because a mother with HIV can pass the condition on to baby. This might happen in pregnancy or it could happen during breastfeeding once the baby has arrived. Special care practices and treatment will be necessary.

Commentary

Question context/content/style:

One condition and a reason for which a pregnant mother's blood will be checked at an antenatal clinic are given.

Requirements:

- Correct condition stated.
- Correct reason given which shows understanding of the condition.

Marks awarded and rationale: 3/3

- The answer is correct and gains three marks.

Learning outcome 3

Understand postnatal checks, postnatal provision and conditions for development

About this Learning outcome

It is extremely helpful for you to be familiar with the postnatal checks, postnatal provision and conditions for development. This will enable you to offer understanding and support to both parents and baby in the early days and weeks after the birth.

Assessment criteria

In this learning outcome you will cover:

3.1 The postnatal checks of the newborn baby.

3.2 The specific needs of the pre-term (premature) baby.

3.3 The postnatal provision available for the mother and baby, and the postnatal needs of the family.

3.4 Conditions for development.

Getting started

Write a list of all of the ideal conditions you think babies need to thrive and develop well, for example warmth.

3.1 The postnatal checks of the newborn baby

Straight after the birth, the doctor and/or midwife will carry out some routine checks to find out if the baby has any obvious physical problems.

Apgar score

The **Apgar score** (see page 35 for definition) is used to evaluate the physical condition of a newborn, by assessing five vital signs:

- heartbeat
- breathing
- muscle tone
- reflex response (when the foot or nostril is stimulated)
- colour.

The score is used to assess how well the baby is doing outside the mother's womb, and whether it needs medical assistance. This quick assessment is carried out one minute after birth, and again at five minutes after birth. If a problem is identified, reassessment may continue every five minutes. Scores are given out of ten (each sign can score between zero and two). The majority of healthy babies score nine – many of them lose a point because they have blue extremities, and this is a condition that

Key term

Apgar score a score given to evaluate the physical condition of a newborn on assessment of their vital signs.

can last several hours after birth. In hospital, a paediatrician will be informed if there is a score of six or under after five minutes. (Low scores at one minute are not so concerning, as many babies will score higher by five minutes.) Babies who score between five and seven will be showing signs of mild asphyxia (lack of oxygen in the blood) and may need treatment. A score of between three and four indicates moderate asphyxia that will certainly need treatment. A baby scoring between zero and two has severe asphyxia and will need emergency resuscitation.

Skin

A newborn baby's skin can be damaged easily because it is very thin. It will take a month or so for it to develop and mature into a protective barrier – longer if a baby is premature.

A baby's skin will be checked for birthmarks.

Salmon patches (stork marks)
Salmon patches are flat red or pink patches that appear on the eyelids, neck or forehead at birth. They can be more noticeable when a baby cries because they fill with blood and become darker, and most fade completely in a few months. On the forehead or the back of the neck they can remain for four years or longer.

Mongolian spots
Mongolian spots are bluish patches of darker pigment, appearing most commonly over the bottom and on black skin. They can be mistaken for bruises, but are completely harmless. They usually disappear by the age of four.

Infantile haemangiomas (strawberry marks)
These are raised marks on the skin that are usually red, and can appear anywhere on the body. They grow in the first six months but then shrink and disappear, usually by seven years of age.

Vernix

Vernix is the white, waxy substance that covers a baby's skin while it is in the womb. Newborns will have this on their skin at birth. It is a natural moisturiser and provides a protective layer that helps to prevent infection, so it should be left to absorb naturally into the skin. If a baby is overdue, the vernix may have been absorbed while in the womb, leading to dry and cracked skin. Avoid creams or lotions, as these can irritate the baby's skin. The top layer of skin will peel off on its own over a few days, revealing perfectly healthy skin underneath.

Lanugo

During pregnancy, at around 22 weeks, a baby begins to become covered in lanugo – a soft, fine hair that is usually unpigmented (it does not have colour). It is thought that this downy hair helps to keep the baby's body at the right temperature. Lanugo is generally shed during months 7–8 of pregnancy, but it is sometimes present in premature babies and full-term newborns. This is no cause for concern though, and the lanugo disappears within a few days or weeks.

Physical checks

After new parents have had time to cuddle their baby and have skin-to-skin contact, which is important for bonding, some more physical checks will be done, and these are outlined below. Within 72 hours of a baby being born, all parents in the UK are also offered a thorough physical examination of their baby, and after that there will continue to be regular checks to monitor a baby's growth and development. This is extremely important, as it enables any problems to be identified and treated as early as possible.

Weight

The baby's weight will be recorded in a Personal Child Health Record (the 'red book'), which is given to all parents. A full-term baby usually weighs 2.7–4.1 kg (6–9 lb). The weight is tracked on **centile charts** (see page 36 for definition), which show the expected pattern of growth of a healthy baby, so that comparisons can be made over the coming weeks and months. Steady

Did you know?

Boys and girls have different centile charts because their growth pattern is slightly different. Baby boys are often heavier and longer than baby girls.

Key term

Centile charts charts showing the expected pattern of growth of a healthy baby, against which comparisons can be made.

weight gain is an important sign that a baby is healthy and feeding well. It is normal for babies to lose some of their birth weight within the first few days, but this should soon be regained – usually within two weeks. Support will be given by a health professional if this does not happen.

Length

As with weight, length is also recorded on centile charts, which allows health professionals to see how the baby is growing. The length of a full-term newborn is usually 50–53 cm.

Head circumference

The shape of the baby's head is assessed and the circumference measured. This will also be used to track the baby's development over the coming weeks and months. A squashed appearance is common, as a result of the baby being squeezed through the birth canal. This usually resolves itself within two days.

Fontanelle

A baby's head has soft spots, called the fontanelles, between the bones in the skull. This is because the skull bones have not yet fused (joined) together when the baby is born. These soft spots are covered by a tough protective membrane, and there is one on the top of the head near the front, and a smaller one towards the back. They will be checked, but it will be a year or more before the bones join together.

Eyes

Eye tests do not reveal how well a baby can actually see – they allow health professionals to check for cataracts and other conditions, by assessing the appearance and movement of the eyes. This involves shining a light into the eyes to check a reflex. If a baby has cataracts, there will be a clouding of the transparent lens inside the eye. The NHS reports that around 2 or 3 in every 10,000 babies are born with problems with their eyes that require treatment.

Mouth

A finger is placed in the mouth to check that the palate (roof of the mouth) is complete and the baby's sucking reflex is working (Also see page 37).

Feet

The toes will be counted and checked for webbing. The natural resting position of the baby's feet and ankles will be observed to check for talipes (clubfoot) – a condition in which the front half of the foot turns in and down. Talipes may already have been identified in an ultrasound scan.

Fingers

Fingers will be counted and checked for webbing. The baby's palms will be checked to see if two creases (palmar creases), run across them. A single palmar crease is sometimes associated with Down's syndrome.

Hips

A health professional will check the baby for 'developmental dysplasia of the hip' – this is a condition in which the hip joints have not formed properly. This can result in joint problems or a limp if it is not identified and treated. Around 1 or 2 in 1,000 babies are born with the condition.

Reflexes

A health professional will observe the newborn baby to see if it is displaying the expected reflexes. If these do not occur naturally, they may stimulate the baby to elicit the reflex they wish to see.

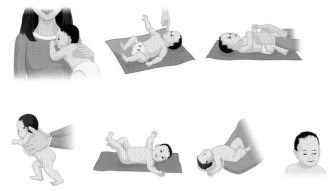

Figure 3.1: Reflexes.

Examples of reflexes are:

- **the sucking reflex –** if you gently touch the roof of a baby's mouth they will make sucking motions. This motion allows them to feed.
- **the rooting reflex –** when a baby's lips or cheek is touched, the newborn will move their head; they are searching for their mother's nipple or a bottle teat so that they can feed
- **the grasp reflex –** if you touch a baby's palm, they will grasp your fingers with their fingers
- **the standing and walking reflex –** when a baby is held upright with their feet on a firm surface, they make stepping movements with their legs (but they cannot yet take their own weight)
- **the startle reflex –** if a baby wakes suddenly or hears a loud noise, they will make a fist with their hands and move stiff arms away from their body.

3.2 The specific needs of the pre-term (premature) baby

Babies that need specific extra care when they are born will be cared for in a special care baby unit. Babies are admitted there for many reasons, but most commonly it is due to them being **pre-term** (born before 37 weeks, also called premature).

> ### 🔑 Key term
>
> **Pre-term** a baby born before week 37 of pregnancy.

Birth before 37 weeks

By around week 12 of pregnancy, a baby is formed. For the remaining weeks, the baby continues to develop and grow. Babies born before 37 weeks are not developed enough to survive outside the womb without medical help. They are likely to have some or all of the following:

- breathing difficulties due to undeveloped lungs
- a weak immune system that makes infection more likely
- inability to suck and swallow, and difficulty digesting milk
- problems regulating body temperature
- low calcium and iron levels
- jaundice (yellow tinged skin) or red wrinkled skin
- weak muscle tone and little movement
- sealed eyes
- low blood-sugar levels
- a head that seems large in proportion to the rest of the body.

Pre-term babies

Pre-term babies often need extra vitamins and minerals for growth, so many are given supplements. Special formula milks are also available, although it is best to breastfeed if possible. A baby that is too weak to feed normally will be fed through a tube into a vein – this is called an intravenous (IV) line. Alternatively, they may be fed through a fine tube that goes into the stomach – either via the nose and throat or through the mouth.

Specific needs

Treatment for infection

Some babies acquire an infection during the birth process, and there is also a risk of acquiring an infection after the birth. In addition to having an immature immune system, babies who need specific care experience interventions that make them vulnerable, including blood tests, intravenous lines and intubation tubes. Treatments may be given for:

- bacterial infections – antibiotics
- fungal infections – anti fungal medications

✔ Good practice

A baby with a contagious infection (such as a respiratory virus) may be cared for in an isolated setting.

- viral infections – supportive measures such as good nutrition (specific treatments to exist for some viruses).

Breathing problems

An unborn baby's lungs are filled with liquid that helps them develop. During labour and birth this fluid is absorbed, so that air can be taken in once the baby is born. In pre-term babies, the lungs are often not mature enough to adjust after birth, so help is needed. Healthcare professionals will provide help that is as gentle as possible, because ventilators (a machine that helps with breathing) can cause lung problems.

Feeding problems

If a gap in the roof of the mouth is picked up during the mouth check, the baby is said to have a 'cleft palate'. This can make feeding very difficult, and surgery will be necessary. If a baby has persistent problems latching on during breastfeeding, they are likely to be checked for 'tongue-tie'. This is when tongue movement is restricted because the tongue is anchored to the bottom of the mouth by a piece of skin that is too short and tight. The baby might need a very simple procedure that generally overcomes feeding problems immediately.

It is very common for parents to experience issues with feeding at some point, and they may need to access information, advice and support (see below).

Figure 3.2: A father needs time to bond with their new baby.

3.3 The postnatal provision available for the mother and baby and the postnatal needs of the family

As you have learnt, having a baby is a very significant life event. A new arrival brings lots of enjoyment, but parents will also be making lots of adjustments to their usual lifestyle, and there will also be an impact on other close family members, such as siblings. The support needed depends on the individual baby and family, but postnatal provision is very important for the wellbeing of all concerned.

The role of the father/partner

The father or partner of the mother has a very significant role, and it is important that they have time to bond with the new baby alongside the mother.

They may also be the person closest to the mother and best placed to support her through the early days and weeks of motherhood, which can be difficult. It can take a great deal of time and energy to take care of the new baby. But the mother needs to take care of herself too, in order to stay fit and healthy, and in some cases to recover from the birth. The father/partner should ensure that the mother has the help and support she needs to achieve this.

The responsibility and tiredness that comes with looking after a new baby can also put a strain on the relationship between the mother and the father/partner. Family and friends can help to relieve this.

Support from other family and friends

Support from other family and friends can be a huge help to new parents, especially if their own relationship comes under pressure as they adjust to their new responsibilities. Practical help and advice are both valuable, from helping with the shopping to sharing childcare tips. Some new parents need a lot of support from family and friends who have more experience in the care of babies and children.

Information, advice and support from the GP, midwife and health visitor

The job of health visitors is to give all families support, from pregnancy until children are five. The Government claims that its Healthy Child Programme – which is spreading more widely in line with an expansion in health visitor numbers – offers every family regular contact with a health professional to make sure that their child is healthy and developing normally, and to support both parents to care well for their child.

When a child is ill, the GP will usually be the first point of contact. GPs work with others, including health visitors and those working in children's centres or nurseries, or childminders, to make sure that families get the treatment, information and advice they need to keep healthy. For details of accessing information, advice and support from a midwife, see pages 19, 25 and 26.

Postnatal check 6 weeks after birth

This check is to make sure that the mother feels well and that she is recovering properly from the birth. This is not offered in every area, but the mother can request an appointment for a check, especially if she has any concerns. There are no set guidelines for what should be covered in the check.

6–8 week review by a health visitor or doctor

This check repeats the baby's newborn physical examination. There are some local variations, but generally a mother can also expect:

- questions about how she is feeling in terms of mental health and wellbeing
- to be asked if she has any vaginal discharge and whether there has been a period since the birth
- a blood pressure check if there were problems at the birth
- to be offered an examination to see if stitches have healed (if relevant)
- to be asked about contraception
- to be weighed if overweight or obese, and to receive weight loss advice, and guidance on healthy eating and physical activity.

If there are concerns or queries at any point, parents can contact their midwife, health visitor or GP to ask for help and advice. They can drop in to local clinics, which may be held at a children's centre, GP surgery or a community venue, to speak to somebody from the health visiting team. For urgent queries that involve the health of a baby, parents should contact their GP, NHS 111 or go to an NHS Walk-in Centre or the nearest accident and emergency (A&E) department as soon as possible.

3.4 Conditions for development

In order for them to successfully thrive, develop and grow, children need certain basic conditions.

The importance of the environment to the child

A positive environment is crucial to a child, and the following needs must be met.

Love and security

All children need to feel loved, wanted and nurtured, and this gives rise to feeling emotionally secure (see page 7). Children also need to be kept physically secure and safe from harm (see page 61).

Warmth

See page 7.

Rest/sleep

See page 7.

Exercise/fresh air

Exercise and fresh air are good for a child's physical health and wellbeing – young children are built to be busy and active. Sufficient exercise builds fitness, robustness and helps strong growth and development. A lack of exercise can have a very negative effect on health, fitness and development.

Cleanliness

Children need clean and appropriately hygienic environments. As their immune systems are less mature, it is much easier for a child to pick up an infection. Cleanliness in kitchen areas is especially important (see page 123). The child must also be bathed daily and kept clean and fresh. Their clothing and bedding should be regularly laundered.

Stimulation/opportunities to play

All children need opportunities to play in ways that are appropriate to their stage of development (see Unit R020). Under the UN Convention on the Rights of the Child, all children have a fundamental right to play.

Opportunities for listening and talking

Listening and talking with a child shows that you care about them and are interested in them. This is very important to their social and emotional development. It is also vital for their intellectual and language development – just think of all the things a child learns in conversation.

Figure 3.3: Listening and talking with a child shows that you care about them.

Routine (for example bedtime, bathtime, feeding)

Routines help young children to feel safe and secure. They also help adults to ensure that all of their care needs can be met effectively every day – for instance, feeding needs to be spread out across the day to ensure that children have the nutrition they need to keep them going (see Unit R019).

Awareness of Sudden Infant Death Syndrome (SIDS)

Parents and carers should know how to take measures to prevent SIDS. See page 89.

The need for acceptable patterns of behaviour and approaches to discipline

Children need to learn how to behave in socially acceptable ways, and adults should always strive to be positive role models for children. A consistent approach to discipline is also needed or a child may become confused, unsure or even worried about the reaction their behaviour will elicit.

Need for boundaries

Children need to be aware of the boundaries set for their behaviour. In other words, they need to know what they can and cannot do. Boundaries should also be consistent – it is unfair to send a child mixed messages. By always explaining why a particular behaviour is unacceptable, you can help a child to think through a situation. Then they will begin to moderate their own behaviour in similar situations in future.

Consideration of others

If you ask a parent what behaviour trait they would like to see in their child, they will often say that they want them to be kind and considerate towards other people. We value this highly in our society. Young children need a lot of support when they are learning how to be considerate, because it is natural for them to notice and act upon their own feelings ahead of someone else's. For instance, they might snatch a toy away from a peer because their desire for the item is greater than their awareness of how this could upset another child. In time and with lots of role-modelling and talking through social situations, children are increasingly able to be considerate

Figure 3.4: Toddlers can be empathetic towards one another.

in more situations. Toddlers can be seen being very empathetic with another child who has hurt themselves, for instance.

Safety

A lot of the rules we make are in place because they keep children safe – from holding hands when crossing the road to not being allowed to stand on the table. It is important that these rules are explained so that children gradually become more aware of how to keep themselves safe independently (also see pages 73–77).

Promoting positive behaviour

Promoting positive behaviour is by far the best way to limit inappropriate behaviour. When adults notice and praise specific positive behaviour, a child tends to feel proud of themselves, and they enjoy the approval they receive. This encourages them to repeat the socially acceptable behaviour, until it becomes an ingrained, normal part of what they do. Verbal praise is the most effective form of praise, and the easiest to give. If there is a behaviour goal in place for a child, a reward chart can also be an effective visual reward system – see the case study below for an example.

Case study

Three-year-old Darius has been having tantrums at bedtime most nights for the past three weeks. His auntie, whom he lives with, has made a sticker chart to try and help Darius settle down for sleep appropriately. She has shown him the chart, which features a picture of a space rocket, one of Darius' favourite things. Each time he goes to bed without a fuss, Darius will be given a sticker to put on the rocket. These feature windows and other details. They talk about how wonderful the rocket will look when all of the stickers have been collected. Within a few days, Darius receives three stickers. By the second week, he receives a sticker five days out of seven.

Questions

1 Why do you think Darius's behaviour is changing?

2 What other sorts of behaviour do you think might be improved with the use of a sticker chart?

3 Can you suggest other ways in which positive behaviour could be promoted in this scenario?

Test your knowledge

1 State five checks carried out on a newborn baby.

2 Explain and discuss the common signs of illness.

3 A baby is considered to be pre-term if it is born before how many weeks?

4 Outline the postnatal provision available for the mother and baby.

5 Outline five conditions for development and state why they are important.

6 Explain and discuss what is meant by promoting positive behaviour.

Question practice

Question

a Postnatal checks are carried out on newborn babies. Explain the five reflexes medical professionals will normally expect to see.

Mark Scheme and Additional Guidance

Expected answers	Marks	Additional guidance
Five required, **one** mark each. ● Sucking: if you gently touch the roof of a baby's mouth, they will make sucking motions. This motion allows them to feed. ● Rooting: when a baby's lips or cheek is touched, the newborn will move their head; they are searching for their mother's nipple or a bottle teat so that they can feed ● Grasp: if you touch a baby's palm, they will grasp your fingers with their fingers. ● Walking: when a baby is held upright with their feet on a firm surface, they make stepping movements with their legs (but they cannot yet take their own weight). ● Startle (Moro): if a baby wakes suddenly or hears a loud noise, they will make a fist with their hands and move stiff arms away from their body.	5	An explanation is given for each of the five reflexes medical professionals will normally expect to see.

Candidate answer

a) **Sucking:**

The newborn will suck anything that goes into its mouth. This reflect allows the baby to feed and is linked to the rooting reflex. Babies find sucking soothing and it doesn't always mean that they are hungry.

Rooting:

When a newborn baby's lips or cheek is touched, he or she will move their head. They do this as they are searching for their mother's nipple or a bottle teat so they can feed.

Grasp:

This can be seen when a newborn baby's palm is touched. He or she will grasp the fingers touching them with their own fingers.

Walking:

This can be seen when a newborn is held upright with their feet on a firm surface. They make stepping movements with their legs and can take their own weight.

Startle:

If a newborn wakes suddenly or hears a loud noise, they will make a fist with their hands and move stiff arms away from their body.

Commentary

Question context/content/style:

Explanation of five reflexes medical professionals normally expect to see during postnatal checks. (Five marks).

Requirements:

Correct explanation of five reflexes.

Marks awarded and rationale: 4/5

- Four reflexes have been explained correctly, gaining four marks.
- The walking answer is incorrect, as newborn babies cannot yet take their own weight when held in the standing position.

Question

b Explain the primary benefit of promoting positive behaviour through praise.

Mark scheme and additional guidance

Expected answers	Marks	Additional guidance
One required. - Verbally praising a specific positive behaviour encourages a child to repeat that behaviour, until it becomes ingrained. Other rewards may also be used occasionally (e.g. stickers). *(This would be a well-developed response.)* - Praise the child verbally because this will make them repeat those things that earned them the praise. *(This would be a developed response.)* - Praise the child by talking to them. *(This would be a basic response.)*	6	An explanation is given for the primary benefit of promoting positive behaviour through praise. Level 3 (5-6 marks): You will include a detailed explanation of the primary benefit of promoting positive behaviour through praise. Your answer will be coherent and use correct terminology. *You will include reasoning and your answer will be structured. The information you include will be relevant and supported by some evidence.* Level 2 (3-4 marks): You will include an explanation of the primary benefits of promoting positive behaviour through praise. Your answer will address some benefits but not all, and include some correct terminology. Level 1 (1–2 marks): In comparison, this will be a basic explanation or the primary benefit of promoting positive behaviour. You will include the benefit but you may include only this, or your answer may be muddled and lack detail. *The information may not include evidence/an example or the relationship to the evidence will be unclear.* *There may be alternative answers and your tutor will be able to guide you on this.*

Candidate answer

b) Promoting positive behaviour helps to limit inappropriate behaviour. Children feel proud when adults notice and praise specific positive behaviour. They enjoy the approval and feel encouraged to repeat the behaviour, until it becomes a normal, everyday part of what they do. Verbal praise is the most effective. Sometimes a reward chart can also be an effective visual reward system – this is mostly used when there is a behaviour goal in place for a child.

Commentary

Question context/content/style:

Explanation of the primary benefit of promoting positive behaviour through praise.

Requirements:

Correct explanation given.

Marks awarded and rationale: 6/6

- The answer is correct.

Learning outcome 4

Understand how to recognise, manage and prevent childhood illnesses

About this Learning outcome

Learning how to recognise, manage and prevent childhood illnesses is a vital part of keeping children safe. Babies and younger children in particular do not have the language to tell you when something is wrong and they are feeling poorly, so knowing the signs and symptoms of illness is important. Illnesses can become progressively worse and even threaten lives if they are not quickly treated, so you need to know what to do should a child become ill in your care.

Assessment criteria

In this learning outcome you will cover:

4.1 How immunity to disease and infection can be acquired.

4.2 How to recognise and treat common childhood ailments and diseases.

4.3 When to seek treatment by a doctor, and when emergency medical help should be sought.

4.4 Diet-related illnesses.

4.5 The needs of an ill child.

4.6 How to prepare a child for a stay in hospital.

Getting started

Think back to when you were young. Working with a partner, discuss a childhood illness that you had, such as chickenpox. Talk about how you felt physically (for example itchy and tired) and emotionally (for example upset to miss out on activities with friends). Now swap over and listen to your partner.

4.1 How immunity to disease and infection can be acquired

Immunity (see page 46 for definition) to disease and infection can be acquired naturally (see babies' natural immunity below) or through vaccines.

Vaccines (see page 46 for definition) make our bodies produce antibodies to fight disease, without actually infecting us with the disease. Then, if we come into contact with the disease, our immune system will recognise it and automatically produce the antibodies needed to fight it.

Key terms

Immunity when an organism has the ability to resist disease.

Vaccine a biological preparation that provides or improves immunity to a specific disease, commonly given via an injection.

Antibodies proteins made by the body that can latch on to foreign viruses and bacteria, making them ineffective.

Babies' natural immunity

During pregnancy, **antibodies** from the mother are passed to an unborn baby through the placenta. Some immunity can also be passed on through breastfeeding. But the mother can only pass on immunity that she has herself. So if a mother hasn't had chickenpox, she will not have developed immunity against it, therefore no chickenpox antibodies will be passed on. Childhood immunisations begin at two months old, because any immunity from the mother is temporary.

Did you know?

Babies receive antibodies in the last three months of pregnancy. So the immune system of premature babies is not as strong because they have had fewer antibodies passed to them. This puts them at a higher risk of disease.

Childhood immunisations and vaccination programmes

Vaccination helps to protect children against a range of serious and potentially fatal diseases. To protect children in the UK, the NHS offers a free programme of immunisations to every child, known as the 'routine immunisation schedule' – you can study an excerpt below.

Reasons for immunisation

The NHS says there are three good reasons to have a child vaccinated:

- Vaccinations are quick, safe and extremely effective.
- Once a child has been vaccinated against a disease, their body can more successfully fight it off.
- If a child is not vaccinated, they are at higher risk of catching and becoming very ill from the illness.

There will always be some children who are unavoidably unprotected because:

- they can't be vaccinated for medical reasons
- they are too young to be vaccinated
- they can't get to the vaccine clinics
- the vaccine doesn't work (although this is rare).

However, if more parents have their children vaccinated, then a greater number of children in the community will be protected against an illness.

Additional and selective vaccinations

Additional vaccines may be offered to children with underlying medical conditions, for example severe asthma, heart failure or diabetes. Selective vaccines may be offered to children with a higher risk of hepatitis B or tuberculosis.

The routine immunisation schedule			from Spring 2016
Age due	**Diseases protected against**	**Vaccine given and trade name**		**Usual site**
Eight weeks old	Diphtheria, tetanus, pertussis (whooping cough), polio and *Haemophilus influenzae* type B (Hib)	DTaP/IPV/Hib	Pediacel or Infanrix IPV Hib	Thigh
	Pneumococcal (13 serotypes)	Pneumococcal conjugate vaccine (PCV)	Prevenar 13	Thigh
	Meningococcal group B (MenB)	MenB	Bexsero	Left thigh
	Rotavirus gastroenteritis	Rotavirus	Rotarix	By mouth
Twelve weeks	Diphtheria, tetanus, pertussis, polio and Hib	DTaP/IPV/Hib	Pediacel or Infanrix IPV Hib	Thigh
	Meningococcal group C (MenC)	MenC	NeisVac-C	Thigh
	Rotavirus	Rotavirus	Rotarix	By mouth
Sixteen weeks old	Diphtheria, tetanus, pertussis, polio and Hib	DTaP/IPV/Hib	Pediacel or Infanrix IPV Hib	Thigh
	MenB	MenB	Bexsero	Left thigh
	Pneumococcal (13 serotypes)	PCV	Prevenar 13	Thigh
One year old	Hib and MenC	Hib/MenC booster	Menitorix	Upper arm/thigh
	Pneumococcal (13 serotypes)	PCV booster	Prevenar 13	Upper arm/thigh
	Measles, mumps and rubella (German measles)	MMR	MMR VaxPRO or Priorix	Upper arm/thigh
	MenB	MenB booster	Bexsero	Left thigh
Two to six years old (including children in school years 1 and 2)	Influenza (each year from September)	Live attenuated influenza vaccine LAIV	Fluenz Tetra	Both nostrils
Three years four months old	Diphtheria, tetanus, pertussis and polio	DTaP/IPV	Infanrix IPV or Repevax	Upper arm
	Measles, mumps and rubella	MMR (check first dose given)	MMR VaxPRO or Priorix	Upper arm

Figure 4.1: The **NHS** routine immunisation schedule. Were you given these immunisations when you were young? See www.gov.uk/government/publications/the-complete-routine-immunisation-schedule for more information

4.2 How to recognise and treat common childhood ailments and diseases

To successfully recognise and treat common childhood ailments and diseases, you need to know about:

- general signs of illness
- common childhood ailments and diseases
- caring for a sick child
- when to seek treatment by a doctor
- when to seek emergency medical help.

This section looks at each of these in turn.

General signs of illness

Children who become ill in your care may display the following signs and symptoms of illness:

- vomiting and diarrhoea
- high temperature
- tiredness/disturbed sleep
- reduced appetite
- flushed or pale complexion/lip area
- irritable/fretful behaviour
- lack of desire to play
- headache
- swollen glands
- runny/blocked up nose
- cough.

You will often see two or more of these signs together. For instance, a child coming down with a cold may have a blocked-up nose, a cough and a reduced appetite. A child displaying any of these symptoms will need monitoring and sympathetic care (see the section on 'caring for an ill child'). Signs of specific ailments and diseases are given below.

Common childhood ailments and diseases

Read through table 4.1 of childhood ailments and diseases carefully. Working in threes, one student can look at the table and read out a specific

ailment/disease along with the symptoms. The other two, working together, can suggest the appropriate treatment.

Caring for an ill child

The following section provides information on emergency situations in which you will need to act calmly and quickly. (See also food allergies on page 51, and the needs of an ill child on page 53.)

4.3 When to seek treatment by a doctor; Key signs and symptoms

You learnt about the general signs of illness on page 48. Children displaying these signs may need treatment from a doctor if the signs worsen, persist, or if there are complications. You should always be cautious with children's health, and if you are worried, it is far better to call the doctor or the NHS advice line 111 for advice than to delay.

Key signs and symptoms – when to seek emergency medical help

The following signs and symptoms of illness indicate that you need to call for urgent medical attention – i.e. that you need to call an ambulance:

- breathing difficulties
- convulsions/seizures/fitting
- child seems to be in significant pain
- child is unresponsive – cannot easily or fully be roused from sleep, or a state of drowsiness
- baby becomes unresponsive and/or their body seems to be floppy or limp
- severe headache which may be accompanied by a stiff neck or a dislike of light
- rash that remains (does not fade) when pressed with a glass
- vomiting that persists for over 24 hours
- unusual, high pitched crying in babies
- high fever/temperature that cannot be lowered
- will not drink fluids – this is most worrying in babies.

Ailment/disease	Spread	Signs and symptoms	Rash or specific sign	Treatment
Common cold	Airborne/droplet, hand-to-hand contact Incubation 1–3 days	Sore throat, sneezing running nose, headache, slight fever, irritability, partial deafness		Treat symptoms
Chickenpox	Airborne/droplet, direct contact Incubation 10–14 days	Slight fever, itchy rash, mild onset then child feels ill, often with a severe headache	Red spots with a white centre on trunk and limbs at first; blisters and pustules	Rest, fluids, calamine on rash, cut child's nails to prevent secondary infection
Food poisoning	Indirect: infected food or drink Incubation 30 minutes – 36 hours	Vomiting, diarrhoea, abdominal pain		Fluids only for 24 hours; medical aid if no better or in babies
Gastroenteritis	Direct contact Incubation 7 – 14 days Indirect: infected food or drink Incubation 30 minutes – 36 hours	Vomiting, diarrhoea, signs of dehydration		Replace fluids – water (or Dioralyte). Medical aid is needed urgently
Measles	Airborne/droplet Incubation 7–15 days	High fever, fretful, heavy cold – running nose and discharge from eyes. Later a cough	Day 1: Koplik's spots (clustered white legions inside mouth) Day 4: blotchy rash begins to spread on face and body	Rest, fluids, tepid sponging, shaded room if light is uncomfortable to eyes
Mumps	Airborne/droplet Incubation 14–21 days	Pain, swelling of jaw in front of ears, fever, eating and drinking painful	Swollen face	Fluids given via a straw (if child is old enough to manage this), hot compresses, oral hygiene
Pertussis (whooping cough)	Airborne/droplet, direct contact Incubation 7–21 days	Starts with a snuffly cold, slight cough, mild fever	Spasmodic cough with whoop sound, vomiting	Rest and reassurance, feed after coughing attack, support during attack, steam inhalations as advised by a doctor
Rubella (German measles)	Airborne/droplet Incubation 7–14 days	Slight cold, sore throat, mild fever, swollen glands behind ears, pain in small joints	Slight pink rash starts behind ears and on forehead – not itchy	Rest if necessary. Treat symptoms.
Scarlet fever	Droplet Incubation 2–4 days	Sudden fever, loss of appetite, sore throat, pallor around mouth	Bright red pinpoint rash over face and body – may peel	Rest, fluids and observe for complications, antibiotics
Tonsillitis	Direct infection, droplet	Very sore throat, fever, headache, pain on swallowing, aches and pains in back and limbs		Rest, fluids, medical aid, antibiotics. Iced drinks to relieve pain

Table 4.1: Childhood ailments and diseases.

Meningitis

A child with meningitis may have the following symptoms:

- a high temperature or fever
- vomiting
- severe headache
- stiff neck
- drowsiness
- confusion
- dislike of bright lights
- seizures (fitting)
- a skin rash of red/purple 'pinprick' spots.

If the spots spread they can resemble fresh bruising, but this is hard to see on black skin. The rash will not fade when the side of a glass is pressed against it. In babies, there may also be restlessness and a high-pitched crying or screaming, a limp or floppy body, swelling of the fontanelle area of the skull (the soft spot on the top of the head) and refusal to feed.

A doctor must be called immediately, because meningitis can be life-threatening, and the child might deteriorate quickly. If they cannot be contacted or are delayed, call 999 (or 112 from a mobile) for an ambulance. Do not wait for all of the symptoms to appear. If a casualty has already seen a doctor but is becoming worse, seek urgent medical attention again. Reassure the casualty and keep them cool until help arrives.

Asthma

When an asthma attack occurs, the airways go into spasm, making breathing difficult. This may occur after contact with allergens such as dust, pollen or pet hair, and can also be caused by the child having a cold, experiencing stress or extreme cold. The severity of attacks varies, but they can be serious and life threatening. They can also be very frightening.

The casualty may cough, wheeze and become breathless. If a child is known to be asthmatic, they should have a 'reliever' inhaler immediately available. These are generally blue, and deliver medication to the lungs to relieve affected airways. Reassure and give the inhaler as

Figure 4.2: A 'reliever' inhaler delivers medication to the lungs.

instructed. Children and young people may also have another type of inhaler used to prevent attacks. Make sure you know which to use in an emergency. Sit the casualty upright and leaning forwards in a comfortable position – they should never lie down. Stay with them. If this is the first attack or the condition persists or worsens, call for an ambulance.

Seizures (fitting)

Seizures (fitting) may be due to epilepsy or a high temperature. There may be violent muscle twitching, clenched fists and an arched back, which may lead to unconsciousness. An ambulance should be called. Instead of trying to restrain the casualty, the immediate area should be cleared and the casualty should be surrounded with pillows or padding for protection. The casualty should be cooled gradually (as for a temperature, see below), and if the seizure stops before help arrives, the casualty can be placed in the recovery position (see Learning outcome 5).

? Did you know?

You can download a free app that will tell you all you need to know about meningitis. It has saved lives, because people can check the symptoms instantly if they are concerned about a child. You can download the app here: www.meningitisnow.org/meningitis-explained/signs-and-symptoms/download-our-mobile-app/.

Did you know?

Children may also have a high or higher temperature after physical activity or having hot food or drinks.

High temperatures

The normal temperature reading for a child is between 36.5°C and 37.4°C. Children may have a higher temperature when they are ill. Taking a child's temperature with a digital or feverscan thermometer helps you to monitor their illness. These come with directions for use.

You should take steps to lower a temperature by:

- ensuring that warm clothing is removed so that just a cool layer is worn
- providing a cool drink, either water or another drink diluted with water.

Some children may be given paracetamol syrup by parents or carers (for example, if a child is prone to convulsions brought on by a high temperature).

4.4 Diet related illnesses

Some children experience illnesses that are related to diet, and these are covered in more detail in this section.

Childhood obesity

Children can be at risk of becoming obese with incorrect nutrition. The NHS tells us that very overweight children tend to grow up to be very overweight adults, which can lead to serious health problems. Children who are of a healthy weight tend to be fitter, healthier, better able to learn and more self-confident. The NHS recommends five key ways to help children achieve a healthy weight:

- encouraging 60 minutes of physically active play each day – for young children this will occur in several short bursts throughout the day
- providing healthy meals, drinks and snacks
- keeping to child-size portions

- sufficient sleep
- being a good role model (e.g. eating healthily and being physically active).

Deficiency diseases

Children can be at risk of developing deficiency diseases if they do not receive the necessary nutrition, including vitamins and minerals. You can read more about this on pages 112 and 113 of Unit R019.

Food intolerances and allergies

Some children have food allergies, intolerances or medical conditions – for example diabetes or an enzyme deficiency – that means their diets have to be restricted. It is very important to ensure that you fully understand children's dietary requirements so that you can meet their needs without error. Here are some key facts:

- In a setting, practitioners should ensure that full details of diet restrictions are recorded on a child's registration form. They must also communicate the child's requirements to everyone involved in caring for them. A list of the child's requirements should be displayed in the kitchen and eating area to remind all staff.
- You must never give a child food or drink without checking that it is safe for them to have. This also applies to raw cooking ingredients or food used in play that is not intended for consumption.
- Common allergens include nuts and cows' milk.
- Some children (for example those with diabetes) may need to eat at certain times of the day.
- Children might take medication daily.
- Children might have medication to take if they show symptoms of their condition or if you become aware that they have eaten – or in the case of some children, even touched – a food they should not have. Often, time is of the essence in these situations. You must ensure that you are absolutely clear about what to do for an individual child, and you must know how to recognise their symptoms. **This could save a life.**

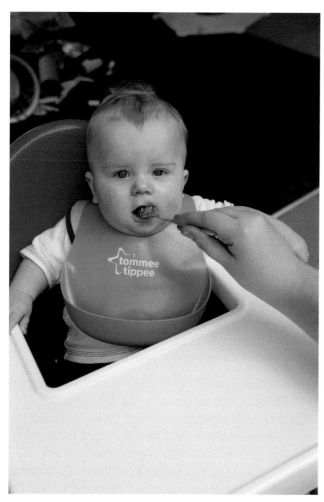

Figure 4.3: Never give a child food or drink without checking that it is safe for them to have.

Anaphylactic shock

Anaphylactic shock is a severe allergic reaction and a life-threatening situation. An ambulance must be called immediately. Anaphylactic shock can be caused by any allergens, but common triggers include nuts, eggs and shellfish.

Signs of anaphylactic shock:

- red, itchy rash or blotchy skin that becomes raised
- swelling of face, hands, feet
- pale or flushed skin
- puffy/red/itchy/watery eyes
- wheezing/difficulty breathing
- swelling of tongue and throat
- abdominal pain

> ### 🔑 Key term
>
> **Anaphylactic shock** a severe allergic reaction, and a life-threatening situation.

- vomiting/diarrhoea
- agitation/confusion
- signs of shock.

To treat anaphylactic shock, a first aider will:

- call for an ambulance
- check if the casualty has their own auto-injector of adrenaline and if so, administer (if trained to do so)
- help the child to sit in a position that aids breathing
- monitor and assess until help arrives
- if casualty becomes pale with a weak pulse, treat for shock – lie them down and raise their legs.

Diabetes

In children with diabetes, the body doesn't produce the hormone insulin, which in turn affects the body's ability to process the sugar or glucose found in food. To counteract this, most children with diabetes will need to have insulin injections at various times of the day. If they have either too much or too little insulin in their body, a child can experience the following serious conditions:

- hypoglycaemia (often called a 'hypo') – the blood sugar level is too low
- hyperglycaemia (often called a 'hyper') – the blood sugar level is too high.

Hypoglycaemia

Signs and symptoms of a hypoglycaemic attack (hypo) include:

- drowsiness with a deteriorating level of response
- feeling weak or faint
- feeling hungry
- confusion or irritability

- behaving irrationally
- palpitations
- muscle tremors (trembling)
- sweating and cold, clammy, pale skin
- rapid pulse.

Managing a hypo

The casualty needs to get sugar into their system to balance out the insulin level, which is incorrect. This is often caused by more exercise than usual or lack of food at the right time. Children with diabetes will have a care plan, and practitioners will know what to give them if they show signs of a hypo. This might be a sugary drink such as orange juice, chocolate or a tube of special glucose gel. The child will bring this to the setting with them.

If impaired consciousness has already occurred, the attack is in an advanced stage and an ambulance is needed. If at an earlier stage, a first aider will:

- sit the child down
- give them their drink/gel as described above
- if they respond, give them more food and drink until they feel better
- encourage the child to rest; they may have the equipment with them (a glucose testing kit) to check their own glucose levels.

If the child doesn't respond, an ambulance is needed. The first aider will monitor and record the level of response, breathing and pulse, and also remain alert to other reasons for the symptoms.

Hyperglycaemia

Signs and symptoms of a hyperglycaemic attack (hyper) include:

- drowsiness, resulting in impaired consciousness/unconsciousness if not treated
- feeling very thirsty
- rapid breathing
- warm, dry skin
- rapid pulse

- fruity, sweet-smelling breath
- passing urine frequently.

Managing a hyper

A hyper develops slowly over a few days. It requires emergency medical treatment to prevent the casualty from falling into a diabetic coma (unconsciousness brought on by diabetes). A first aider will:

- call for an ambulance
- monitor and record the level of response, breathing and pulse. If a casualty loses consciousness, the first aider will open the airway, check breathing and be ready to start CPR if necessary.

4.5 The needs of an ill child

When a child is unwell, they rely on adults to meet all of their needs. These fall into four categories:

- physical needs
- social needs
- emotional needs
- intellectual needs.

Physical needs

When a child is sick, they need plenty of rest, so usual routines often need to be adjusted to allow for extra naps, particularly if night-time sleep has been disturbed (for example through coughing or vomiting). Children's diets may need to be adjusted – if they have an upset stomach for example. But it is always important to ensure that plenty of water (or diluted juice) is taken.

You should always monitor a sick child carefully, as conditions can worsen suddenly, and you should be ready to call for medical help if necessary. You should also make sure that you are aware of a child's medical conditions (such as asthma or diabetes) and that you know what to do should there be a problem. High temperatures or fevers are often seen in young children, so you should know how to care for a child experiencing these (see page 51).

Figure 4.4: If a child is feeling unwell, they need plenty of rest.

Social and emotional needs

An ill child needs empathy and plenty of reassurance, especially when they are too young to understand how they feel. It can be confusing and frightening to suddenly feel unwell. Adults should gently explain the illness to a child, and if appropriate, let them know that they will feel better soon. Talking positively about any medication, naps and healthy eating can also help. Children's desire to have company may be just as strong as ever, so activities you can do together are especially helpful.

 Good practice

Children might need extra physical affection, such as cuddles or sitting on your lap. Also bear in mind that an ill child may also regress in their behaviour, going back temporarily to things they did that brought them comfort when they were younger, for example clinging to an adult's legs or sucking their thumb.

Intellectual needs

Children are likely to need quiet activities to keep them amused and stimulated while they are not up to more active play. Stories, colouring activities and IT devices are popular choices. If a child is ill or will be recovering for a longer period, it will be important to think carefully about activities

that will help their learning and development to continue as expected. If appropriate, visits from friends and family will also be beneficial, as children can miss wider social contact.

4.6 How to prepare a child for a stay in hospital

Going into hospital can be a worrying time for anyone – especially for young children – and sometimes hospital admission happens very quickly in an emergency. When admission is planned, adults have time to prepare the child. This can make a big difference to the levels of anxiety felt by both a child and their family.

Hospital/ward visit

Adults as well as children often worry about the unknown – not knowing enough about a place or a situation in advance can make you nervous. It can also lead you to imagine scary scenarios. This is no different for children, so if a child has not been to hospital before, or they have not stayed on a particular ward before, it is a good idea to arrange a visit with hospital staff. Being able to see where their bed will be, where their toys will be and meeting friendly staff can really put children at ease. If parents will be staying at the hospital, it will help for the child to see where they will sleep.

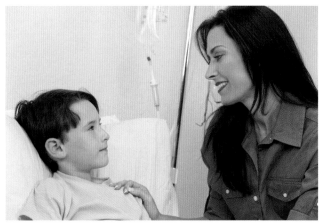

Figure 4.5: You should prepare a child for a hospital stay.

Acting out fears and hospital games

Imaginary play is a wonderful, safe way for children to act out and explore their fears. This helps them to prepare for real life situations, and gives them reassurance. Hospital games can be played with just a few resources, such as a toy doctor's kit with a play stethoscope, thermometer, syringe etc. Teddies or dolls make perfect patients. In group settings, hospital uniforms are popular additions to the dressing up clothes.

Books and DVDs

There are many story books, non-fiction books, DVDs and even children's TV programmes that explore going into hospital (and visiting a doctor's surgery). These have been written especially to help children become familiar with the environment before they have their own experience. The characters featured can also become strong role models for a child.

Explanation and honesty

During a hospital stay, and when preparing for the stay at home, it is very important to explain what will happen in simple terms. You should always be gentle but honest. This includes answering children's questions honestly. It can be tempting not to admit that procedures might leave children feeling uncomfortable or sore. But if a child learns that they cannot trust you, they will feel considerably more anxious in the long

Did you know?

Characters in books and DVDs often show the feelings and emotions a child is likely to experience, for example they may feel poorly and reluctant to go into hospital at first. But then everyone is friendly and perhaps they like the food. There will often be an introduction to some hospital procedures, which will (perhaps after a bit of recovery) make the character feel much better. Typically, they will then say goodbye to their new friends and return home.

term, and might no longer be reassured by the things you say, even when they are true. However, it is important to stress the benefits of going into hospital, and the positive impact that any procedures will have for the child. There is an example of this in the case study below.

Involvement in a child's care

Parents and carers are often able to be quite involved in their child's care while they are in hospital. In some circumstances, they may even be able to sleep on the ward or in the building. Parents can often continue with many aspects of the child's care, such as feeding, bathing and changing nappies. This continuity of care can help young children to feel more settled, secure and relaxed.

Case study

Four-year-old Seth has a chronic medical condition, and he's going to stay in hospital for the third time. He asks his grandad if he will have to have an injection again. His grandad tells him he probably will. Seth wants to know if it will hurt like last time. His grandad says he might feel a scratch but it will be over ever so quickly. He asks Seth if he can remember how well he felt after his last stay in hospital. Seth says he can and asks if his grandad

will tell him stories like last time. His grandad tells him he's bought some new books especially for his stay in hospital.

Questions

1   Do you think Seth's grandad handled the conversation well?

2   Why is that? Give your reasons.

Activity

Find out more about preparing a child for hospital by visiting this NHS website: www.nhs.uk/conditions/pregnancy-and-baby/pages/going-to-hospital.aspx.

- Read the information and watch the video clip.

- Now look at the advice about dealing with health problems and operations on the CBeebies website: www.bbc.co.uk/cbeebies/grownups/helping-your-child-prepare-for-an-operation.

- Read the information, then follow the link to explore the Get Well Soon app.

Test your knowledge

1 Explain the ways in which immunity can be acquired.
2 What are the common signs of illness?
3 Explain when emergency treatment should be sought for a child.
4 Outline a diet-related illness.
5 Outline the social and emotional needs of an ill child.
6 Explain three ways in which you would prepare a child for a stay in hospital.

Question practice

Question

a A child with whom you work will soon be experiencing his first hospital stay. He has already been on a visit to the hospital ward. Explain how you could also help to prepare him for the hospital stay through:

● acting out fears and hospital games
● books and DVDs
● explanation and honesty
● parent/carer involvement in his care.

Mark scheme and additional guidance

Expected answers	Marks	Additional guidance
Four factors identified, **one** mark each.	8	Level 3 (7–8 marks): Answers will provide a detailed explanation of four ways in which you could help a child to prepare him/her for a hospital stay. Answers will be coherent, and use appropriate terminology. You will include reasons and these will be clear and structured logically. The information will be relevant and include evidence or examples.
Acting out fears and hospital games Imaginary play is a safe way for the child to act out and explore his fears, preparing him for the real life hospital situation and giving reassurance. Hospital games can be played with a few resources, such as a toy doctor's kit. Hospital uniforms can also be included amongst a setting's dressing up clothes.		
Books and DVDs Story books, non-fiction books and DVDs that explore going into hospital can help the child become familiar with the hospital environment. The characters featured can also become strong role models for a child.		
Explanation and honesty What will happen in hospital should be explained simply and the child's questions should be answered. Adults must be gentle but honest, including about whether procedures might leave the child feeling uncomfortable or sore, or trust will be lost in the longer term. The benefits of going into hospital should be stressed alongside the positive impact that any procedures will have for child.		
Involvement in the child's care Parents and carers may be able to continue with many aspects of the child's care, such as feeding, bathing and changing nappies. This continuity can help a young child to feel more settled, secure and relaxed. In some circumstances, they may even be able to sleep on the ward or in the building.		

Expected answers	Marks	Additional guidance
Acting out fears and hospital games Hospital games can be played with a few resources, such as a toy doctor's kit. This means children can act out their fears, which will help to prepare them for hospital. **Books and DVDs** Story books, and DVDs about going into hospital can help children to understand what it is like to be in a hospital. **Explanation and honesty** Adults should listen to the child and answer any questions they may have. They should explain why they are going into hospital, and the benefits of this. They should explain what will happen and why and should explain this in a calm and simple way so that the child can understand. **Involvement in the child's care** Parents and carers may be able to continue to take part in some of the child's care while the child is in hospital. For example, they could feed, bath and change nappies. They might even be able to sleep in the building. All of this may help the child to feel relaxed and settled.		Level 2 (4–6 marks): Your answers will be a sound explanation of at least 2 ways you could prepare a child for a hospital stay. Your answer will cover use some appropriate terminology. Your answer will include reasons and there will be some structure. The information is mostly relevant and supported by some evidence.
Acting out fears and hospital games **Books and DVDs** **Explanation and honesty** **Parent/carer involvement in his care**		Level 1 (1–3 marks): Learners will give a basic description of how you could prepare a child for a hospital stay. Your answer may be a list or may not cover all the ways. The information is basic and unstructured. The information you include will be supported by limited evidence and the relationship to the evidence may not be clear.
		0 mark = the response will not be worthy of credit.

Candidate answer

a) Acting out fears and hospital games:

The child can act out his fears during imaginary play. This can be encouraged through providing imaginary play resources such as medical dressing up clothes and a doctor's kit, with dolls and teddies to act as patients. This is a safe, reassuring way for children to prepare for the real life hospital situation.

Books and DVDs:

There are lots of story books, non-fiction books, DVDs and some children's TV programmes about going into hospital. They are good for helping the child become familiar with the hospital environment and the things that routinely happen there. The child characters tend to be good role models who will interact with caring hospital staff. They often feel a bit scared at the start of a story, but soon overcome this and feel better for their hospital stay.

Explanation and honesty:

You should explain what to expect simply and honestly, so that the child knows they can trust you. The child should be encouraged to ask questions and these should also be answered honestly and sensitively, even if they ask if procedures might feel sore. Alongside, you should explain the benefits of going into hospital, such as the positive impact of having an operation. For example, if they have been ill, they may feel a lot better in the long term after they have recovered from the operation.

Involvement in his care:

Parents can stay involved in their child's care needs by explaining to nurses exactly how they do things like feed and change their child's nappies, so the nurses can do this in the same way. This helps to reassure children as things stay very similar to what they are used to.

Commentary

Question context/content/style:

Explanation of how to prepare a child for the hospital stay through four factors – acting out fears and hospital games, books and DVDs, explanation and honesty, parent/carer involvement in the child's care.

Requirements:

Correct identification of four factors

Marks awarded and rationale: 6/8

- Three factors are explained, gaining six marks.
- The explanation regarding parent/carer involvement in his care is incorrect, so does not gain a mark.

Question

b   Some diet related illnesses are shown in the box below

| Food allergies | | Childhood obesity | | Diabetes |

Complete the table to match each illness with the brief description given (3 marks).

Diet related illness	Description
	The body does not produce the hormone insulin. Most children with the illness will need to have insulin injections.
	In the most serious form of this condition, a severe reaction can cause a serious allergic reaction that can cause death. Nuts, eggs or shellfish can cause allergic reactions.
	To combat this condition, the NHS recommends 60 minutes of play each day that involves children being active. They also recommend providing healthy meals, drinks and snacks, keeping to child-sized portions, getting enough sleep and being a good role model.

Mark scheme and additional guidance

Expected answers	Marks	Additional guidance
Three required, **one** mark each. The answers should appear in the table in the following order: ● **Diabetes:** The body does not produce the hormone insulin. ... ● **Food allergies:** In the most serious form of this condition, a severe reaction can cause anaphylactic shock. ... ● **Childhood obesity:** To combat this condition, the NHS recommends encouraging 60 minutes of play each day that involves children being physically active. ...	3	A mark is given for each illness that is matched correctly to its description. No other answers are acceptable.

Candidate answer

b)

Diet related illness	Description
Diabetes	In children with this condition, the body does not produce the hormone insulin. Most children with the illness will need to have insulin injections.
Food allergies	In the most serious form of this condition, a severe reaction can cause a serious allergic reaction that can cause death. Nuts, eggs, shellfish can cause this reaction.
Childhood obesity	To combat this condition, the NHS recommends 60 minutes of play each day which involves children being active. They also recommend providing healthy meals, drinks and snacks, keeping to child-size portions, getting enough sleep and being a good role model.

Commentary

Question context/content/style:

Match the diet related illnesses with the brief descriptions given.

Requirements:

Correct matching of three diet related illnesses with their brief descriptions.

Marks awarded and rationale: 3/3

● Three diet related illnesses have been matched, gaining three marks.

Learning outcome 5

Know about child safety

About this Learning outcome

For anyone looking after a child, the most crucial responsibility is to keep that child safe from harm. When asked, most parents will say that their biggest hope for their children is that they will be 'safe and happy'. Whether a child is safe and happy also tends to be a parent's main concern when they leave them in the care of someone else. So it is vital that you know how to maintain a safe environment for children and how to provide safe equipment. You should also be aware of the most common childhood accidents, and issues relating to social and internet safety.

Assessment criteria

In this learning outcome you will cover:

5.1 How to create a safe, child-friendly environment.

5.2 Safety labelling.

5.3 To be aware of the most common childhood accidents.

5.4 Social safety.

Getting started

Choose one of the following rooms. Now think about possible risks to a young child's safety that might be present in that room in your own home. Thought storm as many as you can think of (for example there might be bleach in the bathroom):

- kitchen
- bathroom
- living room
- bedroom.

5.1 How to create a safe, child-friendly environment

Young children need adults to make the environments in which they spend their time as safe as possible. This means carrying out a risk assessment. To do this, a practitioner will think carefully about a particular space, and identify all of the apparent **hazards** (see page 62 for definition) in that space. They will then take steps to reduce the risk of the hazard causing harm to an acceptable level. There will always be accidents, as we cannot wrap children up in cotton wool. But we can do our best to protect children from foreseeable accidents.

Figure 4.6: Environments should be as safe as possible.

A hazard is an item or situation that could cause harm to a child, and potential hazards are all around us. They include:

- physical hazards – for example unsafe objects, things that may be tripped over
- security hazards – for example insecure exits and windows
- fire hazards – for example heaters, electrical appliances
- food safety hazards – for example a faulty refrigerator, unsafe produce
- personal safety hazards – for example stranger danger, busy roads.

A **risk** is the likelihood of the hazard actually causing harm. For example, whenever we walk along the pavement, road traffic – a significant potential hazard – is very close to us. But the likelihood of actually being harmed by traffic in this situation is low.

 Key terms

Hazard an item or situation that may cause harm.
Risk the likelihood of a hazard actually causing harm.

Within the home

Most accidents occur at home. When thinking about safety, it is best to consider each room or area at a time:

- kitchen
- bathroom(s)
- living room
- bedroom(s)
- stairs.

You need to think carefully about child development when you are carrying out risk assessments. This will help you to consider how aware children are of danger at various ages. It will also help you to think about their skill levels, and the things they are likely to do – for example a 12-month-old is likely to pull themselves up on a chair, which might be unsafe. They could also open low kitchen cupboards when sitting on the floor.

Kitchen

Hazards in the kitchen are likely to include:

- unsafe chemicals children could handle, for example, cleaning products, dishwasher tablets, washing powder
- food safety hazards, for example, raw meat
- dangerously hot equipment, for example, oven, grill, hob, microwave, toaster, kettle, coffee maker (and hot items that are/have been in them, for example, food, water)
- sharp equipment, for example, knives, skewers, scissors, tin openers, graters
- fragile items that become dangerous when broken, for example, crockery, glasses
- electronic food preparation equipment, for example, blenders, tin openers, food processors, juicers
- access to power sockets
- access to hot taps
- access to water (drowning risk)
- a window from which a child could fall.

Bathroom

Hazards in the bathroom are likely to include:

- unsafe chemicals for children to handle, for example, cleaning products, bleach, medicines, toiletries
- sharp equipment, for example, razors
- access to hot taps and hot water
- access to water (drowning risk)
- access to items unhygienic for children to handle, for example, toilet brush, inside of the toilet

- access to items that are slippery when wet, for example, bath, shower tray, floor
- a window from which a child could fall.

Living room

Hazards in the living room are likely to include:

- access to electrical items and their power cords, for example, TV, DVD player, stereo, computers, phone
- access to power sockets
- access to heating source
- access to furniture that could tip, be climbed on or pulled over
- access to glass doors
- access to ornaments, for example, glass, china, small parts
- a window from which a child could fall.

Bedroom

Hazards in the bedroom are likely to include:

- access to power sockets
- access to heating source
- access to TV, DVD player
- access to electric blanket, hot water bottle
- access to furniture that could tip, be climbed on or pulled over (including bunk beds or a cot a child has grown out of but is still in use)
- a window from which a child could fall.

Stairs

Hazards/risks on the stairs are likely to include:

- items left on the stairs that could be tripped over
- risk of tripping
- risk of falling
- faulty or missing handrail.

Garden/play areas

There are some specific things to consider when children play in a garden or outside play areas, including:

- Are gates, sheds and any boundary fences secure?

- Can strangers or animals come into contact with children?
- Are there any problems caused by weather, for example icy patches or waterlogged areas?
- Is there shelter from the sun/will children need sun protection?
- Are there any other risks from water, for example ponds, water courses or gullies?
- Are litter bins and drains secure?
- Is the area free of litter, glass, poisonous plants and animal faeces? (Cats are particularly attracted to an uncovered sand tray.)
- Have any items/equipment that could cause harm been left out?
- Is play equipment assembled safely and is it age appropriate?
- Is safety flooring in good condition? If mats are needed under play equipment, are they present?

Figure 5.1: Play equipment must be age appropriate.

Road safety

Young children should always be under close and direct supervision of adults when walking on the pavement or crossing the road. If you are in charge of a child who is old enough to be walking near a road, you should hold their hand at all times. Follow the five point Green Cross Code and make children aware of it:

1 First find the safest place to cross.
- If possible, cross the road at: subways; footbridges; islands; zebra, puffin, pelican or toucan crossings; or where there is a crossing point controlled by a police officer, a school crossing patrol or a traffic warden.
- Otherwise, choose a place where you can see clearly in all directions, and where drivers can see you.
- Try to avoid crossing between parked cars and on sharp bends or close to the top of a hill. Move to a space where drivers and riders can see you clearly.
- There should be space to reach the pavement on the other side.

2 Stop just before you get to the kerb.
- Do not get too close to the traffic. If there is no pavement, keep back from the edge of the road but make sure you can still see approaching traffic.
- Give yourself lots of time to have a good look all around.

3 Look all around for traffic and listen.
- Look in every direction.
- Listen carefully because you can sometimes hear traffic before you can see it.

4 If traffic is coming, let it pass.
- Look all around again and listen.
- Do not cross until there is a safe gap in the traffic and you are certain that there is plenty of time.
- Remember, even if traffic is a long way off, it may be approaching very quickly.

5 When it is safe, go straight across the road – do not run.
- Keep looking and listening for traffic while you cross, in case there is any traffic you did not see, or in case other traffic appears suddenly.

- Look out for cyclists and motorcyclists travelling between lanes of traffic.
- Do not cross diagonally.

When out walking, toddlers are safest on reins, and babies and children in prams or buggies should wear a harness.

Safety equipment

The table below shows key safety equipment that can prevent accidents:

Equipment	Purpose
Harness and reins	Prevent falls from prams, push chairs and high chairs. Prevent young children escaping and/or running into the road when out walking.
Safety gates	Prevent access to kitchens, stairways, outdoors. Always place a guard at the bottom and top of stairs for babies and young children.
Locks for cupboards and windows	Prevent children getting hold of dangerous substances or falling from windows.
Safety glass/ safety film	Prevent glass from breaking into pieces, causing injuries.
Socket covers	Prevent children from poking their fingers into electrical sockets.
Play pens	Create a safe area for babies.
Smoke alarms	Detect smoke and sounds the alarm.
Cooker guards	Prevent children pulling pans from the cooker.
Firefighting equipment such as a fire blankets or extinguishers	May be used to tackle minor fires.

Table 5.1: Key safety equipment. Can you think of additional safety measures you can take to protect children from harm?

Activity

1   Find out more about road safety by visiting this website: http://think.direct.gov.uk/education/early-years-and-primary/parents/3-to-5s/. Click all of the links in the 0–4 category, and read the information given.

2   Now write down five things you will do to promote road safety when working with young children.

5.2 Safety labelling

Safety labelling tells you whether a product or piece of equipment is safe for use by children. Any relevant additional safety information will be specified. You must always check for safety marks and read safety information before buying or using products for children. You can read more about this in Unit R019, page 91.

BSI safety mark/kite mark

The BSI safety mark/kite mark is a UK product and service quality certification mark, administered by the British Standards Institution (BSI). It is used to identify products where safety is paramount, for example bicycle helmets and smoke alarms. It gives assurance that the product should be safe and reliable, but manufacturers are not legally required to display a kite mark on their products.

Figure 5.2: BSI safety mark/kite mark.

Lion Mark

The Lion Mark appears on toys that have been made by a member of the British Toy and Hobby Association and Toy Fair. This organisation requires members to sign up to a strict safety Code of Practice. Around 95 per cent of toys sold in the UK are supplied with a Lion Mark as many any major UK and European toy manufacturers are members.

Figure 5.3: Lion Mark.

Age advice symbol

This symbol identifies when equipment or a product isn't suitable for children under the age of 36 months (in the opinion of the manufacturer). It is mainly displayed on toys that might not pass a 'choke hazard test'. It is also seen if a product has small parts that could be removed and swallowed by children under three years.

Figure 5.4: Age advice symbol.

CE symbol

This is the most common toy label and it is the first one to look for. By law, it has to be displayed on all new toys on the market in the EU. The CE logo proves that the toy has been tested for compliance with EU standards. It is also the manufacturer's declaration that the item meets all toy safety requirements.

Figure 5.5: CE symbol.

Children's nightwear labelling

Nightwear can burn quickly if set alight by contact with an open fire, gas or electric fire, or another heat source, and this can cause serious injury. As a result, you should look for a label confirming that children's night garments (including dressing gowns) meet the flammability performance requirements. This includes garments for babies.

5.3 Be aware of the most common childhood accidents

Everyone who works with children must always do their best to prevent accidents, injuries and illnesses. But whatever precautions you take, it is a fact of life that these things happen to all children occasionally. Because of this, all practitioners should take a paediatric first aid course. The information in this Learning outcome by no means replaces first aid training.

Sometimes, first aid is all that is necessary – common minor injuries such as grazes can be sufficiently treated. It is important to recognise when medical assistance is urgently required, as this can save a child's life. The most common childhood accidents are shown on the diagram below.

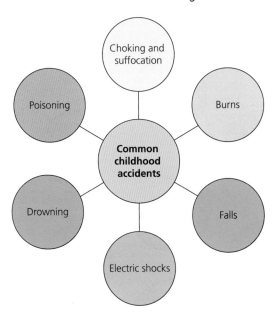

Figure 5.6: Common childhood accidents. Would you know how to respond to each of these?

✔ Good practice

If you ever need to call the emergency services, you should dial 999 (or 112 from a mobile phone). Be prepared to give the nature of the injury, the age of the child and your location. Listen carefully and follow any instructions you are given. Stay on the phone until you are told to hang up.

Choking and suffocation

Babies and children can choke to death on any small object they put in their mouths that blocks their airway, so you must be very careful which objects are left within reach. In addition, children can struggle to breathe or stop breathing due to suffocation. This can happen when the airway is blocked externally, for example if a child puts their head into a plastic bag, if something heavy falls on their chest, or if an item (such as a scarf) gets caught around their neck.

Choking on food is also common, and can be caused in a number of ways:

- laughing or gasping when eating
- trying to swallow a piece of food that is too large
- eating lying down.

Mild or severe obstruction

If there is a minor airway obstruction, breathing will be difficult, but the child will still be able to get some air into their lungs. They will be able to cough. With difficulty, they will also be able to talk, cry or make a noise. If obstruction is severe, the child will not be able to do these things. They may hold their neck – a sign recognised as choking distress. Not being able to breathe will eventually cause the child to lose consciousness. Therefore immediate treatment is needed and you must call an ambulance.

First aid for a choking child

- Encourage the child to cough, as this could clear the obstruction.
- If the obstruction is severe and the child can't breathe – or if coughing fails – bend the child forwards and give up to five sharp back blows between the shoulder blades with the heel of the hand.
- Check the mouth and remove any obvious obstruction.

- If the child is still choking, administer abdominal thrusts – stand behind the child and put your fist between the navel and the lower breastbone, grasp the fist with the other hand and pull sharply in an upwards and inwards movement, up to five times.
- Recheck the mouth as before.
- If the child is still choking, alternate between back blows and abdominal thrusts until the airway is cleared, emergency help arrives or the child becomes unconscious.

First aid for a choking infant

- Lie the baby along the forearm on its front, keeping the head low. Take care to support the head. Give the infant up to five sharp back blows between the shoulder blades with the heel of the hand.
- Turn the infant onto its back along the other arm. Check the mouth and remove any obvious obstruction.
- If the infant is still choking, administer chest thrusts. With two fingertips, give up to five sharp thrusts on the lower part of the breastbone (a finger's breadth below the nipples), pressing inwards and upwards.
- Recheck the mouth as before.
- If the infant is still choking, alternate between back blows and chest thrusts until the airway is cleared, emergency help arrives or the infant becomes unconscious.

? Did you know?

A child or infant who has had abdominal thrusts/chest trusts administered will need to be seen by a doctor to ensure no injuries have been sustained.

Activity

Find out more about common childhood accidents by visiting this website: www.capt. org.uk/safety-advice.

- Imagine that a baby and a young child are coming to stay with you.
- Now take the safety quizzes provided by clicking on each of the links given on the right-hand side of the page. Answer the questions with your own home in mind.
- Make notes on changes you would make to your home to keep the visiting baby and child safe from harm. Give reasons for your changes.

Burns

The causes of burns and scalds are shown on the diagram below.

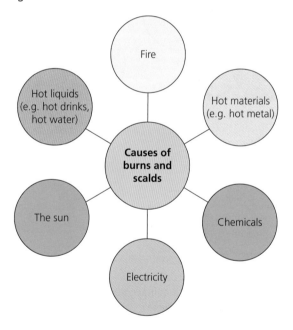

Figure 5.7: The causes of burns and scalds. Are there any chemicals in your home that could scald a child?

? Did you know?

Scalds are caused by liquids. The majority of scalds are caused by hot drinks or hot water. So it is very important to always keep hot drinks and boiling kettles or saucepans out of the reach of young children.

? Did you know?

Blister plasters must not be used on burn/scald blisters, and blisters should not be broken or the injured skin interfered with. Some people used to apply fats such as butter to a burn – this should not be done.

Doctors consider three things when assessing how severe a burn or scald is:

- the size of the affected area – this is expressed as a percentage of the skin, with the palm of the hand equalling 1 per cent. When describing a burn to the emergency services, a first aider may compare the size to a commonly known object, for example, by saying the burn is the size of a postage stamp
- the depth of the burn or scald – 'superficial' burns or scalds affect just the top layer of the skin and redness occurs. 'Partial thickness' means blisters have been caused, while 'full thickness' causes charred skin or 'ash whiteness' of the skin
- the location of the burn or scald – the most serious locations for burns are the hands, feet, face and genital area.

First aid for burns and scalds

Burns and scalds need immediate treatment, as this can limit their effect. An infant or young child with any burn needs to go to hospital straight away.

- Take action immediately.
- Cool the area with water for at least ten minutes, preferably by holding it under gently running tap water.
- Remove any jewellery, watches, belts or restrictive clothing that isn't stuck to the burn/scald before swelling occurs.
- Cover the burn/scald with clean cling film or place a clean plastic bag over a foot or hand. Cling film should be applied lengthways instead of being wrapped around a limb due to the risk of swelling. If cling film/bags are not available, a sterile dressing may be used.

Falls

Falls are a very common form of injury. This is why it is important to fit window locks and stair gates, and to supervise young children carefully whenever there is a risk of falling. Injuries can also occur as a result of a seemingly minor trip or slip. Fractures and head injuries are the most common results of a fall.

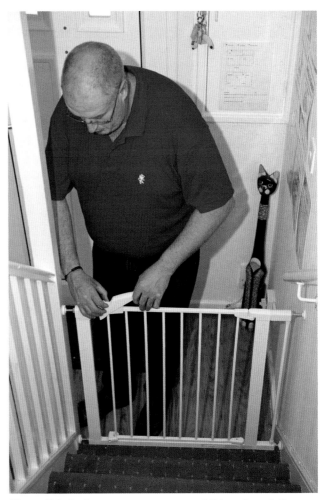

Figure 5.8: Stair gates protect young children from falls.

Head injuries

The brain is wrapped in layers of tissue and encased within the hard, protective skull, which is made of bone. It is important to recognise head injuries as they:

- are relatively common and can be serious
- can result in impaired consciousness or unconsciousness
- may require emergency surgery.

The following head injuries may occur:

- Concussion – caused when a brain is shaken within the skull, usually by a blow to the head. Normal brain activity is disturbed temporarily, but is usually followed by a complete recovery.
- Cerebral compression – occurs when pressure builds up on the brain. This is usually a result of swelling of injured brain tissue or a build-up of blood within the skull, caused by a blow to the head. (It can also be caused by an infection, brain tumour or stroke.) Surgery is generally required to relieve the pressure. Prolonged pressure can cause disability and death.
- Skull fracture – this is a break in the skull, caused by a blow to the head.

Signs and symptoms

Signs and symptoms of a head injury include:

- a bump or other swelling
- bruising
- headache
- drowsiness
- loss of consciousness (may only last seconds)
- vomiting or nausea
- confusion/loss of memory (for example can't remember the accident, or immediately before it)
- dizziness or loss of balance
- seizures
- problems with vision (for example blurred vision)
- pupils of the eyes uneven in size
- blood or clear fluid coming from the nose or ear
- bleeding from the head
- breathing problems

- weakness or paralysis down one side of the face or body (includes weakness in an arm or leg and difficulty walking)
- difficulties talking
- change in behaviour (for example irritable, disorientated).

In babies, there may also be:

- a change in the sound of their cry
- swollen fontanelle (a soft spot on a baby's skull).

Figure 5.9: A change in cry can be a sign of a head injury.

? Did you know?

Cerebral compression can develop hours or days after a head injury. So it is possible that a child could become ill from the effects of a head injury that practitioners caring for them are completely unaware of.

✔ Good practice

If a child has banged their head, they should be watched closely for at least six hours. Adults should also remain alert for the signs of head injury for several days.

First aid for head injuries

- Call for an ambulance.
- Apply a pad and direct pressure to any head wound. The pad may be secured in place with a bandage.
- Lie the casualty down. See below if a spinal injury is suspected or if the casualty is unconscious and should therefore be treated as though there is a spinal injury.
- Monitor and record the level of consciousness, breathing and pulse until the ambulance arrives. Also record symptoms, including how long any loss of consciousness lasted, if blood or fluid has leaked from the nose/ear, pupil size, any vomiting etc.

Protecting the spinal cord

It is common for people with head injuries to also injure their neck (which is part of the spine). The spinal cord contains nerves which take messages from the brain to other parts of the body. If the spinal cord becomes damaged due to broken or dislocated bones in the spine, paralysis and other serious conditions may occur. A first aider will treat an unconscious casualty with a head injury as though they also have a spinal injury, to prevent them from causing further damage. Signs and symptoms of spinal injury include:

- neck or back pain
- abnormal curve of the spine
- loss of sensation
- abnormal sensation
- weakness in or inability to move limbs
- skin feels tender
- loss of bladder/bowel control
- breathing difficulties.

? Did you know?

Spinal injury can be caused when a child falls from a height onto their head, back or feet – for example, a fall from a climbing frame.

First aid for spinal injury or an unconscious child

- Do not move the child; if conscious, tell the child not to move.
- Kneel behind the child and place steady hands on either side of their face. Steady and support the neck and head. Keep holding in place until the ambulance arrives.
- If others are available to help, get them to place padding such as rolled up towels or blankets around the neck and shoulders (without moving the child). This will provide extra support.

Electric shocks

Electricity can be extremely dangerous, and electric shocks can kill by stopping the heart. It is important to fit socket covers that protect children from electric shocks caused by them poking fingers or objects into electric sockets.

If a child has been electrocuted, it is vital to stop the flow of electricity. The child must never be approached until this is undertaken, otherwise the first aider is also likely to receive an electric shock. The power should be turned off at the mains or master switch. If this isn't possible, the child may be pushed or pulled well away from the source using material that will not conduct the electricity. (A first aider will learn how to do this safely on a first aid course.) Techniques may include looping a thick towel around the feet to enable a child to be pulled, or using a wooden broom to push them away from the electricity source.

First aid for electric shocks

Once the electricity has been turned off or the casualty has been safely moved, approach the child. If the heart has stopped, an ambulance is needed. Check the airway, breathing and circulation and start **CPR** (cardiopulmonary resuscitation, sometimes referred to as 'heart massage and rescue breaths').

Electricity can cause burns at the entry and exit points, which must be treated with cold water (see page 69). However, note that the source of electricity must be turned off or the casualty must be well removed from the source, because water and electricity are a very dangerous combination. Urgent or emergency medical attention will be needed, depending on the extent of the burns.

Drowning

Drowning can occur in natural water bodies such as the sea and rivers. It can also occur in manmade places, such as pools, canals, lakes, ponds and baths. These are the places most likely to occur to you when you think about the risk of drowning. However, babies and young children can drown in as little as 2.5 cm of water, which is enough to cover their face should they fall forwards. You must never leave a baby or young child unattended anywhere near water, even for a few seconds. This includes sitting or lying in the bath or paddling pool.

Figure 5.10: Never leave a baby or young child unattended anywhere near water.

First aid for drowning

- Carry the child out of the water with their head lower than their chest.
- Take off their wet clothing.
- Cover the child with a dry towel or blanket.
- If they are unconscious and breathing, put them into the **recovery position**.
- If they are not breathing, give CPR.

 Good practice

First aiders will place an unconscious, breathing child in the recovery position to help keep them safe. If the unconscious child isn't breathing, the first aider will begin CPR to prolong life and to attempt to restart the heart. The recovery position and CPR are just two of the life saving techniques you will learn on a paediatric first aid course. Taking such a course is highly recommended for anyone who spends time looking after children.

 Key terms

CPR cardiopulmonary resuscitation.
Recovery position a safe position in which to position an unconscious, breathing child.

Poisoning

Poisons enter the body when they are swallowed (for example medication, bleach or berries), when they come into contact with the skin (for example poison ivy) or when they are inhaled (for example poisonous gas fumes or dust such as ant powder). Some common household/workplace substances and plants can poison children, and it is important to guard against this. Common items that can poison include:

- cleaning fluids and sprays
- medication, including over-the-counter medication and prescription drugs
- personal care products and make-up
- pesticides (which should never be used around children)

Good practice

Items that could poison must be kept out of children's reach. Cleaning fluids should be kept in a locked cupboard in the kitchen. Gas boilers must be serviced annually to help prevent them from becoming faulty and leaking gas. Plants must not be introduced to a setting unless they can be identified as safe. Care must also be taken about where visitors' bags are stored, as they may have prescribed or over-the-counter medication in them.

- some plants including delphinium, mistletoe (including berries), wild mushrooms and other fungi, foxgloves, daffodil bulbs, poison ivy – berries from bushes and trees should all be regarded as poisonous because it is difficult to tell which are which.

Signs and symptoms of poisoning

The signs and symptoms of poisoning vary according to what the poison is and how it has been ingested; they include:

- vomiting
- pain
- drowsiness or unconsciousness
- burns to the mouth (if chemicals like cleaning fluids have been swallowed)
- blisters on the skin
- swelling
- itchy skin and/or severe rash
- unusual smell on the breath.

Other evidence may also be present:

- smells, for example smell of gas fumes or bleach
- spilt poisonous liquids
- open chemical containers such as cleaning fluid bottles
- open/empty medication blister packs or medicine/pill bottles
- open medicine cabinet

- open cleaning cupboard
- berries or pieces of plant in the vicinity of the child.

First aid for poisoning

As soon as you find that poisoning has occurred, call an ambulance. Try to find out what substance or plant the child has taken or been in contact with, how much they have taken and when.

Pass this information to the emergency services. If a substance or plant has been touched, rinse it from the skin with running tap water. Monitor the child closely, and be ready to act if they become unconscious. (If they do, check the airway, breathing and circulation, place the child in the recovery position and continue to monitor them until help arrives.) You should never try to get a child who has been poisoned to vomit. If chemicals have been swallowed, they will have burnt the child on the way down and will burn again on the way up.

5.4 Social safety

As they grow up, children need to be aware of how to protect themselves, and the ways in which they should and shouldn't be treated. Adults can help by teaching children about their rights in respect of their bodies, what to do if they are in an emergency situation and they are vulnerable, and what to do if they are bullied.

Personal safety awareness

Knowledge of what to do for themselves in an emergency situation helps to keep children safe. It also helps them to develop feelings of confidence and self-reliance. Research has shown that these positive feelings make a child less likely to become a victim of abuse. Children should know:

- what to do if they are lost – stop and look all around for the adult they are with. If they can't see them, they should approach a safe person – a police officer, CPO, crossing point

Figure 5.11 Children should know who they can go home with.

Case study

Creche worker Sahira works with Kierra and Ruby, whose parents are friends – the girls sometimes visit each other's houses. Sahira has noticed that when Ruby's mum arrives to collect Ruby, Kierra often thinks she is going home with her. But Ruby's mum is not authorised to collect Kierra on the creche contact form. Sahira mentions to Kierra's mum that it could be a good idea to talk to Kierra about who she is allowed to leave with.

Questions

1 Kierra's mum asks Sahira why she should talk to her daughter about this. What reason should Sahira give?

- personal details – as soon as they are able, children should learn their full name, address and telephone number.

Awareness of strangers

Children need to know what a stranger is, and what to do if they are approached by a stranger. If an unknown person talks to them, they need not be rude – they can simply walk away quickly, telling an adult if they feel worried. But if a stranger asks or tells a child to go with them, the child should run away and tell a safe adult immediately. They must learn to 'Say no, never go!' If children are touched, grabbed or feel frightened or worried that they are in danger, it is alright to break the usual behaviour rules. They should attract attention by shouting and screaming, and punch and kick, if they feel they need to.

Did you know?

Police officers/CPOs often visit early years settings to talk to children about stranger danger, and being lost. This helps children to see them as safe people who will help if needed.

patrol guard (lollipop person), cashier at a till in a shop or lastly a parent with children. They should wait outside until their adult, parent or a police officer comes to look after them. They should not go anywhere with strangers – not to a phone, workplace or house

- who to go home with – when away from their parent or primary carer, children should know who they are allowed to go home with, for example who is allowed to pick them up from pre-school
- how to answer the door – young children should never answer the door unless an adult is with them

Avoiding inappropriate personal contact – physical and emotional

Children's bodies and feelings are their own. You can help them to understand what this means by ensuring the following:

- Children do not have to show physical affection to anyone if they do not want to – this includes kissing, hugging or sitting on people's laps.
- Children can have help if they need it when toileting, but they have a right to privacy if they want it. You should ask if help is wanted before opening a toilet door.
- Children should know it is wrong for them to be touched in a way that hurts them, frightens them or feels rude. They should also know to tell a safe adult if they are worried about this or if it occurs.
- Children should know that it is wrong for them to be bullied. They should also know to tell a safe adult if they are worried about this or if it occurs.

Internet safety

By the age of five, most children use computers. Via family members, they are likely to have access to a mobile phone, and perhaps a games console that connects to the internet. Technology can enhance a child's life in lots of ways. But being online, playing video games and using a mobile phone also presents some dangers.

Dangers

The possible dangers of using technology include the following:

- Physical danger/contact with strangers who may seek to harm a child – these people may pose as a child online and may target a child by pretending to have similar interests. They may then use this to establish an online 'friendship'. When trust has developed, they may entice the child to meet up with them in person. This is known as **child grooming.**
- Exposure to inappropriate material – material may be pornographic, violent or hateful (for example promoting extreme political, racist or sexist views). It may promote dangerous or illegal behaviour, or may simply be inappropriate for the child's age.

Key terms

Child grooming occurs when someone establishes an online 'friendship' with a child, intending to entice them to meet up when trust has developed.
Cyberbullying occurs when a child is bullied online, for example in a chat room or via social media.

- Divulging personal details – children may unintentionally disclose personal details that may be used to facilitate identity theft or cons. 'Con' is short for 'confidence trick', which is an attempt to defraud after gaining someone's confidence (trust). For example, if a child reveals the names and address of their parents, these details could be used to falsely obtain a credit card in the parent's name. The details may also fall into the hands of people who may harm them.
- Illegal behaviour – users may become caught up in behaviour that is illegal, anti social or otherwise inappropriate. This includes illegally downloading copyrighted material.
- Bullying – **cyberbullying** may occur via the internet, through video games or mobile phones. It can leave victims extremely upset, scared and humiliated.

Talking to children about internet use and how to be safe

It is important that young children understand the dangers of the internet and how to enjoy it safely. So it is up to adults to talk to them about it, answer their questions and put precautions in place to protect them. It can help to make connections between the real world and the online world. For example, you can explain that people online might not be who they say they are and could be dangerous, just like any other stranger. For this reason, children should not give out any personal information online.

Safety strategies

Young children should be made aware of child-friendly search engines, which filter out inappropriate internet sites. Alternatively, safe

? Good practice

It is good practice to monitor children's internet use by checking the history folder on the browser regularly. This contains a list of sites that have been visited.

Figure 5.12: Explore websites and apps together.

search settings can be turned on to allow safe use of traditional search engines.

They should also be told not to:

- give out personal information, for example name, home address, landline and mobile numbers, bank details, PINs and passwords
- supply registration details without asking for permission and help
- visit chat websites or social networking sites without asking for permission and help
- arrange to meet an online friend in person without parental knowledge and permission (if a parent agrees to let them, they should always go along with them)
- give any indication of their age or sex in a personal email address or screen name
- keep anything that worries or upsets them online secret from you
- respond to unwanted emails or other messages.

Explore sites and apps together

Exploring websites and apps together is a great way to teach children how to use technology. It also gives you the opportunity to talk about safe use together. At the same time as guiding children, you can satisfy yourself that the sites and apps are appropriate.

Family discussions

It is important for the whole family to be aware of how to keep children safe online. This particularly applies if there are older siblings in the home who may be accessing sites and apps that are not appropriate for children of a younger age. If a child comes across something that upsets, worries or

shocks them online, it is important to discuss it and to give the child plenty of reassurance. Talking through how to avoid a repeat incident will help a child to rebuild their confidence. If there is a problem, parents are advised to:

- contact their internet service provider if a child comes across inappropriate content or is subjected to any inappropriate contact while online. Worries about illegal materials or suspicious behaviour should also be reported to the Child Exploitation and Online Protection Centre (https://ceop.police.uk/)
- install and regularly update filtering software to protect against inappropriate internet access.

Agree boundaries

Parents and carers should create clear rules for internet use with the child. Examples can include the following:

- The internet-connected computer must be in a family room with the screen facing outward so you can see what is happening.
- If a child accidentally goes to an unsuitable website, they should tell you. This can then be deleted from the 'history' folder and you can add the address to the 'parental control' filter list (see below).
- The child should take breaks from the computer every 30 minutes for health and safety reasons.

- The child should not download files from the internet without your agreement – it is best to never download unknown files at all.
- Children should not download or share files illegally (for example music, films).
- Children should not attempt to buy or order things online.

Using safe search facilities and restrictions
Adults should always use the parental controls available on computers, tablets, games consoles and mobile phones. These help to keep children safe by:

- blocking inappropriate websites and email addresses by adding them to a filter list
- setting time limits for the use of computers and devices
- preventing children from searching certain words.

Test your knowledge

1 Explain the measures you would take to keep a child safe in the kitchen.
2 What safety marks should you look for when buying toys?
3 Explain the circumstances in which a child could be at risk of drowning.
4 Outline how you can help a child to keep themselves safe from stranger danger.
5 Outline measures you would take to keep a child safe online.

Question practice

Question

a Explain three appropriate boundaries you could agree with a child to help to keep them safe online.

Mark scheme and additional guidance

Expected answers	Marks	Additional guidance
Three required. The following are all acceptable: • Only using child-friendly search engines or traditional search engines with safe settings turned on. • Not giving out personal information, e.g. name, address, phone numbers, passwords • Not supplying online registration details without asking for permission and help • Not visiting chat websites or social networking sites without asking for permission and help • Not arranging to meet an online friend in person without parental knowledge and permission • Not giving any indication of their age or sex in a personal email address or screen name • Not keep anything that worries or upsets them online secret from you or their parents • Not responding to unwanted emails or other messages, but telling you/their parents about them. The list is not exhaustive and other appropriate explanations may be accepted. Your tutor will be able to advise you on this.	6	You are able to explain three appropriate boundaries you could agree with a child to help keep them safe online. Level 3 (5-6 marks): Your answer will be detailed as it will include three appropriate boundaries you could agree with a child to help keep them safe online, and will include a reason or examples for each. Your answer will be coherent and use the correct terminology. *You may show reasoning, and the information will be relevant and supported by some evidence.*
		Level 2 (3-4 marks): Your answer will include two appropriate boundaries that you could agree with a child to keep them safe online and will include sound reasons supported with examples for each. Some use of correct terminology will be evident. An example of a level 2 answer has not been included.
Only using child-friendly search engines. Not giving out personal information. Not using chat websites.		Level 1 (1–2 marks): Your answer may include one or two appropriate boundaries. It may be that only one or two are mentioned briefly. Your answer may be a list and very brief without development. They may be muddled and lack detail. The information is basic, and supported by limited or no evidence, and the relationship to the evidence may not be clear.
		0 marks= response is not worthy of credit.

Candidate answer

a) Search engines:

The child should only use safe search engines. The safe settings on a general search engine can be switched on, or a special child-friendly search engine can be used. Then only age-appropriate content will be seen.

Personal details:

The child should never give out their personal details, including their name, age, date of birth, home address, telephone numbers and passwords.

Emails:

Children shouldn't have email addresses.

Commentary

Question context/content/style:

Explanation of appropriate boundaries that could be agreed with a child to help keep them safe online.

Requirements:

Three correct explanations given.

Marks awarded and rationale: 4/6

- The first two answers are correct, gaining two marks each.
- The third answer is incorrect and does not gain marks.

Question

b   Abigail works at a pre-school. To promote personal safety, she has been asked to talk with children about 'stranger danger'. Explain what she should tell children to do if a stranger approaches them.

Mark scheme and additional guidance

Expected answers	Marks	Additional guidance
One required. If a stranger talks to them, a child need not be rude – they can simply walk away quickly, telling an adult if they feel worried. But if a stranger asks or tells a child to go with them, the child should run away and tell a safe adult immediately. They must learn to 'Say no, never go!' If children are touched, grabbed or feel frightened or worried that they are in danger, it is all right to break the usual behaviour rules. They should attract attention by shouting and screaming, and punch, kick, etc. if they feel they need to.	8 marks	You are able to explain what Abigail should tell children to do if a stranger approaches them. Level 3 (7-8 marks): Your answer will provide a detailed explanation of what Abigail should tell children to do if a stranger approaches them. Your answer will be coherent and use the appropriate terminology. *You will show that you have developed your reasons and this will be clear and structured in a logical way. The information you include will be relevant and include some evidence or examples.*

Expected answers	Marks	Additional guidance
If a stranger talks to them, the child should walk away and tell their parents if they feel worried. If a stranger touches them, or the child feels scared, it is okay to shout as this will attract the attention of other people nearby.		Level 2 (4-6 marks): Your answer will provide a sound explanation of what Abigail should tell children to do if a stranger approaches them. Answers will use some appropriate terminology. Your answer will be reasoned with some structure. The information will be mostly relevant, and supported by some evidence.
If a stranger talks to them, the child should walk away and tell their parents If a stranger touches them, or the child feels scared, it is okay to shout.		Level 1 (1-3 marks): You will give a basic description of what Abigail should tell the children. Your answer may be a list. The information is basic and not structured. The information is supported by limited evidence and the relationship to the evidence may not be clear.

Candidate answer

b If a stranger talks to them a child should shout and scream to attract attention, whilst running towards a safe adult such as their parent or carer. They should tell them what happened straight away.

Commentary

Question context/content/style:

Explanation of what to tell children to do should they be approached by a stranger.

Requirements:

Correct explanation given.

Marks awarded and rationale: 0/8

● The answer is incorrect and does not gain a mark.

Read about it

Great Ormond Street Hospital. Visit: www.gosh.nhs.uk/children/staying-hospital

Meningitis Now. Visit: www.meningitisnow.org/meningitis-explained/signs-and-symptoms/meningitis-babies-and-children-under-five/

National Society for the Prevention of Cruelty to Children (NSPCC). Visit: www.nspcc.org.uk/preventing-abuse/keeping-children-safe/

NCT's website, offering information and support in pregnancy, birth and early parenthood. Visit: https://www.nct.org.uk/about-us

NHS Health Scotland's 'Ready Steady, Baby' guide to pregnancy, antenatal care, birth and parenthood. Visit: www.readysteadybaby.org.uk/

NHS labour and birth guide. Visit: www.nhs.uk/Conditions/pregnancy-and-baby/Pages/what-happens-during-labour-and-birth.aspx

NHS pregnancy guide. Visit: www.nhs.uk/conditions/pregnancy-and-baby/pages/pregnancy-and-baby-care.aspx

St John's Ambulance. Visit: www.sja.org.uk/sja/first-aid-advice/first-aid-for-parents.aspx

The Child Accident Prevention Trust (CAPT). Visit: www.capt.org.uk/

The NHS. Visit: www.nhs.uk/conditions/pregnancy-and-baby/pages/going-to-hospital.aspx

The Red Cross. Visit: www.redcross.org.uk/What-we-do/First-aid/Baby-and-Child-First-Aid

Unit R019
Understand the equipment and nutritional needs of children from birth to five years

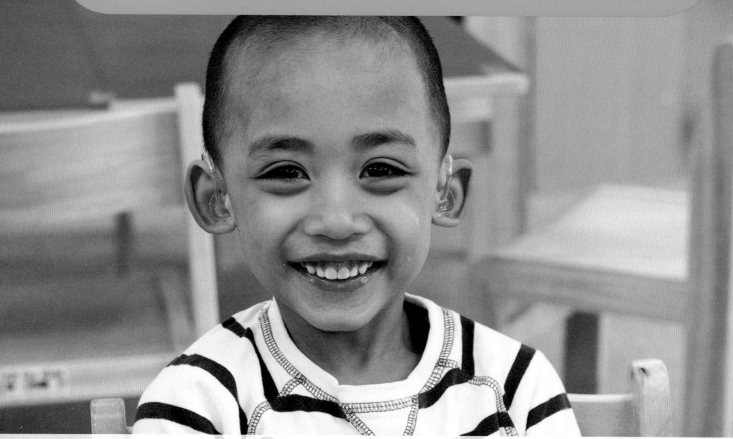

About this unit

There are 30 GLH (guided learning hours) for this unit. This unit is about the different equipment and nutritional requirements of children from birth to five years. It focuses on understanding the key factors to consider when choosing equipment. It also focuses on dietary guidelines, the functions and sources of **nutrients** and the feeding of young children.

Children need a range of equipment, including equipment for travelling, feeding and sleeping, as well as clothes and footwear. For a child's well-being and safety, all items chosen must be both appropriate and cared for hygienically.

Good nutrition is vital to a child's health and development, so it is very important that you learn about making healthy choices for children. This will encourage children to make healthy choices for themselves as they grow and develop.

Learning outcomes

By the end of this unit you will:

- understand the key factors when choosing equipment for babies from birth to 12 months
- understand the key factors when choosing equipment for children from one to five years
- know the nutritional guidelines and requirements for children from birth to five years
- be able to investigate and develop feeding solutions for children from birth to five years.

➡

How will I be assessed?

In Learning outcome 1, you should investigate the main points to be considered when choosing equipment for travelling, feeding and sleeping as well as clothes and footwear for babies from birth to 12 months.

In Learning outcome 2, you should investigate the main points to be considered when choosing equipment for travelling, feeding and sleeping as well as clothes and footwear for children from one to five years.

In Learning outcome 3, you should have knowledge of the function and sources of nutrients and current government guidelines for children from birth to five years. This should include stages of feeding children from 0 to 6 months, 6 to 12 months and 1 to 5 years.

In Learning outcome 4, you should demonstrate their understanding of the nutritional requirements by completing a practical task that involves creating a suitable feeding solution.

Make sure you refer to the current OCR Specification and guidance.

Learning outcome 1

Understand the key factors when choosing equipment for babies from birth to 12 months

About this Learning outcome

Babies develop and grow quickly between birth and the age of 12 months. In fact, their bodies will develop and change faster now than at any other time in their lives. As a result, the equipment needs of babies up to the age of 12 months also changes rapidly. It is up to a baby's parents and carers to respond, ensuring that the equipment they make available always meets the baby's needs at the current moment in time. A good understanding of child development will help you to anticipate what a baby is likely to need next and to plan accordingly. You will learn about child development in Unit R020.

Assessment criteria

In this learning outcome you will cover:

1.1 Key equipment to be considered for babies from birth to 12 months:
- travelling equipment
- feeding equipment
- sleeping equipment
- clothing and footwear.

1.2 Key factors to consider when choosing equipment for babies from birth to 12 months:
- age-appropriateness
- safety
- cost
- design/ergonomics
- durability
- hygiene.

Getting started

How much equipment do you think a baby needs? Choose one of the following categories and thought storm as many items as you can think of for the category:
- travelling equipment (for when parents/carers are travelling with the baby on foot, via car and on public transport)
- feeding equipment
- sleeping equipment
- clothing and footwear.

1.1 Key equipment to be considered for babies from birth to 12 months

In this Learning outcome, you will learn about equipment in the following categories:

- travelling equipment
- feeding equipment
- sleeping equipment
- clothing and footwear.

This unit looks at each of these in turn.

Travelling equipment

Travelling equipment is necessary for when:

- parents and carers are travelling with the baby on foot and on public transport
- parents and carers are travelling with the baby by car.

Prams and buggies

Prams and buggies are among the most expensive pieces of equipment that parents or carers are likely to buy. Not all buggies are suitable for newborns and very young babies, who have different needs to older babies as they cannot yet support their own weight. Some families choose to use a pram at this age and they then switch to a buggy when the baby is a bit older.

Other families choose an adjustable buggy that can be used throughout the first year and beyond. These have a fully reclining element designed for the younger baby. In most adjustable designs, the buggy can also be manoeuvred to become parent facing or outward facing. The first option allows a close eye to be kept on a younger baby, and also enables eye contact and interaction. The second option allows an older baby to look out into the world.

Car seats

It is not only sensible to use a car seat to keep children safe in the car – it is the law. RoSPA (the Royal Society for the Prevention of Accidents) tells us that this law requires that: '... all children travelling in the front or rear seat of any car, van or

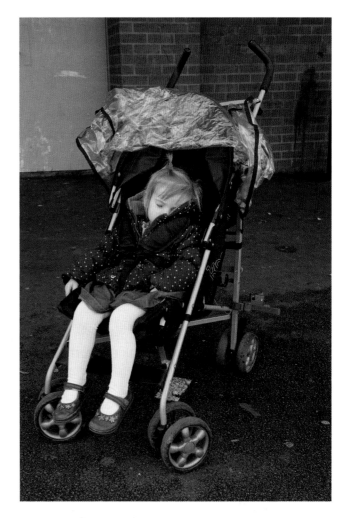

Figure 6.1: Prams and buggies must be age appropriate.

goods vehicle must use the correct child car seat until they are either 135 cm in height or 12 years old (whichever they reach first). After this they must use an adult seat belt. There are very few exceptions.'

Baby seats are only effective when fitted properly in the car, so it is crucial to follow the manufacturer's instructions precisely. Any car seat that has been in a car during an accident must be replaced, even if there is no visible damage. This is because it could have been weakened and might no longer provide the necessary protection.

Baby car seats usually have a weight restriction alongside an age for which they are appropriate, so it is important to consider this when choosing a seat. It is also important to remember to replace

Did you know?

Some buggies have a detachable element that unclips from the frame and can be used as a baby carrier. Some of these also double as a car seat.

it at the specified time. For example, it might say on the packaging of a car seat 'suitable from birth up to 13 kg (29 lbs) or 12–15 months'. Further information is included in the text and table on page 105 of Learning outcome 2. In Autumn 2016, researchers involved in a small study reported that newborn babies may be at risk of developing breathing difficulties when spending a long period of time in a car seat, due to the 40 degree angle at which their body will be positioned. They advised parents to keep a watchful eye on babies during journeys, and to avoid making journeys of more than 30 minutes with a young baby. If a longer journey is necessary, taking regular breaks is advised. Parents are also advised to limit the use of car seats to the car, so you should not remove the car seat for use as a baby carrier. You should not leave babies to sleep, or put them down to sleep, in a car seat. You can read more about this study at http://www.nhs.uk/news/2016/10October/Pages/Warning-over-babies-sleeping-in-car-seats.aspx

Baby carrier

There are two types of carrier – those that resemble car seats and baby slings worn by the parent or carer.

- There will usually be both a weight and age limitation given, and it is important not to exceed these criteria.
- Great care must be taken to ensure that slings are fitted (worn) properly to ensure that the baby doesn't slip or feel uncomfortable.

Most carriers are designed to be used when babies are quite young, typically from birth to four months.

Feeding equipment

It is important for practitioners to support the chosen feeding methods of parents and carers – breastfeeding, bottle feeding or combiation feeding. Quite a lot of equipment is required to support both methods, because it is so important that all feeding equipment is sterilised to ensure that it is hygienic.

Steriliser and sterilising

Feeding equipment must be washed thoroughly before being sterilised. It should be rinsed, washed and rinsed again. Bottle brushes and teat brushes should be used. Equipment to be washed and sterilised includes:

- bottles
- teats
- bottle caps
- measuring spoons
- breast pump
- plastic knives (used for levelling a spoonful of milk powder when making up feeds).

There are different methods of sterilisation. Traditionally, a sterile solution was made up in a steriliser (a small bucket with a lid) by mixing either sterilising tablets or sterilising liquid with water, following the manufacturer's instructions. The equipment was then submerged in the steriliser for a specified amount of time. This method is still used, but now there is the additional choice of an electric steriliser or a steam steriliser.

Figure 6.2: Sterilising equipment.

Bottles

Although only one bottle will be given to a baby at any one time, several bottles are needed in order to always be prepared for feeding. Best practice is to make up fresh feeds as they are required, but parents or carers will sometimes need to make up bottles ahead of time and refrigerate them – see Learning outcome 4 for full details. It is also best to allow for a few bottles to be in the steriliser at any one time.

There are various teats available and these should be selected according to the baby's needs. The younger the baby, the more slowly they will need to receive their milk. 'Slow' teats have a smaller hole in them to restrict the flow. Sometimes, a doctor or health visitor will recommend a teat of a particular shape for a baby who experiences difficulty feeding.

? Did you know?

Bottles may be needed for babies who are breastfed as well as those who are bottle fed. There might be times when the mother expresses her milk to feed to a baby from a bottle rather than from the breast.

Breast pump

Breast pumps allow mothers to express milk that can then be fed to a baby via a bottle. This enables the baby to be fed breast milk even when the mother is away from the baby – for example, a practioner or childminder can give the feed when the mother is at work. It also allows other family members to feed the breastfed baby. This can be important to the well-being of some mothers as well as fathers. For example, it means that the task of waking throughout the night to feed a baby can be shared, allowing the mother to get some rest and sleep. There are two types of breast pump:

- manual
- electric.

Figure 6.3: Feeding bottles.

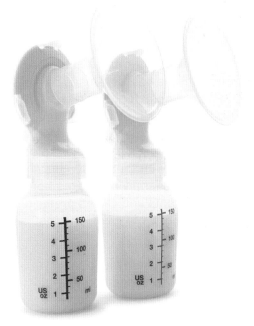

Figure 6.4: Breast pump.

Sleeping equipment

Sufficient sleep is vital to a baby's well-being, growth and development. The younger the baby, the more they will sleep, so comfort is absolutely paramount.

Moses basket and cot

Moses baskets are a suitable option for a newborn baby's first bed, but they will need to move up into a cot by around 3–4 months of age, depending on the basket selected and the baby's rate of growth. The manufacturer's guidelines on this will come with the basket. Moses baskets are designed to be portable. In the early months when a baby is sleeping for much of the time, it is convenient to be able to carry a baby from room to room with you. Moses baskets are also easy for parents to take with them when they go out – for a day spent at a family member's house, for example. Some parents and carers prefer to put their newborn straight into a cot, and that is absolutely fine.

Cots should be sturdy and kept clean. Always ensure that wood is in good condition to avoid splintering. Cots take a lot of wear and tear, especially in a group setting. The side of the cot that slides down for the lifting in and out of the baby can be particularly prone to wear, so check

Good practice

Cots are sometimes heirlooms, passed down through families, or they might be bought second hand. In this situation, it is important to investigate whether the cot is up to current safety standards. This includes the finish of the cot, as varnish or paint used on vintage cots may not be non-toxic and could be potentially dangerous. A new mattress should always be used.

that it is in good working order. If you notice the sliding mechanism starting to feel slacker, report it to the appropriate person straight away, as movement from the baby may cause it to slide down unintended. This presents a risk in terms of a baby's body being pinched or trapped, or they may roll and fall from the cot.

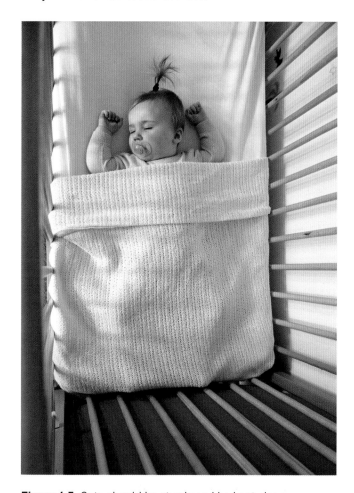

Figure 6.5: Cots should be sturdy and be kept clean.

Mattress

Moses baskets come with their own fitted mattresses, uniquely shaped and sized to fit into individual designs, because there is not a standard Moses basket size. However, cot mattresses are generally purchased separately from the cot itself, presenting the buyer with more choice.

There has been much research into how sleeping position and bedding (including mattresses) may be a factor in cases of Sudden Infant Death Syndrome (SIDS). SIDS occurs when a seemingly healthy baby or toddler dies unexpectedly in their sleep with no medical explanation. This affects around 300 babies in the UK each year. The National Health Service (NHS) advise that to prevent SIDS, babies should sleep on a mattress that is:

- firm
- flat
- waterproof
- in good condition.

Here is the complete list of advice given to parents for the prevention of SIDS:

Do:

- always place your baby on their back to sleep
- place your baby in the 'feet to foot' position (with their feet touching the end of the cot, Moses basket, or pram)
- keep your baby's head uncovered. Their blanket should be tucked in no higher than their shoulders
- let your baby sleep in a cot or Moses basket in the same room as you for the first six months
- use a mattress that is firm, flat, waterproof and in good condition
- breastfeed your baby (if you can).

Do not:

- smoke during pregnancy or let anyone smoke in the same room as your baby (both before and after birth)
- sleep on a bed, sofa or armchair with your baby. This is even more dangerous if you or your partner smoke or take drugs, or if you have been drinking alcohol

Activity

1 Visit this NHS weblink and read more about SIDS: www.nhs.uk/Conditions/Sudden-infant-death-syndrome/Pages/Introduction.aspx.

2 Follow at least two of the weblinks given on the NHS webpage and read the information that you discover. Make notes of any key points that you would like to remember.

- let your baby get too hot or too cold. A room temperature of 16–20 °C, with light bedding or a lightweight baby sleeping bag, will provide a comfortable sleeping environment for your baby.

Clothing and footwear

The first set of clothing bought for a newborn baby is known as the 'layette'. This will generally consist of vests and baby grows, with an outer layer of clothing added depending on the weather. At this age, babies move very little, so all they really need is to be comfortable and neither too hot or too cold.

But babies grow quickly, so their newborn items will not last them for long. Once a baby begins to become more mobile, they will need more from their clothing.

Nappies

There are two types of nappies:

- disposable
- reusable.

Disposable nappies are available in a range of sizes. Some are unisex, but these days, many are shaped to be suitable for boys or girls. Nappies must always be disposed of safely, as bodily waste is potentially harmful to health (see 'Hygiene' on page 94). In the home and some group settings, used nappies are placed into a bag (often known as a 'nappy sack'), which is then tied closed. The bag is placed in a nappy bin with a lid. Some settings will have a special unit which seals a nappy into a plastic wrapping as it is placed inside.

Reusable nappies – shaped and traditional

Shaped nappies are now available. According to one manufacturer, the Cotton Nappy Company, these are, 'shaped for ease of use and available either in different sizes depending on the baby's age, or as "birth to potty" nappies which adjust to fit using poppers. They consist of an absorbent inner part, which is usually made of bamboo, cotton or microfibre, and a waterproof PUL outer. Popular types include pocket nappies, where an absorbent insert is stuffed inside the waterproof outer; two-part systems, where an absorbent inner nappy is covered with a waterproof wrap; and "all-in-ones", which are the most similar to disposable nappies. Nappies and outers are usually fastened with poppers or velcro.' Traditional reusable nappies are made from a rectangle of terry towelling, which is very absorbent. Nappies are folded to fit the individual baby and secured using a nappy pin or clip – these have been designed with a safety feature to ensure that they do not come undone and become unsafe. There are a range of nappy folding techniques to suit babies of different sizes, and some are more suited to boys or girls. In both shaped and traditional nappies, a disposable nappy liner may be used inside the nappy to help keep the baby's skin dry while letting wetness through to the fabric. These can be flushed down the toilet along with stools. Plastic pants with close fitting legs are also placed over the traditional nappy to keep wetness from coming out of the fabric. Used reusable nappies are placed in a nappy bucket with lid when removed, then laundered in the washing machine at 60 degrees. (A machine pre-rinse can also be used in the case of soiled nappies).

Daywear, outerwear and nightwear

All daywear, outerwear and nightwear should be:

- comfortable
- easy to move in
- washable and easily dryable, e.g. suitable for the tumble dryer
- preferably 'non-iron' or 'easy iron'
- made from fabric suitable for purpose, e.g. a crawling baby will benefit from hard-wearing trousers that will protect their knees. Heavier, warm material is ideal for a coat (outerwear).

Very soft, fire retardant material is perfect for nightwear

- suitable for various weather conditions, e.g. sunhat, shorts and T-shirts in the summer; long sleeved top, leggings and cardigan in the winter, plus outerwear (e.g. hat, coat, mittens)
- easy to fasten (e.g. Velcro, poppers, elasticated waist instead of button and zip)
- easy to get on and off, especially for nappy changes.

Unisex clothing is preferred by some families because it can be passed down to siblings more effectively and saves on cost.

Babies do not need shoes until they begin to walk outside at around 12–14 months, unless there are items on the floor inside that may cause harm. (You can read about first shoes in Learning outcome 2.) Walking barefoot indoors when it is safe to do so is good for the natural development of a young child's feet. A baby's feet will need to be kept warm enough, so socks and booties will be needed.

Figure 6.6: Clothes should be comfortable to move in.

1.2 Key factors to consider when choosing equipment for babies from birth to 12 months

The key factors to consider when choosing equipment for babies from birth to 12 months include:

- age-appropriateness
- safety
- design/ergonomics (comfort)
- cost and durability
- hygiene.

This section looks at each of these in turn.

Age-appropriateness

As you have learnt, babies develop very quickly in their first year, and this has a continual impact on the equipment that is suitable for them. So you must always check the safety mark and instructions on a piece of equipment (see below) and take note when an item will become unsuitable for a baby in the future. For example, it is safe to put a very young baby down to sleep in most Moses baskets. But as the baby grows and becomes able to roll over, they may tip a Moses basket, making it no longer safe.

> ? **Did you know?**
>
> On some pieces of large equipment, weight restrictions are given as well as or instead of age restrictions. This applies to high chairs and cots, for example.

Safety

Before using any piece of equipment, it is absolutely vital to check that the item is safe for the child or the children who will use it. This applies to both new pieces of equipment that you are selecting (and perhaps buying) for the first time, and any pieces of equipment that you use regularly.

Safety marks

Before buying an item for a child, practitioners need to check that it has a recognised safety

mark. These are quality assurance standards that tell you that the item is safe for use as directed by the manufacturer. So it is important that you always use equipment in line with the manufacturer's instructions. This includes making sure items are assembled according to directions. An incorrectly assembled item can be very dangerous. For example, a high chair could collapse causing a child to fall, or body parts could be trapped between gaps in a cot.

You must also follow guidelines that appear on boxes and other packaging. For example, it is very common to come across the guideline 'Not suitable for use by children under 36 months due to small parts'.

Safety checks

All equipment is prone to wear and tear over time, even if **durable** items have been selected (see the 'durability' section on page 93). This is especially true in group settings and other professional childcare settings (such as a creche), because over the same period of time, equipment will get much more use than it would in the average family home.

- A previously safe piece of equipment can turn into a hazard when damaged.
- A previously safe baby carrier can become dangerous if the handle stops locking into position.

Figure 6.7: British Standards Institution (BSI) safety mark/ kite mark. Can you suggest a piece of equipment on which you would expect to see each of these marks?

✔ Good practice

Whenever you see a piece of equipment that has become damaged or unhygienic, you should remove it from the vicinity of babies and children right away. This will prevent injuries and/or risks to health. If the problem is with a piece of equipment that cannot easily be moved, ensure that babies or children stay away from it.

You should report any damage or hygiene concerns to the appropriate person right away.

- A broken rattle may have a sharp edge.
- Damaged footwear may cause a child to slip and fall.
- Damaged wood may cause a splinter.

The best way to ensure that equipment remains safe over time is to visually check it over each time it is set out and put away. This works very well for items such as toys and clothing. Pieces of equipment that tend to stay out can be checked the first time you use them each day – this applies to items such as car seats, cots and baby swings. Car seats must be replaced if they have been in a car at the time of an accident - even if damage cannot be seen, they may no longer be safe to use. Second hand car seats should not be bought, as although they may feature a safety mark, you cannot be sure that they have not been in an accident or become otherwise unsafe. You should also consider whether the item is hygienic – see page 94 for more information.

Some items such as feeding equipment and toys (such as teething rings) will need sterilising. See page 86.

Flammability

Flammability is the term used to describe the ability of a substance to ignite or to burn. The more flammable a material is, the greater the fire risk it presents. To promote safety, there are strict regulations around the materials that manufacturers can use in clothing and other key items for babies, including bedding and soft furnishings. Flammability is carefully considered

✔ Good practice

Not all equipment used with babies is manufactured. Some people will make items such as blankets, clothes and soft furnishings. In this case, it is up to parents and carers to make sure that they are made safely from appropriate materials that do not present risk, including a risk of catching fire or burning. It is possible for safety marks to be counterfeited (faked). So equipment should always be purchased from a reputable retailer, such as a shop that you trust.

🔑 Key term

Flammability the ability of a substance to ignite or to burn.

when a product is safety tested for a BSI safety mark/kite mark – this provides another reason for always checking for the safety marks before selecting equipment.

Stability

Stability is another key safety issue. A high percentage of injuries reported in the UK every year come from falls. It is very important to make sure that any item of equipment that takes a baby's weight or supports a baby's body is stable and secure. Items need to be both well made and sturdy. Equipment also needs to be carefully used to ensure stability. For example, if heavy shopping bags are placed on the handles of a buggy, it will become unstable and is likely to tip over backwards, putting the baby at risk. A baby sling not worn according to the manufacturer's instructions could also be unsafe, as the baby's body may become sore and they may even slip. Some pieces of equipment need to be placed on a sturdy flat surface before use, or stability will be affected. This applies to high chairs, cots and baby swings.

There are also many injuries as a result of objects falling onto a child. Parents and carers need to think carefully about how to prevent objects falling onto babies. This is a particular area of concern at this age, as babies will pull themselves to standing position and move around the room by holding onto furniture or other nearby equipment. As well as holding onto items intended for them (such as a baby seat) babies will make use of anything in reach (such as an adult's chair). So it is best practice to make sure that all such items are sturdy. Larger items that could fall onto a baby should they be bumped into (such as shelving units, TVs and wardrobes) should be fixed to the wall.

Figure 6.8: Highchairs must be placed on a sturdy, flat surface.

Activity

Return to the list of equipment you made during the 'Getting started' activity on page 84.

1 Which of the items would you expect to check for safety each time they are set out and put away? Underline them with a coloured pen.

2 Which of the items would you expect to check the first time you use them each day? Underline them in a different colour.

Design/ergonomics

Ergonomics is the science of design, which is applied to make products efficient, safe and comfortable for use. If you look out for it, you will spot evidence of ergonomics being applied to many pieces of equipment. For example:

- some feeding bottles have a distinct shape that makes them more comfortable to hold
- car seats are moulded to keep a baby comfortable in a position, as well as keeping them safe
- some cots are lower to the ground than others, making it easier for a shorter person to lift a baby in and out safely.

Design/ergonomics is particularly important when choosing a pram or buggy. If the handles are not at the right height for the person pushing it, their shoulders, back and neck may become sore with prolonged or frequent use.

It is important to think about design/ergonomics for both babies and adults when selecting pieces of equipment.

Cost and durability

It is always best to select items that are **durable**, or made to last. There is less chance of durable items being broken and becoming potentially dangerous during use. They are most likely to stand up to use by a group of babies or children.

Durable items can be more expensive at the time of purchase, usually because they are made of higher quality materials. But in the long run, they may be more economic (a better buy) because a cheaper alternative may break or become worn out and so may need to be replaced. For example, a high chair with plastic legs may be less durable than one with wooden legs that costs more.

While **durability** sometimes costs a little more, the expense may be warranted. However it is important to recognise when spending more money is not a necessity. For example, there are expensive designer pieces of baby equipment available that are not necessarily more durable than mid-price alternatives. See unit R018, LO1 for more information on finance.

Key terms

Ergonomics the science of design applied to make products efficient, safe and comfortable for use.

Durable made to last.

Durability the ability to withstand wear and tear.

Hygiene

When completing your safety checks on pieces of equipment (see 'Safety checks' on page 91), you should consider whether the item is hygienic. If it is visibly dirty or otherwise unhygienic, you should remove the item for cleaning. In the case of large pieces of equipment such as cots, you should remove babies from the vicinity or area and then clean the item.

Easy to clean

Selecting equipment that is easy to clean helps enormously in terms of keeping things hygienic. Practitioners will have a planned schedule for washing or sterilising appropriate materials and equipment, even if they do not appear to be dirty to the eye. (They will also be washed in between times if necessary as described above.)

Some items such as nappy changing equipment (e.g. a changing mat), feeding equipment and baby toys will need cleaning each time they are used. Whenever you are cleaning and washing equipment, always make sure that you only use cleaning products that are safe for use with very young children. All cleaning products must be kept out of reach of children.

Washable

Items made from fabrics such as a baby's clothes or bedding will need to be washed frequently, and in some cases after every use. Items close to a baby's skin such as a baby grow or vest will only be worn once before washing, while outerwear such as a coat will need washing less often. However, it is often necessary to change a baby's clothes partway through the day – if they are sick or if a nappy leaks. It is sensible to buy fabric items that can be washed easily, ideally in a washing machine. It is also helpful if they can be tumble dried.

Figure 6.9: Equipment must be easy to clean.

Good practice

Bodily waste is a potentially harmful substance, since it can pass on infections such as hepatitis and HIV. Early years settings will have strict procedures in place for handling nappies, vomit and blood, and for clearing up after toileting accidents. These include wearing disposable gloves and using designated disposal bins.

Good practice

Whenever you see a piece of equipment that has become damaged or unhygienic, you should remove it from the vicinity or area where the babies and children are right away. This will prevent injuries and/or risks to health. If the problem is with a piece of equipment that cannot easily be moved, ensure that babies or children stay away.

You should report any damage or hygiene concerns to the appropriate person right away.

Test your knowledge

1 What does the term 'ergonomic' mean?
2 Give five examples of pieces of equipment that should be sterilised.
3 What is a safety mark?
4 When should you replace a car seat?
5 What does the term 'durability' mean?

Assessment preparation

The OCR model assignment will ask you to investigate the main points to be considered when choosing:

- Clothing and footwear
- Feeding equipment
- Sleeping equipment
- Transport equipment

for babies from birth to 12 months of age. You should support your evidence by considering the following features when making your decision:

- Suitability for age and growth
- Safety aspects
- Costs
- Design
- Practicality
- Durability
- Ease of cleaning.

1. Outline the safety aspects you would consider before selecting a buggy.
2. Explain why durability should be a key consideration when selecting feeding equipment.
3. Outline hygiene factors might you consider when selecting sleeping equipment.
4. Explain why age-appropriateness (including a baby's weight) should be a key consideration when selecting a baby carrier.

Assessment guidance

Learning outcome 1: Understand the key factors when choosing equipment for babies from birth to 12 months

Marking criteria for LO1

Mark band 1	Mark band 2	Mark band 3
1.1 A **limited range** of examples are given for some types of equipment needed for babies from birth to 12 months. **1.2 Outlines** the key factors for consideration for the types of equipment with **limited reasons** for the choice of equipment selected. Draws upon **limited** skills/knowledge/understanding from Unit R018.	**1.1** A **range** of examples are given for most types of equipment needed for babies from birth to 12 months **1.2 Explains** the key factors for consideration for the types of equipment with **clear reasons** for the choice of equipment selected. Draws upon **some relevant** skills/knowledge/understanding from Unit R018.	**1.1** A **wide range** of examples are given for all types of equipment needed for babies from birth to 12 months. **1.2 Explains in detail** the key factors for consideration for the types of equipment with **well-developed reasons** for the choice of equipment selected **and** rejected. **Clearly** draws upon **relevant** skills/knowledge/understanding from Unit R018.

 Top tips

Command words

- A limited range – the work produced is small in range and scope and includes only a part of the information required, it evidences partial rather than full understanding. A limited range is one or two.
- A range – the evidence presented is sufficiently varied to give confidence that the knowledge and principles are understood in application as well as in fact. A range is two or three.
- A wide range is at least three.

The evidence you need to produce:

- equipment needs for children from birth to five years.

Examples of evidence format:

- written/typed report
- online/shop visit log
- information booklets/leaflets
- PowerPoint presentation with notes
- storyboard/article.

When creating this evidence, it may help to:

- look at more than one example of each type of equipment. This will enable you to compare items and choose the one with the best features.

A wide range for mark band 3 is at least three. At least three factors from the list of six in the specification must be evidenced.

Learning outcome 2

Understand the key factors when choosing equipment for children from one to five years

About this Learning outcome

Young children continue to develop and grow at pace between the ages of one and five years. During this time, they will become increasingly mobile – walking, running, climbing and riding tricycles. They will become more independent too – learning to feed and dress themselves and making the move from nappies to underwear.

They will also move from a cot to a bed, generally sleeping in a different room from their parents/carers.

The equipment selected for young children needs to keep up with their changing needs throughout this period. A good understanding of child development will stand you in good stead and help you to plan ahead. (See Unit R020 for more on child development.)

Assessment criteria

In this learning outcome you will cover:

2.1 Key equipment to be considered for children from one to five years:
- travelling equipment
- feeding equipment
- sleeping equipment
- clothing and footwear.

2.2 Key factors to consider when choosing equipment for children from one to five years:
- age-appropriateness
- safety
- cost
- design/ergonomics
- durability
- hygiene.

Getting started

How much equipment do you think children aged one to five years need? Choose one of the following categories and thought storm as many items as you can think of for the category:
- travelling equipment
- feeding equipment
- sleeping equipment
- clothing and footwear.

2.1 Key equipment to be considered for children from one to five years

In this Learning outcome, you will learn about equipment in the following categories:

- travelling equipment
- feeding equipment
- sleeping equipment
- clothing and footwear.

This unit looks at each of these in turn.

Travelling equipment

Travelling equipment is still necessary when parents and carers are travelling with a child on foot, on public transport and by car.

Stroller/buggy

In Learning outcome 1, you learnt about buggies that can be used throughout the first year of a child's life and beyond. Many children will use this type of buggy throughout the toddler stage. From the age of around two and a half years, many families choose to switch to a stroller-style buggy or pushchair. This is much lighter weight, making it easier to fold and to pack away when not in use, or when going on a journey by public transport, car, plane or boat. At this age, a child no longer needs the more supportive and heavier buggy because they have the strength and body development to hold themselves upright indefinitely when sitting. They will also spend less time being pushed along by adults, and more time walking alongside them.

Reins

Once a baby learns to walk and can do so outside, they are generally keen to explore and to walk independently. They very quickly begin to pick up speed. However, they are still finding their feet and will often fall at first. It is exciting for a child to be able to head off instantly towards anything that takes their fancy. However, this means that their movements are rather unpredictable – they can shoot off in any direction and will have little awareness of what they should or should not do or interact with. This can make it challenging to keep a toddler safe when you are out walking in the world together, especially when you are using the pavement.

Reins can be a very good solution. They fit around the child's chest and the ends are held by a parent or carer. Reins still give a child a feeling of independence as they walk out in front, and as long as they are safe, you can simply follow their lead. But it is very easy to 'put the brakes on' by standing still when they are heading somewhere inappropriate. Also, when on reins, you can often save a child should they begin to fall, by taking their weight. Backpack style reins are also available. The child wears a backpack in the normal way, and detachable reins can be clipped onto the bottom of the bag section, as shown below.

At around the time a child begins to have more reliable control over their walking, they are usually calmer about being out in the world, and happy to hold an adult's hand on a walk. At this stage, the reins will no longer be needed.

Figure 7.1: Reins help to keep a toddler safe on a walk.

Car seat

You were introduced to car seats in Learning outcome 1. Children must normally use a child car seat until they are 12 years old or 135 cm tall, whichever comes first. Only EU-approved child car seats can be used in the UK. These have a label showing a capital 'E' in a circle. You can choose a child car seat based on a child's height or weight. Here is a summary of the two types of car seats available:

Height-based car seats – these are known as 'i-Size' seats. They must be rear-facing until your child is over 15 months old. Your child can use a forward-facing car seat when they are over 15 months old. You must check the seat to make sure it is suitable for the height of your child.

Weight-based car seats – here, the seat your child can use (and the way they must be restrained in it) depends on their weight. You may be able to choose from more than one type of seat.

Figure 7.3: Weight-based car seat.

Child's weight	Car seat
0 kg to 9 kg	Lie-flat or 'lateral' baby carrier, *rear-facing baby carrier, or *rear-facing baby seat using a harness
0 kg to 13 kg	*Rear-facing baby carrier or *rear-facing baby seat using a harness
9 kg to 18 kg	*Rear- or forward-facing baby seat using a harness or safety shield
15 kg to 36 kg	*Rear- or forward-facing child seat (high-backed booster seat or booster cushion) using a seat belt, harness or safety shield

* You must also:

- deactivate any front airbags before fitting a rear-facing baby seat in a front seat
- not fit a child car seat in side-facing seats.

Table 7.1: Different types of car seats.

Figure 7.2: Height-based car seat.

Feeding equipment

In this age range, children will become fully weaned onto solid food, and will be growing in confidence as they learn to feed themselves independently.

Trainer cup

At around 15 months of age, children will be ready for a trainer cup. These have a handle at either side, making it easier for a child to hold the cup level and to take it to and from their mouth. Trainer cups also have a secure lid to prevent spillages, and a spout to drink from. The spout delivers a much faster flow of liquid than a bottle teat, which children can now cope with. When a child has mastered the training cup, the lid can be removed, and they can experience drinking straight from the rim of the cup. Spillages are to be expected, but the use of the two handles will help. Once a child can lift the training cup to and from their mouth fairly reliably without the lid, they will be ready to switch to a plastic cup with one handle.

> **(?) Did you know?**
>
> Learning to self-feed is very challenging for a young child. It requires mastering some complicated fine motor movements that are unlike any learnt so far.

Cutlery

Babies will start trying to feed themselves by 'helping' their parent or carer with the plastic feeding spoon from the time they are able to sit up in a highchair. They will begin to feed themselves with finger foods (such as cut pieces of fruit) from around 10–12 months and will eventually manage the spoon alone from about 13–15 months.

Once they've mastered this and they are also ready to sit up at the table, it is time to introduce a plastic fork alongside the spoon. A child will generally get used to a fork reasonably quickly, using it to spear soft foods and alternating between the spoon and fork by 15–18 months. They can generally use the two together with precision from around three years.

The next stage is to introduce a knife, and it may also be time to switch over to a nursery set of small metal cutlery with plastic handles. Now things get much more complicated. Using a knife and fork requires a child to make a different movement with each hand at the same time, plus hand-eye co-ordination. Learning to use cutlery like an adult is essentially learning to use very tricky tools. Most children have mastered it by the time they are four years of age.

Figure 7.4: Trainer cup.

Figure 7.5: Cutlery.

Weaning bibs

Weaning is a messy affair! Young children will frequently miss their mouths with a spoonful or forkful of food as they learn to master the complicated hand-eye co-ordination and fine motor skills required to get it there safely. You should always be relaxed otherwise, children may become tense about eating and begin to dread mealtimes. In the interests of children's well-being and health, it is very important to avoid mealtimes becoming a battleground or standoff. One of the best ways to achieve this is to make sure that a mess doesn't matter by protecting the child's clothes with a weaning bib. Plastic bibs curl at the end to catch any spilt food or drink, can be disposed of after the meal and can be washed with the dishes.

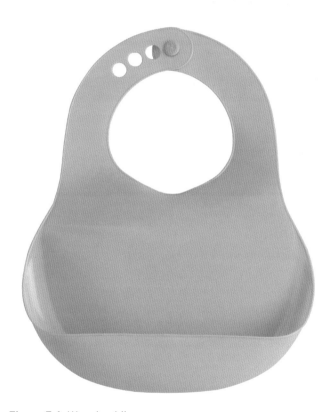

Figure 7.6: Weaning bib.

 Good practice

If you are feeding the child in a carpeted area, protect the floor by placing a wipe-clean mat underneath the child's chair.

 Did you know?

You may hear weaning bibs being called 'pelican bibs'. Originally, the bibs with a curl at the end were named after the shape of a pelican's beak.

Figure 7.7: Most children master eating with cutlery by the age of four.

Sleeping equipment

Sufficient sleep remains vital to a child's well-being, growth and development. Comfort is also still very important. However, in this age range, the amount of daytime sleep needed will slowly decline, with children eventually going throughout the day without a nap around the age of three. However, new experiences (such as starting pre-school) and busy days (such as a day trip) will still wear children out, and they may well nod off to sleep - on the ride home in the car for instance.

Cot bed/bed

Some children may have been sleeping in a special kind of cot known as a 'cot bed'. This means that the cot has been specially designed to turn into the child's first bed with some adjustments when required. Generally, this involves the base of the cot being lowered and the removal of the sides. This can be of comfort to the child, because although sleeping in a bed is a new experience, the bed still retains a familiar feel.

Other children will go straight from their cot into a new child's bed. Either approach is acceptable. The main focus should be on the bed being sturdy, clean and safe.

Bed guard

After the safe boundaries of a cot with high sides, there is a risk that a child may fall out of their bed. Bed guards are designed to prevent this when children make the **transition**. Bed guards fit onto the bottom of the mattress, and are generally made from a steel frame covered with fabric mesh, so the child can see through the guard. Many guards are double sided, but single sided ones are available (for beds next to a wall). It is also possible to find wooden versions.

While bed guards are widely available and are used by many families, caution must be used. Please see the RoSPA guidelines http://www.rospa.com/rospaweb/docs/advice-services/home-safety/rospa-home-safety-position-statements.pdf (If you are unable to access this document using the link, you could look for it using a search engine.)

Good practice

Adults always need to remember that any sort of transition (change) can be challenging for young children. Getting used to a new bed, and possibly sleeping in their own room for the first time (their cot may have been in the parental bedroom) certainly falls into this category. Patience, support and understanding are needed. Special bedtime stories often help, as they encourage a positive connection between comfort and being in bed.

Key term

Transition a process or a period of change from one state or condition to another, through which young children usually need support, e.g. moving from a bed to a cot, starting to eat solid foods, starting pre-school, sleeping in their own bedroom.

Sleeping bag and duvet

A feeling of comfort helps a child to settle down into bed and to get ready for sleep, therefore bedding should be soft to the touch. Just as when they were babies, it is important that young children do not get too hot or too cold at night (see Learning outcome 1). However, once a child is big enough for a bed, they will also be big enough to throw the covers off should they feel too warm. This means that a child's single duvet or child's single sleeping bag can now be introduced safely.

Did you know?

Young children love to choose their own bedding, and there are many vibrant options, e.g. superheroes and space rockets. However, it may be better not to make a bedroom *too* stimulating overall. Soothing colours and designs are more likely to encourage rest, relaxation and sleep.

Good practice

As in Learning outcome 1, you must always check equipment for safety marks and age/weight guidelines. This includes cot/beds, beds, bed guards, sleeping bags and duvets.

Clothing

You were introduced to clothing in Learning outcome 1. In this age range, children will continue to grow out of clothes quickly. As children begin to move around more frequently and to play inside and out for longer periods, harder-wearing clothes suitable for every weather condition will be required.

Footwear

In this age range, children will begin to wear proper shoes. If possible, these should be of good quality and:

- well made, with flexible leather uppers, slip resistant soles and adjustable fastenings
- well fitted by a specialist with training (in a shoe shop), with room for the toes to move and for some growth

- give good support
- protect the foot
- be practical for everyday wear.

You should avoid:

- heels (flat shoes are required)
- second-hand shoes
- shoes with hard inside seams or decorative fixings that can be felt inside the shoe.

While the 'proper' shoes described above are paramount, children will wear a range of other footwear, depending on the weather and circumstances:

- wellington boots
- trainers
- slippers
- sandals.

These are fine for a short while, but they do not give the same level of support and protection as proper shoes. Use them for limited periods only.

Figure 7.8: Consider the weather and circumstances when choosing footwear.

Nappies

Until they are ready to begin toilet training, children will continue to wear nappies. Children can only become clean and dry, or 'toilet trained', when they have control over their bowel and bladder. This happens at different times for different children, but usually from about 18 months to 3 years. Most children are clean and dry in the daytime by the time they are three.

? Did you know?

It takes longer for a child to gain control of their bowel and bladder at night. Many still have accidents up to the age of six or seven. Some children have accidents beyond this age.

Trainer pants

Once a child is ready to toilet train, nappies will be switched for training pants during the day. Some parents or carers opt for disposable pulls-ups at first. These are shaped like pants but are made from a nappy-like material, which will absorb accidents. Some people say these feel too similar to nappies when worn, and prefer to put children straight into fabric pants. Whichever method is chosen, there will need to be a good supply of spares, as accidents will be frequent at first.

Daywear, outerwear and nightwear

In Learning outcome 1, you learnt about the important features of daywear, outerwear and nightwear (see pages 89–90) and the majority of these still apply. But in addition, children will now need clothing that is:

- easy for them to fasten themselves as they become independent dressers
- easy to get on and off during toilet training, when a few seconds sometimes means the difference between an accident and a success.

Case study

Child minder Karen is toilet training two-year-old Lennon in partnership with his parents. Today, he asked for the potty twice. On one occasion, Karen struggled to get Lennon out of his dungarees in time, and he had an accident. Lennon became quite upset about it.

Karen has decided to speak to Lennon's dad about this when he comes to pick up Lennon. She plans to say how well Lennon has done today overall. Then she will explain the circumstances of his accident, and ask that Lennon be bought some clothes that are easier to remove for toileting next time.

Questions

1 Do you agree with Karen's approach?

2 Give reasons for your answer.

2.2 Key factors to consider when choosing equipment for children from one to five years

The key factors to consider when choosing equipment for children from one to five years include:

- age-appropriateness
- safety
- design/ergonomics
- cost and durability
- hygiene and cleanliness.

Age-appropriateness

You learnt about age-appropriateness in Learning outcome 1 (see page 91). You might like to recap that information now.

Safety

You learnt about safety in Learning outcome 1 (see page 91). It is a good idea to take a few minutes to reread that information.

Did you know?

Age-appropriateness remains important beyond the age of five, and right through to adolescence.

Good practice

As a child gets older, it is good practice to make them increasingly aware of safety issues. This helps them to develop an awareness of how to make good decisions to keep themselves safe. This will become more and more important as children's independence increases. For example, you might say on a trip to the park, 'Please do not climb up there. That bench is not very sturdy and you might fall'.

Safety marks, safety checks, flammability and stability

We covered information on the following in Learning outcome 1 (see pages 91–92).

- safety marks
- safety checks
- flammability
- stability

This still applies to this age band. You may want to recap that information.

Design/ergonomics

You learnt about design/ergonomics in Learning outcome 1 (see page 93). This continues to be an important consideration. As children move through the age band, it is particularly important that equipment of the appropriate size is available for them.

Cost and durability/durable materials

You learnt about cost and durability in Learning outcome 1 (see page 93). You may like to recap that information.

Hygiene and cleanliness

You learnt about the following in Learning outcome 1:

- hygiene
- the necessity of equipment that is easy to clean
- the necessity of equipment that is easy to wash.

This still applies to this age range. You may like to reread this information now (see page 94). In addition, young children can increasingly help with hygiene matters such as wiping off the table at home after a meal, or washing the play food in the kitchen sink.

 Good practice

You can increasingly encourage children to develop good hygienic self-care, for example when they go to the toilet and wash their hands afterwards.

Stretch activity

Key factors to consider when choosing equipment for children from one to 5 years

Search the internet to find two websites selling children's:

- beds
- bed guards
- sleeping bags/duvets.

1 Compare the available products for a child transitioning from a cot to their first bed, considering these factors:
   - age-appropriateness
   - safety
   - design/ergonomics
   - cost
   - durability.

2 Decide which items you would buy. Write down the details of each item (or copy and paste the information into a word document and print it out).

3 Give reasons for each of your choices.

Test your knowledge

1 At what age would you expect a child to:
   a feed themselves with a spoon and fork?
   b feed themselves with a knife and fork?
2 Give five examples of items of clothing that should be provided.
3 When would you expect to use a bed guard?
4 Explain why child-sized equipment is important in terms of ergonomics.
5 What are weaning bibs and why are they beneficial?

Assessment preparation

The OCR model assignment will ask you to investigate the main points to be considered when choosing the following:

- travelling equipment
- feeding equipment
- sleeping equipment
- clothing and footwear.

for children from one to five years. You should support your evidence by considering the following features when making your decisions:

- suitability for age and growth
- safety aspects
- costs
- design

- practicality
- durability
- ease of cleaning.

1 Young children in this age range are able to switch from a buggy to a stroller. Explain why and give reasons for your answer.

2 Discuss why age-appropriateness should be a key consideration when selecting feeding equipment.

3 Outline the law regarding the use of car seats for children aged one to five years.

4 Assess the safety reasons for using reins with a toddler.

Assessment guidance

Learning outcome 2: Understand the key factors when choosing equipment for children from one to five years

Marking criteria for LO2

Mark band 1	Mark band 2	Mark band 3
2.1 A **limited range** of examples are given for some types of equipment needed for children from one to five years.	2.1 A **range** of examples are given for most types of equipment needed for children from one to five years.	2.1 A **wide range** of examples are given for all types of equipment needed for children from one to five years.
2.2 **Outlines** the key factors for consideration for the types of equipment with **limited reasons** for the choice of equipment selected. Draws upon **limited** skills/knowledge/ understanding from Unit R018.	2.2 **Explains** the key factors for consideration for the types of equipment with **clear reasons** for the choice of equipment selected. Draws upon **some relevant** skills/knowledge/ understanding from Unit R018.	2.2 **Explains in detail** the key factors for consideration for the types of equipment with **well-developed reasons** for the choice of equipment selected **and** rejected. **Clearly** draws upon **relevant** skills/knowledge/ understanding from Unit R018.

 Top tips

Command words

- A limited range – the work produced is small in range and scope and includes only a part of the information required, it evidences partial rather than full understanding. A limited range is one or two.
- A range – the evidence presented is sufficiently varied to give confidence that the knowledge and principles are understood in application as well as in fact. A range is two or three.
- A wide range is at least three.

The evidence you need to produce:

- equipment needs for children from birth to five years.

Examples of evidence format:

- written/typed report
- online/shop visit log
- information booklets/leaflets
- PowerPoint presentation with notes
- storyboard/article.

When creating this evidence, it may help to:

- look at more than one example of each type of equipment. This will enable you to compare items and choose the one with the best features.

Learning outcome 3

Know the nutritional guidelines and requirements for children from birth to five years

About this Learning outcome

Good nutrition is at the heart of maintaining a healthy body. This is crucial for children's well-being, growth and development. Sadly, children who do not receive good nutrition are at a huge disadvantage, so it is very important that you understand how to meet children's requirements in order to give them the best possible start.

Children's nutritional needs change a great deal in their early years.

Assessment criteria

In this learning outcome you will cover:

3.1 Current government dietary guidelines:
- The Eatwell Guide
- making healthy choices.

3.2 The functions and sources of nutrients:
- macronutrients – protein, fats, carbohydrates
- micronutrients – vitamins, A, B group, C, D, E, K, minerals – calcium and iron
- functions of each nutrient
- sources of nutrients
- vitamins
- minerals
- additional dietary requirements.

3.3 Nutritional requirements for stages of feeding children:
- nutritional requirements from 0 to 6 months
- nutritional requirements from 6 to 12 months
- nutritional requirements from 1 to 5 years.

Getting started

Thought storm all that you know about the following:

- protein
- carbohydrates
- fat
- vitamins
- minerals
- fibre
- water.

3.1 Current government dietary guidelines

The Government issues dietary guidelines to help people understand what constitutes a healthy diet. This empowers them to make healthy choices, both for themselves and for their children.

The Eatwell Guide

To help people to get the balance of foods right, the Government have designed the Eatwell Guide (see the image below). The Eatwell Guide is a pictorial representation of the proportion that different food groups should form in the diet. This representation of food intake relates to people over the age of five, but it is still a very handy visual representation to draw on.

Although most people should be able to get all the nutrients they need from following a healthy balanced diet, certain groups in the population may need to take supplements:

● Women who could become pregnant or who are planning a pregnancy are advised to take an additional 400 micrograms (mcg) of folic acid per day as a supplement from before conception until the twelfth week of pregnancy. They should also eat folate-rich foods such as, green vegetables, brown rice and fortified breakfast cereals (making a total of 600 mcg of folate per day from both folate rich foods and a supplement). Pregnant and breastfeeding

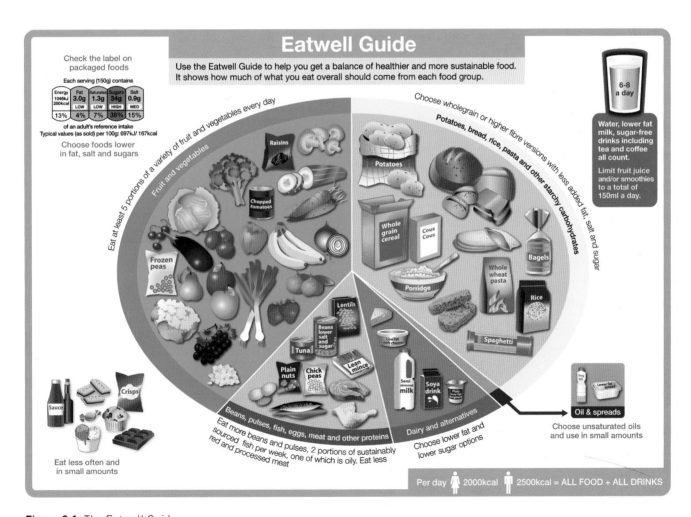

Figure 8.1: The Eatwell Guide

women should also take a daily 10 mcg supplement of vitamin D.

- Children under the age of five who are not good eaters may need to take a supplement containing vitamins A, D and C. Children who have a good appetite and eat a wide variety of foods, including fruit and vegetables, might not need vitamin drops. Parents who are concerned about their child's diet should talk to their GP or health visitor for further advice. Sunlight on the skin is the major source of vitamin D. You can read more about this at http://www.nhs.uk/conditions/pregnancy-and-baby/pages/vitamins-for-children.aspx?tabname=Babies%20 and %20 toddlers

Making healthy choices

Making healthy choices for yourself and your children is very important in terms of health, growth and development. In their Healthy Eating Advice, the Government recommends that all individuals consume a diet that contains:

- plenty of starchy foods such as rice, bread, pasta and potatoes (choosing wholegrain varieties when possible)
- plenty of fruit and vegetables – at least five portions of a variety of fruit and vegetables a day
- some protein-rich foods such as meat, fish, eggs, beans and non-dairy sources of protein, such as nuts and pulses
- some milk and dairy, choosing reduced fat versions, eating smaller amounts of full fat versions or eating them less often
- just a little saturated fat, salt and sugar.

This is the healthy diet that all children should be moving towards. You will learn more about all of these foods as you work through this Learning outcome.

> ### ? Good practice
>
> Children below the age of five with small appetites, who need energy-dense diets, should not be restricted in their fat intake.

> ### Stretch activity
>
> #### Current government dietary guidelines
>
> Find a partner to work with and look at the current government dietary guidelines. Label yourselves A and B.
>
> 1 A should explain to B what is meant by making healthy choices.
>
> 2 B should explain the Eatwell Guide to A.
>
> 3 Together, look through the guidelines – did either of you miss anything out? If so, make notes about the missing information. This will help you to remember it.
>
> 4. Together, now create a leaflet to inform busy parents with young children about the importance of making healthy choices. Include details about the Eatwell Guide.

3.2 The functions and sources of nutrients

Nutrients are the nourishment that come from the food you eat. In this section, you will learn about the function of nutrients – what each nutrient does for the body. Functions of various nutrients include:

- producing energy
- growth and repair
- prevention of disease.

You will also learn about sources of nutrients, or the types of food that contain certain nutrients. For example, under the heading 'Protein', you will see that sources of protein include meat and beans.

Nutrients can be divided into two categories:

- macronutrients
- micronutrients.

The body needs both macronutrients and micronutrients, as well as water, to promote growth and development, and to regulate body processes. Read on to find out more about them.

Macronutrients

Macronutrients are the structural and energy-giving calorie components of food. They include:

- proteins
- fats
- carbohydrates.

Proteins

Protein foods are made up of amino acids.

Sources of protein can be divided into two categories:

- Animal sources – including meat, poultry, fish, milk and eggs
- Vegetable sources – including soya, tofu, beans, pulses and textured vegetable protein (TVP).

The functions of all proteins are:

- to aid growth and repair of the body
- to provide secondary energy.

Fats

Sources of fats can be divided into three categories:

- saturated fats – including butter, milk, cheese, meat (all animal sources), palm oil (vegetable source)
- unsaturated fats – including olive oil and nut oil (vegetable sources)
- polyunsaturated fats – including oily fish (animal sources), corn oil, sunflower oil (vegetable sources).

Saturated fats are solid at room temperature and come mainly from animal fats. Unsaturated fats and polyunsaturated fats are liquid at room temperature and come mainly from vegetable oils and fish.

 Did you know?

TVP is a high-fibre, high-protein meat substitute made from soya flour. You can buy it in flavoured and unflavoured forms. It comes in a variety of sizes, from chunks to small flakes.

 Good practice

Too much saturated fat can increase the amount of cholesterol in the blood, which can increase the risk of developing heart disease. Regularly consuming foods and drinks high in sugar increases the risk of obesity and tooth decay.

The functions of fats are:

- producing energy
- producing warmth
- storing fat-soluble vitamins
- protecting internal organs.

Carbohydrates

Sources of carbohydrates can be divided into two categories:

- starches – including bread, pasta, potatoes, rice, cereals, beans
- sugars – including fruit, honey, sweets, beet sugar, cane sugar.

Carbohydrates are broken down into glucose before the body can use them. Sugars are easily converted and are a quick source of energy. Starches take longer to convert so they provide a longer-lasting supply of energy.

The functions of carbohydrates are:

- producing energy
- producing warmth.

Good practice

The NHS tells us that starchy foods should make up just over one third of everything we eat. This means we should base our meals on these foods. They advise trying to choose wholegrain or wholemeal varieties of starchy foods, such as brown rice, wholewheat pasta and wholemeal or higher fibre white bread. They contain more fibre, and usually more vitamins and minerals than white varieties.

Micronutrients

Micronutrients enable necessary chemical reactions to occur in the body, but they are only required in minute amounts. Micronutrients include the vitamins and minerals that are essential for good health:

- vitamins A, B group, C, D, E, K
- minerals such as calcium and iron.

Vitamins A, B group, C, D, E, K

The body needs a regular supply of water-soluble vitamins, as these cannot be stored in the body. Fat-soluble vitamins can be stored in the body, but intake should still be regular. Table 8.1 sets out the sources and functions of the main vitamins. Many are key in the promotion of health and prevention of disease.

 Key terms

Macronutrients the structural and energy-giving calorie components of food.

Micronutrients micronutrients enable necessary chemical reactions to occur in the body.

Nutrients the nourishment that comes from the food we eat.

Vitamin	Source	Function	Type	Deficiency
A	Cheese, butter, eggs, oily fish, tomatoes, carrots.	Promotes growth and development. Maintenance of good vision and healthy skin.	Fat soluble (Pregnant women must avoid too much vitamin A).	Deficiency may lead to skin conditions and vision impairment.
B group	Meat, chicken, eggs, fish, green leafy vegetables, dates, pulses. Some breakfast cereals are fortified with vitamin B (meaning it is added to them).	Promotes healthy functioning of the nerves and muscles.	Water soluble. Very regular intake required.	Deficiency may lead to anaemia and wasting of the muscles.
C	Fruit: oranges, strawberries and blackcurrants have a high content.	Maintenance of healthy tissue and skin. Prevention of disease.	Water soluble. Daily intake required.	Deficiency leads to decreased resistance to infection and can result in scurvy.
D	Oily fish and fish oil, egg yolk. Milk, margarine and some breakfast cereals are fortified with vitamin D. Sunlight on the skin can cause the body to produce vitamin D.	Maintenance of bones and teeth. Assists body growth.	Fat soluble.	Deficiency in children may lead to bones which do not harden properly (rickets). Also leads to tooth decay.
E	Cereals, egg yolk, seeds, nuts, vegetable oils.	Promotes blood clotting and healing.	Fat soluble.	Deficiency may result in delayed blood clotting.
K	Whole grains, green vegetables, liver.	Promotes healing. Necessary for blood clotting.	Fat soluble.	Deficiency may lead to excessive bleeding due to delayed blood clotting. Usually given to babies after birth as a deficiency is sometimes seen in newborns, although rare in adults.

Table 8.1: Vitamins: how regularly do you take in these vitamins?

Minerals

Minerals are needed for a variety of bodily functions. For example:

- building strong bones and teeth
- healthy blood, skin and hair
- nerve function
- muscle function
- metabolic processes such as turning food into energy.

So in turn, minerals are necessary for:

- the body to work properly
- growth and development
- maintaining normal health and preventing disease.

Table 8.2 sets out the sources and functions of the main minerals.

? Did you know?

Nuts are considered a choking hazard for young children, and they are a common food allergy. Therefore many settings have a 'no nut policy'. They do not use nuts or nut products, and children may not bring them in, even to eat themselves. Nuts should not be included in any form during the weaning stage. Grapes should be cut in half to lessen the risk of choking.

Additional dietary requirements

In addition to all the nutrients mentioned, the body also has some extra dietary requirements:

- fibre
- water.

Fibre

Fibre is an important part of a healthy balanced diet. It adds roughage to food. Its functions are to:

- encourage the body to pass out the waste products of food after it has been digested, by stimulating the bowel muscles
- help prevent constipation, piles, diverticulitis, irritable bowel syndrome and cancers of the bowel
- improve digestive health.

Sources of fibre include:

- fruit, e.g. bananas, apples
- dried fruit
- wholemeal pasta
- beans and lentils
- peas
- sweetcorn
- carrots
- oats

Mineral	Source	Function	Deficiency
Calcium	Milk, cheese, eggs, fish, pulses, wholegrain cereals. White and brown flour are fortified with calcium	Required for growth of teeth and bones. Also for nerve and muscle function	Deficiency may lead to rickets and tooth decay.
Iron	Red meat and offal, eggs, green vegetables, dried fruits	Required for the formation of haemoglobin in the red blood cells, which transport oxygen around the body	Deficiency may lead to anaemia.
Sodium chloride (salt). Too much salt is bad for children. **It must not be added** to food for babies or young children during food. preparation or at the table.	Salt, meat, fish, bread, processed food	Essential for water balance in the body. Also involved in nerve function.	

Table 8.2: Minerals: how regularly do you take in these minerals?

- wheat bran
- wholegrain cereals
- corn.

Water

All the main systems in the body depend on water. It maintains fluid in the cells of the body and in the bloodstream. It also contains some minerals. The human body is up to 70 per cent water, and much of it is lost through urine and sweat. It is also lost in the form of vapour from the lungs during breathing, and it is used to turn food into energy. So water needs to be replaced very regularly. Without any water, all life forms will die. The functions of water include:

- regulating body temperature
- carrying nutrients and oxygen to cells

Figure 8.2: Children must stay hydrated.

- flushing waste products from the kidneys
- lubricating joints
- moistening the eyes, mouth and nose
- dissolving minerals and other nutrients, making them accessible for the body
- protecting organs and tissues
- preventing constipation.

In addition to plain water, sources of water include:

- fruit juice
- milk
- fruit.

Activity

In the 'Getting started' activity you considered all the factors that you had learnt about protein, vitamins, minerals, fibre and water. Now look at the functions and sources of nutrients.

1 Read through what you have written.

2 In a different colour pen, add all you know about protein, vitamins, minerals, fibre and water.

3 Did anything you have learnt surprise you? If so, underline this.

4 Now write a paragraph explaining the functions and sources of protein, vitamins, minerals, fibre and water to parents. This should be suitable for inclusion in a pre-school's newsletter.

3.3 Nutritional requirements for stages of feeding children

You have learnt that young children grow and develop very quickly in their early years. This means that their nutritional requirements are continually changing, as they depend on children's age, weight and height. It is important to know how to respond to these needs. Until the age of around six months old, babies will be fed only on milk, and will receive no solid food at all. Milk can provide them with all the nutrients they need at this age. Read on to learn more.

Nutrition requirements from 0 to 6 months

At this age, children will be fed either:

- breast milk
- formula milk
- soya milk – this is a popular solution when a baby is lactose intolerant (lactose is present in breast milk and formula milk)
- a combination of breast milk and formula milk.

By the age of around six months, a baby's digestive system will have developed fully, meaning that he or she can cope well with solid foods. Newborn babies only take a small amount of milk to start with, but by the time they are a week old, most will need around 150 to 200 ml of milk per kilo of their weight per day until they are six months old. But, this amount will vary from baby to baby.

Good practice

The weight gain of a baby indicates whether the baby is getting enough milk. Babies are generally weighed at birth and between 5–10 days. After this, babies aged 0–6 months should be weighed once a month. The weight is recorded in the Personal Child Health Record (PCHR), provided for parents by the NHS.

Did you know?

If parents are concerned about their baby's weight gain, they can speak to their health visitor, who will offer advice and support.

You will find further information about feeding babies aged 0–6 months in Learning outcome 4.

Nutritional requirements from 6–12 months

At around six months, babies are ready to begin the **weaning** (see page 116 for definition) process. This is the process in which babies are introduced to solid foods. There are three stages:

- Weaning stage 1 – Babies are introduced gradually to solids, generally starting with baby rice and moving onto pureed fruit and vegetables.
- Weaning stage 2 – Babies are introduced to minced foods such as chicken, and finger foods such as rusks and toast.
- Weaning stage 3 – Babies are introduced to solid foods such as pasta and cheese.

Weaning stage 1

At first, babies should be offered a small amount of bland, warm food of a loose or sloppy consistency. This should be free of salt, gluten and sugar. Baby rice or banana mixed with milk from the baby's bottle are ideal. Half to a full teaspoon is enough to start with. This can then be gradually increased. As the baby begins to take more food and moves onto pureed fruit and vegetables, the amount of milk they receive should be decreased.

Weaning stage 2

Once they are used to the foods in stage 1, babies can have soft cooked meat such as chicken, pasta, noodles, toast, lentils, rice and mashed hard-boiled eggs. They are also ready for full-fat dairy products such as yoghurt, fromage frais or custard with no added sugar or less sugar. Whole cows' milk can be used in cooking or mixed with food from six months. Finger food allows a child to learn to chew. It should be cut into pieces big enough for

Figure 8.3: Finger foods help children learn to chew.

a baby to hold in their fist with a bit sticking out (pieces about the size of your own finger).

Weaning stage 3

By the age of 12 months, a baby will have gradually moved towards eating three meals a day that include solid foods. Their diet should consist of a variety of fruit and vegetables, bread, rice, pasta, potatoes and other starchy foods, meat, fish, eggs, beans and other non-dairy sources of protein, as well as milk and dairy products. At 12 months, a baby can drink whole cows' milk.

? Did you know?

Full-fat dairy products should be selected for children under two - they need the extra fat and vitamins found in them. From two years old, good eaters who are growing well can have semi-skimmed milk. From five years old, skimmed milk can be provided.

🔑 Key term

Weaning the process by which babies are introduced to solid foods.

You will find further information about weaning in Learning outcome 4.

Special dietary requirements

Some people have special dietary requirements from birth and throughout adult life. These may be due to food allergies, which can be severe and life-threatening (such as a nut allergy). They can also relate to medical conditions, culture, ethnicity or religious or ethical beliefs. Therefore it is very important to check whether a child has special dietary requirements, and if so, you must be sure that you fully understand them.

💼 Case study

Gen is a nanny. She has just started working with ten-month-old Ted, who is lactose intolerant and drinks soya milk. She has not come across this before. Gen asks to sit down with Ted's parents to fully talk it over. At the end of the conversation she considers that she understands how to meet Ted's dietary needs. She wants to make sure that she understands how to use soya milk in recipes, as Ted will soon be ready to eat a wider range of foods. She starts off by searching the NHS website (www.nhs.uk) and the Government's food advice website (www.food.gov.uk).

Questions

1   Do you think Gen is looking in the right place for further information? Give reasons for your answer.

2   What else do you think Gen could do to help her meet Ted's dietary needs?

Nutritional requirements from one to five years

Planning menus is the best way to meet the nutritional requirements of children from one to five years. Menus should cater for main meals, snacks and drinks. They should promote the nutritional balance that is needed for a healthy diet overall, so it is important to look at the bigger picture, rather than thinking about each meal or snack in isolation. For example, what did a child eat for their last meal? What will they eat next? Other considerations are shown in the diagram below:

Figure 8.4: Menu planning considerations. Why do you think families should be consulted about menus?

You will learn more about planning menus in Learning outcome 4. You may like to skip ahead and read that information (see page 128).

Main food groups

The meals, snacks and drinks that feature on a menu should be drawn from the main food groups. This includes the following staples:

- bread, other cereals, potatoes, rice, pasta, beans
- fruit and vegetables, e.g. oranges, apples, peas, carrots

- milk and dairy, e.g. cheese, yoghurt
- meat, fish and alternative, e.g. poultry, eggs, Quorn.

Fatty and sugary foods

Fatty and sugary foods, e.g. chocolate, crisps, biscuits and sweets may be offered in small portions as an occasional treat. But they should not feature regularly in a young child's diet. Fatty and sugary foods offer little in the way of good nutrition, and too many fatty and sugary foods are bad for children's health. Some parents or carers may permit the occasional sugary fizzy drink. However, they are full of sugar and so are particularly harmful to children's teeth. It is beneficial not to introduce fizzy drinks to children aged 1– 5 years.

Activity

1   Visit this NHS weblink and read more about what to feed young children: www. nhs.uk/Conditions/pregnancy-and-baby/ Pages/understanding-food-groups.aspx.

2   Follow at least four of the weblinks given on the NHS webpage, and read the information you come across. Make notes of any key points that you would like to remember.

Test your knowledge

1   What does the term 'macronutrient' mean?

2   What does the term 'micronutrient' mean?

3   What is the Eatwell Guide?

4   Describe a 'healthy diet'.

5   Explain the term 'function of nutrient'.

6   Discuss the key considerations that apply when planning a menu for children.

7   Describe how to ensure that a child's dietary requirements are safely met.

Assessment preparation

The OCR model assignment will ask you to have knowledge of the nutritional and current government guidelines for children from birth to five years. This should include stages of feeding children aged:

- 0–6 months
- 6–12 months
- 1–5 years.

Additional aspects of the diet should also be covered. These are:

- fibre
- water.

1 Outline the functions of a) protein, b) carbohydrates and c) fats.

2 Explain why the body needs vitamins and minerals.

3 Outline sources of fibre.

4 Explain the three stages of weaning. Provide diagrams to support your answer.

Assessment guidance

Learning outcome 3: Know the nutritional guidelines and requirements for children from birth to five years

Marking criteria for LO3

Investigate the main points to be considered when choosing clothing and footwear, feeding, sleeping and transport equipment for babies from birth to 12 months.

Mark band 1	Mark band 2	Mark band 3
3.1 Outlines some of the functions and sources of some nutrients.	**3.1 Outlines most** of the functions and sources of **most** nutrients.	**3.1 Describes in detail all** of the functions and sources of **all** nutrients.
3.2 Outlines some of the nutritional requirements for the stages (0–6 months, 6–12 months, 1–5 years).	**3.2 Briefly describes most** of the nutritional requirements for the stages (0–6 months, 6–12 months, 1–5 years).	**3.2 Describes in detail** all of the nutritional requirements for the stages (0–6 months, 6–12 months, 1–5 years).
3.3 Outlines some elements of government guidelines relating to healthy eating.	**3.3 Describes** government guidelines relating to healthy eating.	**3.3 Explains** government guidelines relating to healthy eating.

 Top tips

Command words:

- outline – set out main characteristics
- describe – set out characteristics.

The evidence you need to produce:

- nutritional requirements for children from birth to five years
- current government guidelines for birth to five years.

Examples of evidence format:

- nutritional analysis/food programme
- Recommended Nutritional Values (RDVs/RDIs)
- interviews/questionnaires
- witness statement.

When creating this evidence, it may help to:

- recap the text on government guidelines
- think carefully about additional aspects of the diet (fibre and water).

Learning outcome 4

Be able to investigate and develop feeding solutions for children from birth to five years

About this Learning outcome

As well as understanding the theory of nutrition for children from birth to five years, you need to know how to perform the practical tasks of deciding what to feed a child, preparing and storing food,

and then feeding the child. All of these things are part of providing a **feeding solution** (see page 120 for definition).

This Learning outcome links closely with Learning outcome 3. Links are provided throughout this section.

Assessment criteria

In this learning outcome you will cover:

4.1 • How to investigate feeding solutions.
   • How to develop feeding solutions for babies aged 0 to 6 months.
   • How to develop feeding solutions for babies aged 6 to 12 months.

   • How to develop feeding solutions for children aged 1 to 5 years.
   • How to evaluate feeding solutions.

Getting started

Mealtimes, or feeding times for babies, provide opportunities for children and adults to be close and to bond. Children place a lot of trust in the adults who feed them, especially when they are physically being fed. You can explore this for yourself.

• Pair up with someone else.
• Choose a food you like that can easily be eaten from a spoon, e.g. yoghurt.

• Place your trust in the other person and allow them to feed you a few spoonfuls.
• Swap roles and feed your partner a few spoonfuls.
• Discuss how it felt. Did you trust the other person? Did you feel a little vulnerable? Did they feed you at the right speed? Discuss and justify all your answers.

4.1 How to investigate feeding solutions

When developing feeding solutions, it is good practice to investigate:

- nutritional analysis
- factors for consideration
- hygiene practices.

This unit looks at these in turn.

Nutritional analysis

Nutritional analysis is the process of researching and understanding the nutritional value of specific foods and meals. This analysis allows you to plan menus that promote healthy eating for children. As part of the process you can consider:

- labelling (of commercially produced foods)
- software/apps (usually called nutritional analysis programmes, that help with working out nutritional values)
- Eatwell Guide/healthy eating (food guidelines recommended by the Government – see Learning outcome 3).

Labelling

Food labelling enables you to see what is in commercially produced (manufactured) food, to help you to make healthy choices. The Food Standards Agency traffic light labelling system shows the amount of fat, sugar, saturates and salt in grams. This corresponds to a traffic light colour, as shown in Figure 9.1.

> #### 🔑 Key terms
>
> **Feeding solution** the process of deciding what to feed a child, preparing and storing food and feeding a child.
>
> **Nutritional analysis** the process of researching and understanding the nutritional value of specific foods and meals.

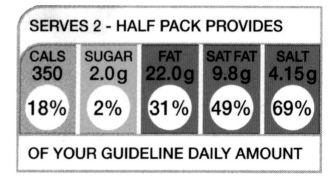

Figure 9.1: Traffic light label.

- Red = a high quantity
- Amber = a medium quantity
- Green = a low quantity

You will see that the number of calories contained is also included on the label.

Calories

Once children are fully weaned, at around 12 months old, it is time to think about the number of calories they consume. The chart below shows the estimated number of calories needed by children each day. You will see that boys require more calories than girls. The calories for adults are also included so you can make a comparison.

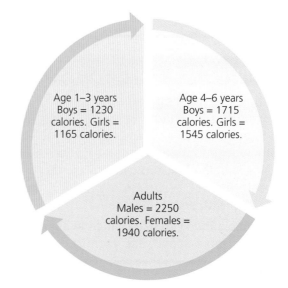

Figure 9.2: Estimated number of calories needed by children each day. Are you surprised by the recommendations? Explain, with reasons.

Software/apps

A range of software and apps are available to help adults with nutritional analysis. Some are more comprehensive than others, and some provide a breakdown of nutritional information for foods that are not manufactured (such as fruits and vegetables) like the type of information you would expect to see on a food label. This is extremely helpful. Others go as far as providing menus for children of various ages, based on their age, weight and growth.

Activity

You are going to investigate software/apps for nutritional analysis.

1 With a partner, follow this link to software that assists organisations such as schools, hospitals and settings for under-fives, to plan nutritious menus: www.nutmeg-uk. com/register.asp.

2 At the bottom of the page, select 'web edition' from the product demo option in the menu (on the left-hand side of the webpage).

3 Watch the demonstration video to understand how the menu options offered give a breakdown of nutritional values for children of various ages.

4 Type 'apps for child nutrition' into a search engine. Investigate the results, looking for apps that are suitable both for planning and tracking nutrition.

Stretch activity

How to investigate feeding solutions

With a partner, follow this link and download the Eatwell Guide: www.gov.uk/government/uploads/system/uploads/attachment_data/file/551502/Eatwell_Guide_booklet.pdf.

1 Read the guide.

2 Discuss how the guide differs from the Eatwell Plate.

3 Why is it helpful to know about the guide as well as the Eatwell Plate?

You may also want to look at the British Nutritional Foundation website, which has lots of useful resources, and is up-to-date.

Eatwell Guide/healthy eating

You were introduced to the Eatwell Guide and healthy eating (making healthy choices) in Learning outcome 3. You may like to recap that information.

Factors for consideration

When providing feeding solutions to children from birth to five years, there is a lot to consider. The key factors for consideration are shown in Figure 9.3.

Nutrition

Nutrition is a key factor for consideration because a balanced diet that meets nutritional requirements is vital for a child's health. You learnt about this in Learning outcome 3.

We also covered nutritional analysis on page 120, and you may want to recap this.

Cost

Cost is an important factor when choosing feeding solutions. Most people need to compare the cost of the food items they wish to buy, and then choose the best quality available within their budget. For example:

- Organic fruit and vegetables are more expensive than non-organic varieties, but may have benefits.
- Lots of meats come in cuts with a range of different prices, e.g. steak is much more expensive than minced beef.
- Commercially produced food brands will usually be more expensive than the supermarket own-brand equivalent.
- Fruit and vegetables in season are often cheaper.

? Did you know?

It can sometimes be cheaper and it is much healthier to make meals from scratch, rather than buying the ready-made versions. These can contain high levels of salt, fats, sugar and possibly contain unwanted additives.

Time

People tend to lead very busy lives, so time can be a factor when choosing feeding solutions. For example, a family may choose quicker, easier meals during the week, but spend more time preparing and cooking them at the weekend. Choices that are quick and easy can still be healthy. For example:

- A side salad or frozen vegetables are a quick alternative to fresh vegetables that take more preparation and cooking.
- Fresh meals can be made ahead of time and frozen for use when time is short.
- Fruit is a quick and healthy snack option.
- A banana smoothie can make a quick nutritious breakfast.

Practicalities/convenience

Sometimes practicalities and convenience influence food choices. Thinking about this is really helpful when planning menus. It helps to consider:

- when it will be possible to go shopping for particular ingredients
- when a meal will need to be eaten outside of the home or school environment, e.g. on a day trip
- who will be eating together – foods that everyone likes
- special dietary requirements
- if there are leftovers to use up (you should not reheat food that is intended for children).

Attractiveness/appealing meals

Have you heard the expression 'We eat first with our eyes?' It means that we tend to be keen to eat food that is presented in an attractive way. It is best to appeal to children by providing food you know they like already, while introducing new foods, flavours and textures gradually alongside the familiar ones. You will learn more about this on page 130.

You can make food attractive by:

- setting the table so it looks pleasant, with all the right utensils in place
- creating a calm atmosphere – quiet, gentle background music can help settle children at lunch time if they've had a busy or exciting morning

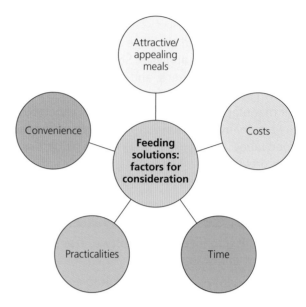

Figure 9.3: Feeding solutions key factors. Can you think of any additional factors to consider?

- considering the portion size and not putting too much food on a child's plate – you do not want them to be hungry, but too much can be off-putting
- considering the way food looks on the plate, in the bowl, etc, for example you could roll slices of ham into an attractive tube shape and place it next to colourful salad vegetables
- involving children in the food preparation process – children tend to be keener to eat something that they have helped to prepare or even grow.

Hygiene practices

Effective food hygiene practices are crucial to children's health and well-being because they prevent food poisoning. Practitioners handling or preparing food in a group setting should attend a course on food hygiene to gain a Basic Food Hygiene certificate.

You need to know how to ensure that food is stored, prepared and cooked safely, and that food areas are kept hygienically. Hygiene practices fall into these three categories:

- personal hygiene
- room/equipment hygiene
- sterilisation.

Figure 9.4: Fridges must be kept at the correct temperature.

Personal hygiene

This includes your own personal hygiene, because you will be handling food for consumption, as well as the personal hygiene of the children who will be eating and drinking. You should:

- wash your hands with antiseptic soap before and after handling food
- use waterproof dressings to cover any cuts or grazes on your hands
- never cough or sneeze over food
- wear protective clothing (such as an apron) that is only used for food preparation.

Children should be taught the following:

- They must wash hands thoroughly with antibacterial soap before eating and drinking. In group settings, children's hands must be

dried with paper towels or a hand drier. Open wounds on hands must be covered with a plaster.

- They must only touch the food they are going to eat, so they should not pick up food and then put it back. It is fine to leave food they do not want to finish on their plate.
- Food and drink should not be taken from other people's plates or cups. They should not share cutlery or eat food someone else has bitten.
- They must not eat food that has fallen on the floor, or eat from cutlery or plates that have been on the floor.
- They should avoid blowing their nose, coughing or sneezing near food.

Room/equipment hygiene

Both kitchen and eating areas should be kept clean at all times. All equipment used, from kitchen appliances to cutlery, must also be kept hygienically. It should be washed thoroughly after use. The following are guidelines for safe food storage:

- Ensure that food in the fridge and freezer is cold enough – use a thermometer to check. Fridges should be below 5°C. Freezers should be –18 °C maximum. They must be cleaned and defrosted regularly.
- Cool food quickly before placing it in the fridge.
- Cover stored food, or wrap it with cling-film.
- Label items with a correct use-by date if necessary.
- Separate raw and cooked food. Store raw food at the bottom of the fridge, and cooked food higher up, so that raw juices (should they spill) will not contaminate cooked food.
- If food has started to thaw, never refreeze it.
- Ensure food is fully thawed before cooking.

The following are guidelines for safe food preparation for children:

- Cook food thoroughly, e.g. cook eggs until firm, and cook meat all the way through.
- Test chicken to check it is cooked properly.
- Do not reheat food.

Sterilisation

In Learning outcome 1, you learnt that it is necessary to sterilise all feeding equipment for babies up to the age of 12 months. This includes the equipment needed to feed expressed milk to babies. You learnt that you will need to:

- choose the sterilising method (e.g. steam or water)
- wash the equipment to prepare it for the steriliser
- follow manufacturer's instructions for your selected sterilising method (see the case study example below).

Case study

Jurgen is a child minder. After feeding ten-month-old Nell, he washes his hands and washes the feeding equipment he used. He rinses it, washes it and rinses it again. He makes up some sterilising solution by following the manufacturer's instructions. He measures out the right amount of water in a jug, and pours it into the steriliser unit (a pail with a lid). He adds the right number of sterilising tablets and they dissolve. He submerges the equipment in the water, and leaves them for the amount of time as per the instructions. When the time has passed, he washes his hands again and places the items on the drainer to dry. He then stores them in a container with a lid.

Questions

1 Why did Jurgen wash his hands twice?
2 Why do you think the sterilised items are kept in a container with a lid?

How to develop feeding solutions for babies aged 0 to 6 months

Did you know?

Babies will not get sufficient nutrition if their formula doesn't contain enough powder, but too much powder is also unhealthy. It is important to get the amount exactly correct.

It is very important to follow directions when feeding babies aged 0 to 6 months. Directions for making formula must be closely followed so that they get the nutrition they need. Babies must be bottle fed safely, hygienically and in an unrushed, caring manner.

Bottle feeding

The amount of milk given to babies will depend on their weight. Over a 24-hour period, babies generally need around 150 ml of milk for each kilogram of their weight. So the bigger a baby gets, the more milk they will need.

Babies should be fed when they are hungry at first, known as 'feeding on demand'. Babies will then settle into a routine with feeds at regular intervals. Every baby is different, but newborns need around eight feeds a day at approximately four-hour intervals.

To calculate how much milk babies need, divide the amount of food needed each day by the number of feeds. Babies should be bottle fed following current best practice guidelines and the parent or carer's wishes.

How to bottle feed

The steps to follow when bottle feeding are shown on the chart below.

Bottle feeding babies

1 Check the formula has not passed the sell-by date and that the tin has been stored correctly – in a cool, dry cupboard. Read the instructions on the tin.

2 Boil some fresh water in the kettle and allow to cool.

3 Wash hands and nails thoroughly.

4 Take the required sterilised equipment (rinse this with cool, boiled water if taken straight from a water sterilising unit).

5 Following the instructions on the tin, fill the bottle to the required level with water.

6 Measure out the exact amount of powder using the scoop provided in the tin. Level with a sterilised knife. Do not pack the powder down.

7 Add the powder to the measured water in the bottle.

8 Screw on the bottle cap and shake well to mix.

9 Test the temperature of the milk on the inside of your wrist before feeding a baby. The milk should feel just warm. Babies will take cold milk but they prefer it warmed (as it would come from the breast).

10 It is best practice to make up a fresh bottle as and when it is needed.

How to bottle feed

Bottle feeding is a time for closeness and bonding, so it shouldn't be rushed. Aim to establish a comfortable and calm environment. Take time to talk to the baby and to make eye contact.

1 Gather together everything you'll need – bottle, bib and for younger babies, a muslin cloth.

2 Before feeding in a group setting **check that you have the right feed and bottle for the right baby.** If the wrong feed is given to a child with an allergy they could become seriously ill or even die. Also, different bottle teats are used to suit the needs of different babies.

3 Test the temperature of the milk (as described above).

4 Place a soft bib on the baby and sit together comfortably.

5 Hold the baby in a semi-reclining position with one arm, so that the head rests in the crook of your arm. The baby's head should be higher than the rest of the body.

6 Hold the bottle at an angle with your opposite hand so that the teat fills with milk, and allow the baby to latch on to the teat (take the teat into the mouth). Continue to tilt as the baby drinks the milk. The baby may curl a hand around yours.

7 Go at the baby's pace. Some babies like a break or two during a feed. You can wind the baby during this time as well as at the end of their feed (see below).

8 Wind can be uncomfortable for babies. Because a baby's mobility is limited, it can be difficult for a baby to pass wind, so you must always wind them at the end of a feed. Hold the baby on your lap in the sitting position, with the body leaning slightly forward. Gently rub the back. Sometime babies bring up a little of their feed – you can anticipate this by having the muslin cloth (or other suitable material, such as disposable kitchen towel) ready.

9 After feeding, gently wipe the baby's face and settle them in a comfortable position. You can then clear everything away. In a group setting, take care to ensure that other children cannot access the feeding equipment at any stage of the feeding process.

Figure 9.5: How to bottle feed. Are you confident you know about bottle feeding? Could you arrange to watch a baby being bottle fed?

 Good practice

It is good practice to warm a bottle of milk in lukewarm water. Using a microwave to heat up any sort of milk, or to defrost breast milk, can cause hot spots, which might burn a baby's mouth.

Types of formula

You learnt about different types of formula in Learning outcomes 1 and 3. It is a good idea to read these sections again to refresh your memory.

Bottles and teats

You learnt about bottles and teats in Learning outcome 1. You might like to recap this topic.

Storage and transportation

Guidelines for the storage of prepared formula have changed recently. The current NHS advice is to make up feeds at the time they are required as far as possible, in order to minimise the risk of food poisoning.

If a baby needs to be fed away from home, it is best to take a measured-out amount of formula in a small dry container, plus a flask of boiled water and an empty sterilised bottle. This will enable a fresh feed to be made up – the water must still be hot when it is used. The bottle should be cooled under running water before the baby is fed. Or, ready-to-use formula could be used instead.

If this is not possible, or you need to take a ready-prepared feed to another location such as a nursery, the feed should be prepared at home and cooled at the back of the fridge. It should be taken out just before leaving home and transported in a cool bag with an ice-pack.

Prepared formula should be used within four hours. If you reach your destination within four hours, the feed should be taken out of the cool bag and stored at the back of the fridge, if there is one.

Breastfeeding

Breastfeeding has long-term benefits for babies, which can last right into adulthood. The NHS recommends that nothing but breast milk is given for around the first six months of a baby's life. After that, they recommend that giving a baby breast milk alongside family foods for the first two years, or for as long as the mother and the baby want, will help a baby to grow and develop healthily.

Breastfeeding reduces the risk of the following:

- infections, with fewer visits to hospital as a result
- diarrhoea and vomiting, with fewer visits to hospital as a result
- SIDS
- childhood leukaemia
- type 2 diabetes
- obesity
- cardiovascular disease in adulthood.

The NHS offers pregnant women the following advice about breastfeeding:

- Breast milk is perfectly designed to feed a baby.
- Breast milk protects babies from infections and diseases.
- Breastfeeding provides health benefits for the mother.
- Breast milk is available for the baby whenever it is needed.
- Breastfeeding can build a strong emotional bond between mother and baby.

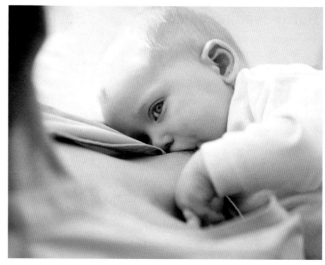

Figure 9.6: Breast milk protects babies.

? Did you know?

The latest figures show that more than 73 per cent of UK mothers start off by breastfeeding their baby.

Expressing

You learnt about expressing breast milk in Learning outcome 1. Reread that section.

Breast pumps must always be sterilised before use. It is also possible for mothers to express milk by hand, and in this case, the milk should be caught in a sterilised feeding bottle or container.

Storage and transportation

Once expressed, breast milk can be stored in a sterilised container. It can be stored:

- in the fridge for up to five days at 4 °C or lower
- for two weeks in the ice compartment of a fridge
- for up to six months in a freezer.

If milk has been frozen:

- defrost it in the fridge
- once defrosted, use it straight away
- do not re-freeze milk once it is thawed.

? Did you know?

If a baby doesn't finish a bottle of breast milk, it should be used within the hour. Anything leftover beyond this time must be thrown away.

Expressed milk can be taken from the home fridge, transported (e.g. to nursery) in a cool bag with deep-frozen ice-packs, then transferred to the fridge on arrival. Wrapping the ice-packs in kitchen roll first prevents the milk becoming frozen. Previously refrigerated breast milk can be kept cool (10 °C or below) for up to 24 hours when in a well-insulated bag with deep-frozen ice-packs.

Depending on what a baby prefers, expressed milk can be given either straight from the fridge, or warmed to body temperature. To warm milk, place the bottle in lukewarm water (a jug of water works well).

Combination feeding

'Combination feeding' is the term used to describe when a baby is:

- breastfed and also given some expressed milk in a bottle
- breastfed for some feeds and given formula milk for some feeds
- bottle fed, but the mother wishes to start breastfeeding.

The introduction of formula milk reduces the amount of breast milk produced by the mother. This can make breastfeeding more difficult, especially at first – therefore formula milk should be introduced gradually.

When introducing a bottle to a baby who is used to breastfeeding, it helps to give the first few bottles when the baby is happy and relaxed (rather than when they are very hungry) as it may take them a little while to get used to the teat and get a flow of milk). Try having someone other than the mother give the first few feeds (so that the baby is not expecting breast milk). Give the baby time to get used to the bottle. Keep trying if necessary, but never force a baby to feed.

Natural-feel bottle teats

Natural-feel bottles and teats are designed to mimic the feel of natural breastfeeding as closely as possible. Some even have a skin-like, soft and squeezable bottle, and some have teats with a natural flex, stretch and softness in them. Anti colic teat valves can also help to avoid trapped wind.

Reduction in breastfeeds and timing

Often, mothers choose to stop breastfeeding when their child begins to eat more solid foods. It is important to note that cow's milk cannot be drunk until a child is 12 months old, so if breastfeeding stops before then, the baby will need to be introduced to formula or soya milk. It is best to reduce breastfeeds and introduce bottle feeds gradually if possible. As well as getting them used to their new food, this will help a baby emotionally, as babies breastfeed for comfort as well as food. It is also best for mothers because it helps to prevent problems such as engorged breasts. Health visitors can provide mothers with help and advice if necessary, and can also put mothers in touch with a breastfeeding specialist.

Activity

Undertake some research into real life experiences of breastfeeding.

1 Follow this weblink: www.healthtalk.org/peoples-experiences/pregnancy-children/breastfeeding/topics.

2 Watch the video on the homepage to find out what it is like to breastfeed.

3 Visit at least three of the web pages that interest you, selecting from the menu on the left-hand side of the screen.

4 Make detailed notes of any information that you might need for future reference to help with completing your set assignment for this unit.

How to develop feeding solutions for babies aged 6 to 12 months

You learnt about feeding solutions for babies aged 6–12 months in Learning outcome 3 (Nutritional requirements from 6–12 months). You may like to go back and reread this information.

Homemade foods

Suitable food for babies aged 6–12 months can be made easily at home, but planning menus ahead of time will help with organisation. The biggest advantage of preparing homemade food is that you are always aware of exactly what has gone into it. For this age range, food falls into the following three categories:

- pureed foods
- minced foods
- finger foods.

Pureed foods

Vegetables and hard fruits are very simple to puree into homemade baby food. Once prepared (e.g. peeled and sliced), cook the food by boiling or steaming. Then puree with a blender, food processor or stick mixer. You can add a little boiled water or breast milk/formula milk to make a loose enough consistency. It is fine to puree more than one item together, e.g. sweet potato and cauliflower. Soft fruits such as bananas can simply be mashed with a fork.

Minced foods

Chicken and turkey are often a baby's first meats. Beef is good because it is high in protein and iron, and also contains calcium and folate. It is also easily digested. Meat can be roasted or baked, then pureed as described above. Again, boiled water or breast milk/formula milk can be used to make a loose enough consistency. As babies get older, they need to get used to eating lumpy food as well as smooth puree, so at this stage, meat can be minced, which will give a coarser texture.

Figure 9.7: Adapt the feeding solution according to the child's age

If it is too coarse, a little more mashing can be done with a fork.

Finger foods

Finger food give babies the opportunity to feed themselves independently and learn how to chew. Ideal foods include lightly buttered strips of bread or toast, slices of carrot, pieces of banana or melon, plain rice cakes, pieces of cheese, chunks of apple, peach or pear and slices of avocado or cucumber. See page 129 for information on equipment and storage.

Purchased foods

Many families use purchased baby food at times, generally for convenience. You should always carefully follow the manufacturer's instructions for storing and preparation.

Figure 9.8: Purchased food.

Food in jars

Baby food in jars include both savoury options and desserts. It is generally a blend of pureed vegetables, meats and fruits.

Figure 9.9: Food in jars.

Food in packets

Packets of dry baby food need to be mixed with boiled water or warmed baby milk. A baby's first food is often baby rice. This comes in a packet and is mixed with the baby's usual milk, giving it a familiar taste.

Figure 9.10: Food in packets.

Tinned and frozen food

There's been much debate over whether it is appropriate to use tinned and frozen fruit or vegetables in homemade baby food. There can be some differences in nutrients, but as long as you carefully check the ingredients, these are safe to use. Items should be sodium (salt) free and sugar free (look out – there can even be sugar in tinned vegetables). Fruits should be tinned in their own natural juice – not syrup. It is possible to buy tinned food especially for babies, which is often organic.

Food in pouches

Pouches of prepared baby food are designed to be given directly to a baby – the baby will eat the food by sucking on the pouch. This is clearly very convenient when on the go as there's no need to carry around feeding equipment such as spoons. The pouches can also be kept as an emergency back-up in a parent or carer's baby bag. However, the experience for the baby is more like taking a bottle than it is eating, and they are also expensive. Therefore pouches are best used infrequently, and for older babies alongside plenty of minced food and finger foods. The contents of pouches can also be transferred to a bowl and given with a spoon.

Equipment and storage

Key items of equipment include:

- feeding bowls and spoons
- blender or food processor
- masher
- containers for storage (freezer proof is advantageous).

Babies only require a small amount of each food item, but it often makes sense to make up a batch of food, divide it into portions and then freeze it until it is required. It is possible to buy specially designed freezer proof containers with several sections for this purpose. Ice cube trays can also be used.

When storing food, always take notice of food labels and use by dates. Most foods can be stored safely in the fridge for 24 hours. (Also see Learning outcome 3.)

Case study

Grandma Gemma is preparing some food in advance for eight-month-old Nathaniel. She peels, slices and boils three carrots. She purees them with a blender and cools them quickly. She divides the puree between the compartments of an ice cube tray with a lid, and freezes it. When she wants to use the food at a later date, Gemma will remove a few cubes of puree - just enough for one feed - and thaw them out in the fridge.

1 Why do you think this food preparation method is appealing to Gemma? Support your views with detailed reasons.

How to develop feeding solutions for children aged one to five years

You learnt about good nutrition for children aged one to five years in Learning outcome 3. You may like to go back and reread the information.

Planning balanced meals

In Learning outcome 3, you learnt how important it is to ensure that a child has a balanced diet. This should include nutritious foods from each of the main food groups. Children should also eat five servings of fruit and vegetables per day and drink plenty of water.

Portion size

What a child eats is not the only thing that matters. The correct portion size is also key. If a child eats too little, they will not receive sufficient nutrients. However, if a child eats too much they will become overweight, even if they are eating food that is generally healthy, and this has health implications. It is very easy to overlook the extra calories contained in healthy drinks such as smoothies, fruit juices and fizzy drinks for older children.

If you are concerned that a child is eating too much or too little, track their food intake for a few days, recording everything they eat and the portion sizes. Foods can be weighed out if necessary. Then, using food labels and calorific tables, or using software/

Good practice

It is good to make children aware of healthy eating habits, but if there's a concern over the weight of a young child, they should not be made aware of it. If children become stressed, anxious or feel guilty about what they do or do not eat, psychological issues with food can develop at the time, or later. These sometimes last into or throughout adulthood.

apps, you can work out how many calories children have eaten. If the calorie intake is too high or too low, future portion sizes can be adjusted.

Introducing new foods/flavours/textures

Children need to become familiar with new foods, flavours and textures over time, and these can be introduced gradually alongside familiar foods. If a child does not like a new option, or leaves it altogether, it is best not to comment at the time. Wait for a few days, then try the food again. Repeat several times if necessary. Sometimes all it takes for a child to accept a new food is for it to become more familiar. Make a small variation /change to an ingredient to make it more exciting or palatable for a small child.

How to evaluate feeding solutions

It is important to evaluate feeding solutions so that improvements can be made over time. It is helpful to consider:

- verbal or written feedback you receive from practitioners, parents and carers
- feedback from children themselves
- whether a child is enjoying the foods they are given
- whether a child is fit and healthy on their current diet.

Comparisons

When evaluating feeding solutions, it helps to make comparisons, considering:

- whether current guidelines for a balanced nutritious diet are being met, e.g. 5 a day, the Eatwell Guide, calorie recommendations

Figure 9.11: Are the children enjoying the foods they are given?

- whether menus are coming within budget.

Evaluating choices

Strengths/weaknesses

The next part of the evaluation process is to think carefully about the feedback you have gathered to identify strengths and weaknesses. For instance, if a child doesn't always get their five fruit and vegetables each day, this is a weakness. If they usually enjoy their meals and eat well, this is a strength.

Improvements/changes

Now it is time to identify what improvements or changes you should make to address the weaknesses. For example, you might decide to increase the amount of fruit eaten by introducing a breakfast fruit smoothie to a child's diet, and accompanying their usual piece of fruit at snack time with a fresh juice drink.

Conclusions

With all of the information and feedback you have gathered, you can start to draw conclusions about how effectively you are providing feeding solutions. You can then identify problem areas, and find ways to deal with these. For example, if you are not giving a vegetarian child a sufficient variety of food, you could research new meals and snacks to try. You might carry out this research online and at the library for example, as well as asking the child's parents for tips.

Test your knowledge

1 What is 'nutritional analysis'?
2 Explain what is meant by combination feeding.
3 Explain how to transport expressed breast milk safely.
4 Discuss in detail all you can about baby food in pouches, how it is used, and its advantages/disadvantages.

Assessment preparation

The OCR model assignment will ask you to:

In Learning outcome 4, you will need to demonstrate your understanding of the nutritional requirements by completing a practical task, which involves creating a suitable feeding solution. The task is for one of these age ranges:

- 0–6 months
- 6–12 months
- 1–5 years.

When undertaking the practical investigation, you should include the following in your evidence:

- nutrition analysis
- factors to consider
- hygiene practices
- comparisons
- evaluation
- conclusions.

1 Outline the personal hygiene practices you should follow when preparing and serving food to babies and children.

2 If a breastfeeding mother has chosen to start combination feeding, what tips would you suggest to help introduce the bottle to the baby effectively?

3 Outline how you would approach devising a menu for a child aged 1–5 years.

4 Explain the process you would follow to evaluate feeding solutions.

Assessment guidance

Mark band 1	Mark band 2	Mark band 3
Limited investigation and development of a feeding solution for **one** age range (0–6 months, 6–12 months, 1–5 years). Needs support to investigate and develop a feeding solution with **limited** consideration of factors and **basic** nutritional analysis. Hygiene practices **may** be followed but not always **effectively**. Evaluation is **brief** with a **basic** comparison. There may be **some** errors in spelling, punctuation and grammar.	**Detailed** investigation and development of a feeding solution for **one** age range (0–6 months, 6–12 months, 1–5 years). Needs **minimal** support to investigate and develop a feeding solution with **detailed** consideration of factors and basic nutritional analysis. Hygiene practices **mostly** followed **effectively**. Evaluation is **detailed** with **sound** comparison. There may be **minor** errors in spelling, punctuation and grammar.	**Thorough** investigation and development of a feeding solution for **one** age range (0–6 months, 6–12 months, 1–5 years). The investigation and feeding solution are developed **independently** with **comprehensive** consideration of factors and **thorough** nutritional analysis. Hygiene practices followed **thoroughly** and **effectively**. Evaluation is **comprehensive** with through comparison. There will be **few, if any**, errors in spelling, punctuation and grammar.

Table 9.1: Grading explanation bands.

 Top tips

Command words:

- Consider – review and respond to given information
- Evaluate – make a qualitative judgement taking into account different factors and using available knowledge/experience.

The evidence you need to produce:

- feeding outcome for one stage from birth to five years
- evaluation.

Examples of evidence format:

- nutritional analysis/food programme
- Recommended Nutritional Values (RDVs/RDIs)
- interviews/questionnaires
- witness statement.

When creating this evidence, it may help to:

- recap the text on feeding solutions shortly before undertaking the feeding outcome task
- make notes and the evaluation soon after the feeding outcome, while details are still fresh in your mind.

Read about it

Childcare and Education 6th ed., Carolyn Meggitt, Tina Bruce, Julia Manning-Morton (Hodder Education, 2016)

OCR Home Economics for GCSE: Child Development 2nd ed., Jean Marshall, Sue Stuart, Lindsey Robins (Hodder Education, 2009)

Healthy Eating: What Young Children Need. BBC webpage. Visit: www.bbcgoodfood.com/howto/guide/healthy-eating-what-young-children-need.

The Child Accident Prevention website. Visit: www.capt.org.uk.

The Development Matters guidance. Look through the development tables from page 8 onwards. Visit: www.foundationyears.org.uk/files/2012/03/Development-Matters-FINAL-PRINT-AMENDED.pdf.

The Eatwell Guide. Visit: www.nhs.uk/Livewell/Goodfood/Pages/the-eatwell-guide; www.gov.uk/government/publications/the-eatwell-guide.

The Government's food advice website. Visit: www.food.gov.uk.

The NHS website. Visit: www.nhs.uk.

The Royal Society for the Prevention of Accidents website. Visit: www.rospa.com.

Understand the development of a child from birth to five years

About this unit

There are 30 GLH (guided learning hours) for this Unit. This unit is about the development of children from birth to five years. It focuses on the impact of play on developmental norms, how children learn through play, providing play activities and evaluating play activities.

Developmental norms tell us when children are generally expected to reach key milestones, such as learning to walk and talk. It is important that you understand these, so you can support children's learning. The best way for young children to learn is through play.

Children benefit in various ways from different types of play activity. Therefore, it is important to provide the right opportunities at the right time. For instance, you might provide dressing up clothes for a child who is learning to dress themselves.

You can also support children by observing their development during play activities, then comparing this to the developmental norms. This helps us to track children's development over time, and to notice where they may need extra help or support.

Learning outcomes

By the end of this unit you will:

- understand the physical, intellectual and social development norms from birth to five years
- understand the benefits of learning through play
- be able to plan different play activities for a chosen developmental area with a child from birth to five years
- be able to carry out and evaluate different play activities for a chosen developmental area with a child from birth to five years.

How will I be assessed?

In Learning outcome 1, learners should explain physical, intellectual and social developmental norms from birth to five years.

In Learning outcome 2, learners should explain the types of play from birth to five years and provide examples of the benefits of learning through play.

In Learning outcome 3, learners should produce plans for different play activities on a chosen developmental area. Learners should carry out an initial **observation**, in order to meet the child they will be observing and to inform the choice and planning of activities.

In Learning outcome 4, learners should carry out, observe, record and evaluate the planned play activities for the chosen developmental area. It is advised that learners study a child of an appropriate age – not a young baby – in order to get the best out of the activities.

Make sure you refer to the current OCR specification and guidance.

Learning outcome 1

Understand the physical, intellectual and social developmental norms from birth to five years

About this Learning outcome

Developmental norms tell us approximately when a child is likely to achieve certain developmental milestones, for example, learning to crawl, learning to read and learning to communicate. Understanding developmental norms is very important, because it enables you to provide appropriate activities and support for children throughout their early years. In this learning outcome, you will learn about development norms from birth to five years – **physical development**, **intellectual development** and **social development**.

Assessment criteria

In this learning outcome you will cover:

1.1 The developmental norms from birth to five years:
- physical development
- intellectual development
- social development.

Getting started

How many important developmental milestones did you go through as a child? Make a list of the developmental milestones from birth to five that you went through. For example, you may start with a baby learning to roll over.

Now take three different pens. Underline all the **physical development** milestones in one colour, all the **intellectual development** milestones in another colour and all the **social development** milestones in a third colour.

Key terms

Physical development the development of **gross motor skills** (large movements) and **fine motor skills** (small, delicate movements).
Intellectual development the development of the way the child's brain processes information received from the surroundings and other people.
Social development the development of the ways in which children experience and learn to handle their own emotions and relationships with others.

1.1 The developmental norms from birth to five years

Once you understand the developmental norms, you will have insight into the learning and skills that a child is currently acquiring. You will also be aware of what they are likely to learn next. This will inform your activity planning, and help you to provide activities that are appropriate for that child.

It also enables you to monitor a child's development and to notice if it is not in line with the expected developmental norms. This is important, because a child may need outside support with an aspect of their development, and if so, it is beneficial for them to receive this support as soon as possible. You will learn more about this in Learning outcomes 3 and 4. However, it is crucial to understand that children develop at different rates, and that the norms are just an approximate guide. Children will not all reach the same milestone at exactly the same time. It is to be expected that some children will reach the milestones a bit later than the norms specified in some developmental areas. Yet the same child may well be ahead in others. For instance, a child may learn to walk and run early, but start to read comparatively late.

In this Learning outcome, you will learn about the developmental norms for children's:

- physical development
- intellectual development
- social development.

Sequence of development

Children tend to develop in broadly the same sequence (or order). So even though the time at which they meet developmental norms might fluctuate or vary, they still tend to learn to sit up before they learn to crawl, and to crawl before they learn to stand. However, there are still some exceptions. For example, a child with a disability may be expected to develop differently in some areas.

Figure 10.1: Children develop in broadly the same sequence.

Physical development

Physical development is the term we use to refer to how children gain physical control of the movements made with their bodies. These movements fall into three categories:

- reflexes
- gross motor skills
- fine motor skills.

Reflexes

When a baby is newly born, they make physical movements or reactions with their bodies without consciously meaning to do so. We call these **reflexes** (see page 138 for definition). You may have noticed a baby displaying some of these. See Unit R018 for more details.

Gross motor skills

The word 'gross' means large. **Gross motor skills** (see page 138 for definition) are the large movements made by the whole body, such as crawling, walking, jumping and balancing. Children develop many of these skills very quickly between birth and five years of age.

? Did you know?

Learning to walk involves mastering a series of gross motor skills. Usually a child will learn to crawl, then to pull themselves up to a standing position. They will go on to learn to walk with both hands held by an adult, then with one hand held. Finally, they will learn to walk alone.

Figure 10.2: Balancing is a gross motor skill.

Figure 10.3: Threading beads requires hand-eye co-ordination.

Fine motor skills

Fine motor skills are the small, delicate manipulative movements made by the fingers. There are links between the development of fine motor skills and the development of vision. We call this **hand–eye co-ordination** (see page 138 for definitions). A good example of this can be seen when children are threading cotton reels onto a piece of string – they need to look to see where the hole is, then position the string in the right place in order to manipulate it through the hole.

> **?** **Did you know?**
>
> You use hand–eye co-ordination in the same way yourself whenever you thread a needle – and you know how tricky that can be sometimes.

Hand–eye co-ordination is also needed to achieve simpler fine motor tasks, for example seeing where an object is and picking it up.

Learning to manipulate involves mastering a series of fine motor skills. First of all, a baby will generally hold and explore objects given to them using their whole hand. They will progress to picking things up themselves using a whole hand grasp called a 'palmar grasp'. Soon, they will develop a more delicate palmar grasp involving the thumb. Next, they will begin to pick items up between their fingers and thumb, known as an 'inferior pincer grasp'. They will then begin to explore objects with just the index finger, poking at things that interest them. This will progress into a 'delicate pincer grasp' when they can pick objects up using just the thumb and their index finger.

137

Key terms

Reflexes the physical movements or reactions newborn babies make with their bodies without consciously meaning to do so.
Gross motor skills the large movements children make with their whole bodies.
Fine motor skills the small, delicate manipulative movements children make with their fingers.
Hand–eye co-ordination using the vision system to control, guide and direct the hands to carry out a manipulative task.

Table 10.1 shows the expected physical developmental norms from birth to five years of age. Study it carefully.

Approximate age of child	Aspect of physical development	
	Gross motor skills	Fine motor skills
Birth – 3 weeks	Reflexes (see pages 36–37) Lies with head to one side when in supine position (lying with torso face up). Lies with head to one side and tucks knees up under the abdomen when in prone position (lying with torso face down).	Holds hands tightly closed.
1 month	Still shows reflexes, but startle reflex is shown less frequently. Posture is more 'unfurled'. When sitting, the head falls forward (head lag) and the back curves. Gazes attentively at faces, especially when talked to, fed, or when care needs are attended to (e.g. nappy changes).	Hands generally kept in a fist or slightly open.
3 months	Turns from side to back. In supine position, the head is central. In prone position, supported by the forearms, the head and chest can be lifted off the floor. When sitting, head lag is slight and the back is straighter. Can wave arms. Legs can be kicked separately and together. Alert and moves head to watch people.	Can bring arms togethe. Can hold rattle briefly before dropping. Engages in finger and hand play.
6 months	Turns from front to back and may do the reverse. In supine position, head can be lifted and controlled when pulled into sitting position by adult. In prone position, supported by arms with the hands flat on the floor, the head and chest can be fully extended. Sits unsupported and plays for some time in this position. May take feet to mouth. Can bear own weight in standing position when held up by an adult.	Uses hands to play with feet. Uses palmar grasp to pick up objects. Takes objects to mouth for exploration. Passes objects from hand to hand.

Table 10.1: Physical development chart. Can you think of activities or resources that would be good for promoting development at each of these stages? (Continued)

Approximate age of child	Aspect of physical development	
	Gross motor skills	**Fine motor skills**
9 months	Sits unsupported on the floor. Gets onto hands and knees, may crawl or find another way to scoot around. Pulls self to standing position using furniture for support. Cruises (side-steps) around the room using furniture for support. Takes steps when both hands are held by an adult. Explores objects with the eyes, looking meaningfully.	Picks up objects with inferior pincer grasp (see page 137 for definition). Points to and pokes at objects of interest with index finger.
12 months	Sits down from standing position. Stands alone briefly and may walk a few steps alone. Throws toys intentionally.	Clasps hands together. Uses sophisticated pincer grasp and releases hold intentionally. Feeds self with a spoon and finger foods.
15 months	Walks independently. Crawls upstairs. Crawls downstairs feet first. Sits in a child sized chair independently.	Tries to turn the pages of a book. Makes a tower of two blocks. Makes marks with crayons. Holds own cup to drink.
18 months	Walks confidently and attempts to run. Walks up and down stairs with hand held by adult. Bends from the waist without falling forwards. Balances in the squat position. Pushes and pulls wheeled toys. Propels ride-on toys with legs. Rolls and throws balls, attempts to kick them.	Uses delicate pincer grasp to thread cotton reels. Makes a tower of three blocks. Makes big scribbles with crayons. Can use door handles.
2 years	Runs confidently. Climbs low apparatus. Walks up and down stairs alone, holding a handrail. Rides large wheeled toys (without pedals). Kicks stationary balls.	Makes a tower of six blocks. Joins and separates interlocking toys. Draws circles, lines and dots with a pencil. Puts on shoes.
3 years	Walks and runs on tip-toes. Walks up and down stairs confidently. Rides large wheeled toys using pedals and steering. Kicks moving balls forward. Enjoys climbing and sliding on small apparatus.	Makes a tower of nine blocks. Turns the pages of a book reliably. Draws a face with a pencil, using the preferred hand. Attempts to write letters. Puts on and removes coat. Fastens large, easy zippers.
4 years	Changes direction while running. Walks in a straight line successfully. Confidently climbs and slides on apparatus. Hops safely. Can bounce and catch balls, and take aim.	Makes a tower of ten blocks. Learning to fasten buttons and zips. Learning to use children's scissors and cuts out basic shapes. Draws people with heads, bodies and limbs. Writes names and letters in play – begins to develop awareness that print carries meaning.
5 years	Co-ordination increases. Controls a ball well. Plays ball games with rules. Rides a bike with stabilisers. Balance is good, uses low stilts confidently. Sense of rhythm has developed. Enjoys dance and movement activities.	Controls mark making materials well (e.g. pencils, felt-tip pens). Writing is more legible. Writes letters and short familiar words. Learns to sew with children's sewing materials.

Table 10.1: Physical development chart. Can you think of activities or resources that would be good for promoting development at each of these stages?

Intellectual development

Intellectual development is the term we use to describe the way the brain processes the information children constantly receive from their surroundings and other people. It is a big area of a child's development. The chart below shows aspects included within the area of intellectual development:

Language

Language is part of intellectual development – in order to communicate, children need to listen and understand the communications from other people. They also need to understand what they want to communicate themselves. Communication, therefore, relies heavily on thinking skills.

See section on communication (on page 141) for more information on body language, listening, and talking.

Did you know?

Once communication is acquired, it actually helps children's thinking processes. You may sometimes find yourself 'thinking aloud', or in other words, talking out loud to yourself. People often do this unintentionally when they are problem solving or thinking creatively.

Reading and writing

Together, the skills of reading and writing are known as **literacy** (see page 141 for definition). Children start to develop their literacy skills in the early years; many will go on to master the basics of reading and writing by age seven, and will be fluent in both by age 11. However, there are wide variations. Some children experience difficulty learning to read and write, and they may continue to struggle with this throughout their education and beyond.

Figure 10.4: You can foster a love of books.

Did you know?

Children with strong language skills tend to become more confident readers and writers. So it is important that we give young children lots of varied language opportunities.

Good practice

You can support young children's future literacy by fostering a love of books and stories, which increases their motivation to read. This motivation can also be fuelled with access to appropriate electronic devices. For example, you can share text messages and emails from loved ones with children, who are usually very keen to find out what has been said. You can also interest children in appropriate online activities and games that require an element of reading – quizzes are a good example of this. You should also provide lots of mark making activities such as painting and drawing, as these help to develop the skills needed to write.

Communication

Communication covers the way in which children master speech and other methods of communicating with others, including:

- **body language** – this is when physical behaviour expresses feelings. It includes body posture and movement, touch, facial expressions, eye movement and the use of space (if a child chooses to stand away from someone for instance)
- **listening** – listening is just as important as talking. Without listening, conversations are often ineffective. The ability to listen is connected to a child's attention span
- **verbal** – talking and other sounds – young children learn vocabulary at a very rapid rate, which enables them to talk with increasing sophistication. Other sounds such as crying, laughing, shrieking and groaning also communicate how a child is feeling
- **gesture** – it is common for children and adults to gesture without being aware that they are

doing so, as it is an ingrained part of behaviour. Children also gesture intentionally when they do not have the words to communicate what they want – they may point to their favourite toy for instance, if it is out of reach

- **sign language** – children who are deaf or have a hearing impairment may learn to communicate in sign language. Children with learning difficulties that impact on their communication skills may learn a simplified sign language called Makaton
- **reading and writing** – reading and writing are extremely important communication skills. Children who struggle to read and write can be at a disadvantage throughout education and beyond. Therefore, practitioners must provide plenty of opportunities to promote the learning and development of literacy skills.

Number skills

The development of number skills is closely related to the development of problem solving and reasoning skills. Together, these skills are often referred to as **numeracy**. There are many aspects to the development of numeracy, including:

- saying and using numbers
- counting
- recognising numbers
- using mathematical ideas to solve problems (e.g. sharing out toy cars fairly)
- recognising and drawing shapes
- recognising and making patterns
- using vocabulary relating to adding and subtracting (e.g. saying 'take one away,' or 'add one more')
- beginning to do simple calculations such as adding one or taking one away
- using language such as 'more', 'less', 'heavier' or 'lighter' when making comparisons.

Key terms

Literacy the ability to read and write (young children will be developing this ability).
Numeracy the ability to recognise, understand and work with numbers (young children will be developing this ability).

Figure 10.5: You can promote number skills through rhymes and games.

? Did you know?

Practitioners sometimes use teaching devices known as 'number lines' or 'magic number squares' to help children with number skills. These are lines or square grids that feature numbers in ascending order. Children can touch the numbers to help them to do simple number operations such as adding and subtracting. Beyond the early years, children can eventually progress to mathematic puzzles, which involve working out a number sequence using specially designed magic number squares.

Activity

Using these weblinks, browse the range of number lines and magic number squares available:

- www.hope-education.co.uk/products/ curricular/mathematics/number-lines- squares
- www.sparklebox.co.uk/maths/counting/100- squares.html#.V9fTtg1TF2t
- www.puzzles-to-print.com/number-puzzles/ magic-square-worksheets.shtml.

Which of the magic number squares do you think are suitable for children under five years of age?

Which of the magic number squares do you think are suitable for children over the age of five?

Table 10.2 shows the expected intellectual developmental norms from birth to five years of age. Study it carefully.

Approximate age of child	Aspect of intellectual development
Birth – 3 weeks	Recognises mother's voice. Cries to communicate hunger, tiredness and distress.
1 month	May be soothed when crying by a familiar voice or music. Uses senses for exploration. Communicates needs through sounds and crying. Communication occurs through physical closeness. Begins to coo and gurgle in response to interaction from carers.
3 months	Through use of senses, begins to understand that he or she is a separate person. Begins to notice objects in his or her immediate environment. Recognises and links familiar sights and sounds, such as the face of their carer with the voice of their carer. Will hold 'conversations' when talked to by making sounds and waiting for a response Can imitate or copy high and low sounds. Returns a smile when smiled at – may smile often.
6 months	Interested in bright, shiny objects. Very alert – watches events keenly. Takes objects to mouth for exploration. Sounds are used intentionally to call for attention. Babbling is frequent. Plays tunefully with the sounds he or she can make. Rhythm and volume are explored vocally. Enjoys rhymes and accompanying actions.
9 months	Likes to explore immediate environment (as long as primary carer is within close proximity). Begins to look for fallen objects. Initiates a wider range of sounds and recognises a few familiar words, including 'no' Knows own name. Greatly enjoys playing with carers and 'holding conversations'. Makes longer strings of babbling sounds. Intentionally uses volume vocally.
12 months	Looks for objects that fall out of sight, understanding that they still exist but cannot be seen. Memory develops. Remembering a past event enables anticipation of future events (e.g. may show excitement when placed in highchair for lunch). Begins to anticipate what comes next in the daily routine (e.g. a bath before bed). Increasingly understands basic messages communicated by family members. Can respond to basic instructions. Babbling sounds increasingly sound like speech, leading to first single words being spoken. Shows understanding that particular words are associated with people and objects by using a few single words in context.
15 months	Will put away/look for familiar objects in the right place. Uses toys for their purpose (e.g. puts a doll in pram). Shows a keener interest in the activities of peers. Understands the concepts of labels such as 'you', 'me', 'mine' and 'yours'. Use of single words increases and more words are learned.
18 months	Uses trial and error in exploration. Understands a great deal of what carers say. More words continue to be spoken and learned. Begins to use other people's names.

Table 10.2: Intellectual development from birth to five years. Can you think of activities or resources that would be good for promoting development at each of these stages?

⇒

Approximate age of child	Aspect of intellectual development
2 years	Completes simple jigsaw puzzles (or 'play-trays'). Understands that actions have consequences. Builds towers of bricks. Will often name objects on sight (e.g. may point and say 'dog' or 'chair'). Vocabulary increases. Joins two words together (e.g. 'shoes on' or 'all gone'). Short sentences used by 30 months, with some words used incorrectly (e.g. 'I goed in' rather than 'I went in').
3 years	Child is enquiring. Frequently asks 'what' and 'why' questions. Uses language for thinking and reporting. Can name colours. Enjoys stories and rhyme. Vocabulary increasing quickly. Use of plurals, pronouns, adjectives, possessives and tenses. Longer sentences used. By 43 months, most language is used correctly. Can match and sort into simple sets (e.g. by colour). Counts to ten by rote. Can count out three or four objects. Beginning to recognise own written name. Creativity is used in imaginary and creative play.
4 years	Completes puzzles of 12 pieces. Memory develops, recalls many songs and stories. Attention span increases. Fantasy and reality may be confused. Imagination and creativity increases. Problem solves ('I wonder what will happen if ...') and makes hypothesis ('I think this will happen if ...'). Sorts objects into more complex sets. Number correspondence (counting out) improves. Begins to do simple number operations. Uses language more fluently. As understanding of language increases, so does enjoyment of rhymes, stories and nonsense. Speech is clear and understood by those who do not know the child. Begins to recognise more written words, fuelling interest in books and electronic devices. Writes own name and copies other words and letters.
5 years	Options and knowledge of subjects are shared using language for thinking. Vocabulary is also still growing fast. Enjoyment of books and electronic devices increases further as he or she learns to read. Spends longer periods engaged in activities and shows perseverance. Learns from new experiences at school. Learning style preferences may become apparent.

Table 10.2: Intellectual development from birth to five years. Can you think of activities or resources that would be good for promoting development at each of these stages? (Continued)

Social development

Social development considers the ways in which children experience and learn to handle their own emotions. The relationships children have with others and the way they relate to them also comes under this area of development. This includes the attachments (or bonds) that children make with the key people in their lives, including their parents, carers and other close family members.

Communicating

Communication is closely linked with the intellectual development of language and communication that you read about on pages 140–141.

Communicating is at the heart of the relationships you have with the people who are most significant in your life. It is also central to your daily interactions with all the other people that you encounter. In many ways, your ability to communicate affects the quality of your relationships and interactions. The same is true for young children, who crave closeness and affection from those who care for them.

Therefore, it is important to always allow a child the time they need to say something – it can take a while for them to form their thoughts and speak at the same time. Try to work out what a younger child may be trying to say to you through body language or sounds – you can help them to feel heard by vocalising this. For instance, if at meal time a child points at their cup and whines, you might say, 'Would you like your drink? Here you go ...'.

Acceptable behaviour

The way in which children handle their emotions gives rise to their behaviour. For example, when a child experiences frustration at not being able to do something, they might cry, throw something or show aggression. Children gain increasing control of their emotions as they develop, and this impacts on the behaviour they are likely to display.

Toddlers are a good example, as when a child is unable to indicate that they need help or want something specific, they may become frustrated and exhibit unacceptable behaviour. But as their language and communication skills develop, they will learn to handle their frustration by asking for help, and this will enable them to behave in a socially acceptable way.

Manners also develop alongside language, as a large part of politeness for young children is connected with using terms such as 'please', 'thank you' and 'sorry'. This is fuelled by the desire to behave in socially acceptable ways, and to receive approval from others.

 Good practice

You always need to be aware of the fact that children will look up to you, and you have a duty to be a positive role model whenever you are with them. This means behaving in socially acceptable ways yourself, and demonstrating good manners. You must not lose your temper and raise your voice. If you do, young children can be expected to display similar behaviour towards you or others sooner or later. (You would also be likely to frighten a child, which is also unacceptable behaviour.) Never use language that would be inappropriate for a child to repeat.

Sharing

Sharing can be difficult for young children. For instance, it can be very hard for them not to be able to play with a toy they want right away because another child has it. They may well experience frustration and jealousy in this situation, which can give rise to inappropriate behaviour.

This is because it involves something called 'delayed gratification' – or in other words, having to wait for something that will bring them pleasure or satisfaction. The same applies when children must wait their turn in a game. The opposite side of the coin can be just as tricky – a child may be quite happily engaged in play when an adult takes an item away from them to give to another child because it is 'their turn'. This can also cause frustration and jealousy.

? **Did you know?**

Children who do not have siblings at home can find sharing a particularly hard thing to get used to when they first start attending a group setting such as nursery. Staff typically find that they mediate between various children who are having difficulty sharing several times each day.

Case study

Anna works in an early years setting. She sees two children – Max and Ava – tussling over a water wheel at the water tray. She approaches and asks if they have a problem. Ava says, 'I want it!' and tries to pull the toy away from Max. He says, 'I need it!'. Anna asks if either of them has already had a turn with it. Ava says she has, but then Chelsea played with it. Now it is her turn to have it back...

Anna says, 'Max has not had a turn yet, so we will let him play with it first. And after five minutes, you can have another go, Ava. Does that sound fair?'. Both children nod and Ava lets go of the water wheel. As Max starts to play with it, Anna says, 'Ah, so you have got the bucket, Ava. How many yoghurt pots of water does it take to fill it up?'.

Questions

1 Do you think Anna handled the situation well? Why is this?

2 Why do you think Anna asked Ava the question about the yoghurt pots and the bucket?

Key terms

Self-esteem this is when a child has a sense of self-worth or personal value.
Self-confidence this is when a child has a feeling of belief and trust in their own ability.

Independence/self-esteem

Children gradually become more able to do things independently as they develop. Each time this happens, children are likely to feel proud and clever – especially when we praise them. This has a positive impact on their **self-esteem**, which in turn gives them **self-confidence**.

For young children, everyday routines that promote independence are valuable, particularly when it comes to gradually learning how to care for their own bodies. For instance, a child can be encouraged to help the adult as the child is washed, dressed and so on. You might also praise a child for their attempts at self-care, for example brushing their own hair. You can also encourage children to take care of their environment, by asking them to help with the tidying up.

Activity

Think back to the first time in your own life that you were able to do something significant independently. Most of us cannot remember much about our early years, so this can be an example from your more recent life – perhaps you can remember the first time you were allowed into town with just your friends, or the first time you used public transport alone.

Write a paragraph about how you felt. Include details about the impact the event had on your self-esteem and self-confidence.

Good practice

Children need to be provided with opportunities to experience increasing independence in line with their needs, abilities and stage of development, in order to keep them safe.

Figure 10.6: Children with good levels of self-esteem are more likely to feel happy.

Approximate age of child	Aspect of social development
Birth – 3 weeks	Begins to bond with primary carers from birth. Needs close physical contact with primary carers for security and when care needs are met. Totally dependent on others.
1 month	Smiles from about five weeks. Begins to respond to sounds heard in the environment by making own sounds. Engaged by people's faces.
3 months	Begins to discover what he or she can do, and this creates a sense of self. May cry if primary carer leaves the room, not yet understanding that the person still exists and will return. Shows feelings such as excitement and fear. Reacts positively when a carer is kind, caring and soothing. If a carer does not respond to a baby, the baby may stop trying to interact.
6 months	Shows a wider range of feelings more clearly and vocally. May laugh and screech with delight, but cry with fear at the sight of a stranger. Clearly tells people apart, showing preference for primary carers/siblings. Reaches out to be held and may stop crying when talked to. Enjoys looking at self in the mirror. Enjoys attention and being with others.
9 months	Enjoys playing with carers (e.g. peek-a-boo games and pat-a-cake). Offers objects but does not yet let go. Increasing mobility allows baby to approach people. Begins to feed self with support. Understands that carers who leave the room will return.

⇒

Approximate age of child	Aspect of social development
12 months	The sense of self-identity increases, as self-esteem and self-confidence develop. Waves goodbye (when prompted at first, and then spontaneously). Content to play alone or alongside other children for increasing periods of time.
15 months	Curious – wants to explore the world more than ever, as long as carers are nearby. May show signs of separation anxiety (e.g. upset when left at nursery). May 'show off' to entertain carers. Can be jealous of attention/toys given to another child. Emotions can change suddenly – quickly alternates between wanting to do things alone and being happy to be dependent on carers. May respond with anger when told off or thwarted (e.g. may throw toys or have a tantrum). Can be distracted from inappropriate behaviour. Possessive of toys and carers – reluctant to share. Child 'is busy' or 'into everything'.
18 months	Has a better understanding of being an individual. Very curious and more confident to explore. Becomes frustrated easily if incapable of doing something. Follows carers, keen to join in with their activities. Plays alongside peers (not interacting with them) and may imitate them Still very changeable emotionally. May show sympathy for others (e.g. putting arm around a crying child). Can be restless and very determined, quickly growing irritated or angry. May assert will strongly, showing angry defiance to adults. Can still be distracted from inappropriate behaviour.
2 years	Begins to understand own feelings. Identifies happy and sad faces. Experiences a range of changeable feelings that are expressed in various behaviours. More responsive to the feelings of others. Often responds to carers lovingly and may initiate a loving gesture (e.g. a cuddle). Peals of laughter and sounds of excitement are common for some. May use growing language to protest verbally. May get angry with peers and lash out on occasion (e.g. pushing and even biting them).
3 years	Can tell adults how he or she is feeling. Empathises with the feelings of others. Uses the toilet independently and washes own hands. Can put on clothes. Imaginary and creative play is enjoyed. Enjoys the company of peers and making friends. Wants adult approval. Is affected by the mood of carers/peers. Less rebellious. Less likely to physically express anger because words can be used.
4 years	May be confident socially. Self-esteem is apparent. Aware of gender roles if exposed to them. Friendship with peers are increasingly valued. Enjoys playing with groups of children. Control over emotion increases. Can wait to have needs met by carers. As imagination increases, child may become fearful (e.g. of the dark or monsters). Learning to negotiate and get along with others through experimenting with behaviour. Some considerate, caring behaviour shown to others. Experiences being in/out of control, feeling power, having quarrels with peers. Distracting the child works less often, but they increasingly understand reasoning. Co-operative behaviour is shown. Responds well to praise for behaviour, encouragement and responsibility.

⇒

Approximate age of child	Aspect of social development
5 years	Starting school may be unsettling. Enjoys group play and co-operative activities. Increasingly understands rules of social conduct and rules of games, but may have difficulty accepting losing. Increasing sense of own personality and gender. Keen to 'fit in' with others – approval from adults and peers desired. Friends are important and many are made at school. Many children will have new experiences out of school (e.g. play clubs, friends coming for tea). Increasingly independent, undertaking most of their own physical care needs. May seek attention, 'showing off' in front of peers. Often responds to the 'time out' method of managing behaviour.

Table 10.3: Social development chart. Can you think of activities or resources that would be good for promoting development at each of these stages?

Stretch activity

Understand the physical, intellectual and social development norms from birth to five years

1 Find yourself a partner to work with.

2 Imagine that you work at a toddler group, and you have been asked to give a presentation to parents on child development from birth to five years of age.

3 Choose one area of development to focus on – physical development, intellectual development or social development.

4 Prepare a presentation consisting of slides and notes. (The notes should consist of what you would say.)

Test your knowledge

1 What does the term 'gross motor skills' mean?

2 Language is an example of a type of intellectual development. Give two further examples of types of intellectual development.

3 At what age would you expect a baby to begin sitting up unsupported?

4 Name three different types of number skills.

5 How are independence and self-esteem connected? Explain your answer in detailed written prose.

Assessment preparation

The OCR model assignment will ask you to:

For Learning outcome 1, you will need to outline and explain the physical, intellectual and social developmental norms from birth to five years of age.

1 Outline the gross motor and fine motor skills that make up the area of physical development.

2 Explain these aspects of development that come within the area of intellectual development – language, reading and writing, communication, number skills.

3 Explain these aspects of development that come with the area of social development – communicating, acceptable behaviour, sharing, independence/self-esteem.

Assessment guidance

Learning outcome 1: Understand the physical, intellectual and social developmental norms from birth to five years

Marking criteria for LO2

Explain or outline the physical, intellectual and social developmental norms from birth to five years.

Mark band 1	Mark band 2	Mark band 3
1.1 Outlines some of the physical, intellectual and social developmental norms from birth to five years.	**1.1 Explains most** of the physical, intellectual and social developmental norms from birth to five years.	**1.1 Explains all** of the physical, intellectual and social developmental norms from birth to five years.

 Top tips

Command words:
- outline – set out the main characteristics
- explain – set out the purposes or reasons.

The evidence you need to produce:
- physical, intellectual and social developmental norms from birth to five years
- sequence of development norms.

Examples of evidence format:
- presentation slides with notes
- wall chart poster
- collage
- leaflets/booklet.

When creating this evidence, it may help to:
- think about your target audience
- think carefully about how to present the information concisely
- make use of images that match your explanations of the developmental norms.

Learning outcome 2

Understand the benefits of learning through play

About this Learning outcome

To develop well, children need to learn and understand many things, and they learn best through play, which they love to do. When children are given good, fun play experiences, they will learn naturally *and* have a great time.

This will encourage a love of learning and discovering new things, which will be of huge benefit to children when they move on to formal learning at school. In this learning outcome, you will learn about the different types of play and the benefits of this for children, including the physical, intellectual, social and creative benefits.

Assessment criteria

In this learning outcome you will cover:

2.1 Types of play:
- manipulative play
- co-operative play
- solitary play
- physical play
- creative play.

2.2 Benefits of play:
- physical
- intellectual
- social/social skills
- creative.

Getting started

Think back to when you were a young child. Thought-storm the ways in which you liked to play. You can include activities such as dancing or playing hide and seek. You can also include playing with favourite toys, such as dolls or a train set.

Use a coloured pen and underline all of the activities and toys that you played with alone. This type of play is known as **solitary play**. In a different coloured pen, underline all of the activities and toys that you played with alongside other children. This is known as **co-operative play**. If there are some activities or toys that you played with both solitarily and co-operatively, underline them in both colours.

Key terms

Solitary play when a child plays alone.
Co-operative play when a child plays alongside one or more other children.

2.1 Types of play

Children initiate play instinctively or on impulse because they find it enjoyable, exciting and fun. To a certain extent, the way in which children play is influenced by the activities and play resources they have available. But children can find ways to play virtually anywhere and with anything. You may have seen children finding ways to play in the supermarket or when waiting for a bus.

Children enjoy and learn from different types of play in very different ways. By understanding these, parents and carers can provide a broad range of play activities to ensure that a child's development is well rounded.

Manipulative play

Manipulative play (see page 153 for definition) occurs when children engage in an activity that involves making delicate operating movements with their fingers. Learning and practising these fine movements is part of a child's physical development.

At first, a young child's manipulative movements are crude – young babies use their whole hand to pick up objects such as rattles. But in time, they will be able to pick up smaller objects using just their index finger and thumb. Many skills that children will use throughout their lives depend on manipulative skills – for example writing and using tools.

Manipulative movements are linked to the development of vision. Children need to look carefully at the object they want to manipulate, then move their fingers accordingly – using hand–eye co-ordination.

Puzzles, drawing and painting

Puzzles, drawing and painting are good examples of activities that require manipulative skills. Puzzle pieces need to be carefully manipulated in order for them to fit together. Children's drawings and paintings will become increasingly sophisticated as their manipulative skills improve.

Activities that promote manipulative play

- puzzles
- mark making, such as drawing, painting, writing and chalking
- shape sorters
- threading beads
- malleable materials (materials that can be squeezed and shaped), e.g. clay, playdough, cornflour paste, jelly and modelling clay
- craft activities, e.g. collage, making recycled models, making things from paper or card (such as planes or hats)
- construction toys, e.g. blocks, interlocking bricks and popping beads
- cooking alongside adults
- gardening
- activities that require tools such as scissors, a computer mouse, utensils and cutlery.

Figure 11.1: Mark making promotes manipulative development.

Key term

Manipulative play physical play involving delicate, operational movements made with the fingers.

Activity

Browse a supplier of children's art and craft materials. You could do this in a shop, online or by looking at a catalogue. Make a list of the art and craft tools available that would require children to use their manipulative skills. (Only include those suitable for children aged three to five years of age.)

Co-operative play

Co-operative play begins from the time children are around three years of age. It occurs when two or more children play together, interacting with one another, with shared goals in mind. A child who is playing co-operatively will be interested in the children they are playing with, as well as the activity they are doing.

Board games

Board games and circle games (such as 'Here we go round the mulberry bush') are a very good example of co-operative play, especially when children are required to follow rules essential to playing well together, such as taking turns. Pair or group imaginary games also require co-operative play, and might involve children organising themselves into roles, for example: 'You work in the shop, and I will be the customer...'.

 Good practice

Young children need plenty of support when playing co-operatively. They will at times need adults to help them manage problems or conflicts that arise due to tricky issues such as sharing, patience, give and take or handling emotions when they lose a game. Through these experiences and lots of practice, children increasingly learn to successfully play co-operatively with others.

 Good practice

It is important to have realistic expectations about young children's co-operative play. Whatever our age, we all struggle at times to get on well with our peers.

Activities that promote co-operative play

- board games (e.g. Lotto, Snakes and ladders)
- circle games (such as 'Here we go round the mulberry bush', 'The farmer's in his den)
- playground games (e.g. 'What's the Time Mr Wolf?', 'Traffic lights')
- imaginary role play (may include props such as dressing up clothes, imaginary areas such as a home corner, or toys such as teddies or tea sets)
- imaginary play with small world toys (e.g. cars and a road play mat, a farmyard set, toy figures, a doll's house).

Figure 11.2: Co-operative play with small world resources. What other small world resources do you think this child would enjoy?

Solitary play

All children, whatever their age, will frequently engage in **solitary play**, or playing on their own. At times this is probably because friends to play with are not available, but often it is their choice. When playing alone, children can set their own pace and explore their own thoughts or ideas. They may also concentrate for longer periods.

Solitary play is the first type of play that babies and young children experience. From birth until the age of around two years, children only play alone. From around two to three years of age, children will enjoy playing alongside one another at the same activity, but will not actually interact or play together – this is known as **parallel play**. From around three years of age, children begin to play co-operatively (as you learned above). At the same age, children will often engage in **onlooker play**. This means they will happily watch other children play, and may copy them. They may eventually join in, or may prefer to keep watching. Together, these different ways of playing are often referred to as the 'stages of play'.

Imaginative play

Imaginative play is an important way in which children learn and make sense of the world. It occurs when a child acts out an experience they have had in their play, or when they pretend to be having an experience that interests them. This allows them to explore various roles in life.

Activities that promote solitary play

- imaginary play (e.g. role play, small world play)
- puzzles
- books
- video/computer games

Key terms

Solitary play when a child plays alone.
Parallel play when children play alongside one another but do not play together.
Onlooker play when a child happily watches other children at play.

Activity

Try to arrange a visit to a playgroup (ensuring you have gained permission from your teacher teacher and the childcare setting). Watch children of different ages playing. Can you spot examples of solitary play and co-operative play? Make a notes of what children are doing while engaged in this play. In your next lesson discuss the types of play you observed with a partner.

- mark making (e.g. drawing, painting and writing)
- construction play (e.g. blocks and interlocking bricks).

Physical play

We have looked at manipulative play, which is an aspect of **physical play**. In addition, physical play also includes:

- activities that require children to use their large motor skills – the movements they make with their arms, legs, feet or their entire bodies
- activities that develop balance and/or co-ordination
- activities that develop the **senses**
- activities that exercise the body and limbs (promoting fitness).

In order to thrive, young children need a balance between physical play opportunities and more restful activities. Many children's settings, such as nurseries and pre-schools, now allow children to move freely between indoors and outdoors during many of their play sessions. This helps children to choose when they wish to use lots of space to play physically – for example, to run or ride a tricycle.

Key terms

Physical play this happens during activities in which children use their manipulative or large motor skills, develop balance or co-ordination, develop the senses or exercise the body and limbs (promoting fitness).
Senses sight, smell, hearing, taste and touch.

Ball games and climbing

Ball games promote many physical skills, such as kicking, throwing, catching and bouncing balls. In later years, children will learn how to use the skills to participate in sports and team games.

As well as promoting climbing skills, climbing helps children to develop strength and fitness. It is important to allow a young child's climbing skills to develop at their own pace. Some children may feel a little anxious at first when leaving ground level.

Activities that promote physical play

- ball games (e.g. involving kicking, throwing, catching, bouncing)
- different ways of travelling (e.g. running, jumping, skipping, hopping, rolling, crawling, climbing)
- playground equipment (e.g. slides, swings, climbing frames)
- ride-on toys and bikes
- push and pull toys
- stepping stones
- tunnels
- mini trampolines
- dancing
- feely bag games (based on touch)
- sound lotto
- gardening.

Also see page 152 for activities that promote manipulative play.

Creative play

Children are engaged in **creative play** (see page 156 for definition) when they express themselves by responding to something that sparks their imagination. For example, a child might make something with materials or objects, for example:

- art and craft resources
- household items (such as cereal boxes or blankets)
- natural objects (such as leaves or twigs).

Figure 11.3: Climbing is a key physical skill for children to develop. Do you think climbing successfully impacts on a child's self-confidence?

? Did you know?

Young children are often more interested in the process of their creative play than in the end product. They may very much enjoy making something, but not want to keep it.

A child might also express themselves in other ways, such as:

- dancing
- singing
- making music
- making up a story.

Good practice

Sometimes, the end product of a child's creative play may not be recognisable, but it is very important to praise their handiwork. Disapproving or making fun of a child's efforts can have a negative effect on their self-esteem and well-being. It might also discourage them from engaging in creative play, which could eventually impact on their development.

Key term

Creative play this is when children express themselves by creatively responding to something that sparks their imagination.

Music and dancing

Making music is a wonderfully creative play experience. Children can express themselves by playing musical instruments. They can also respond creatively to the music that they hear – by dancing along for instance, in their own unique way.

Activities that promote creative play

- music
- dance
- mark making (e.g. painting, drawing, printing)
- collage
- making models (e.g. with recycled objects or malleable materials)
- sand play
- water play
- exploring nature (e.g. playing with leaves, collecting conkers, looking at shells)
- stories
- imaginary play.

Case study

Ali works in an early years setting. He is approached by three-year-old Marlie. She is holding out a model she has made from recycled objects, including yoghurt pots and cardboard boxes. To Ali, it looks like a tower. Marlie says, 'Look at this! It is the donkey I saw on the beach ... I do not know what his name was.' Ali replies, 'So it is! Well done, Marlie. Perhaps we could think up a name for him. Have you got any ideas?'

Questions

1 Do you think Ali's response was positive? Explain your reasons.

2 If Ali had said, 'I could not tell it was a donkey,' how might Marlie have felt?

Activity

Types of play

1 List as many specific examples of types of play as you can.

2 Now look back over pages 152–156 to see if there are any you have missed. If so, add them to your list.

2.2 Benefits of play

Children benefit *hugely* from play. It allows them to:

- develop and learn
- have fun
- relax
- be active.

Let's look at the developmental and learning benefits of play in more detail. These fall into four main categories: physical, intellectual, social and creative.

Figure 11.4: Developmental benefits of play: What area of development is being promoted here?

Physical benefits

Physical benefits of play include the development of:

- fine manipulative skills
- large motor skills
- balance and co-ordination
- fitness and strength.

(Also see pages 154–155).

Hand–eye co-ordination

Physical play helps children to develop hand–eye co-ordination. As children become more experienced in manipulating the objects they see, their hand–eye co-ordination becomes more sophisticated. For instance, a pre-school child will thread large beads onto string, but in their primary school years, they will be able to thread a needle.

Promotes fitness

Physical activity promotes fitness. This is vital to children's health and well-being. Young children are built to be physically active and enjoy the opportunity to run around and move freely. Being fit and active also helps children to avoid becoming overweight.

Intellectual benefits

The intellectual benefits of play fall into three categories: mental stimulation, problem solving and communication.

Mental stimulation

Children can have new ideas and thoughts and explore them during play. They can also make their own discoveries. They can learn about the world, and learn to understand concepts such as counting. They can also develop awareness of mental processes, such as reading. When high quality play activities are provided, children's **attention span** and their memory will both develop.

Problem solving

Through play, children can experiment and test things out. For instance, a child playing at a water tray might discover which objects sink and which float. Or, through trial and error, a child might work out the best way to stick two items together, or to transport many objects from one place to another. This makes learning a real and vivid experience.

Figure 11.5: Through play, children can work things out.

Communication

Play strongly promotes children's communication and language skills, especially when children spend time in a language-rich environment. This is a place (at home, or at a childcare setting perhaps), where adults and peers talk frequently with a child. They will expose them to songs, rhymes, stories and new vocabulary.

Children can also be encouraged to:

- ask questions
- listen
- follow instructions during play activities
- talk about their own experiences and ideas.

Remember that some young children will be learning more than one language through their play.

Key term

Attention span the amount of time for which a child can concentrate on a particular activity.

Social skills and benefits

Play is vital to well-being; children need it to thrive and to feel happy. Play can impact positively on children in several ways.

Independence

When children go off to play with their peers, they are independent of their parent or carer (even if they are supervising from across the room). This is a big step for a young child. In addition, a playgroup will be many children's first experience of being cared for by someone other than a close family member. Play also helps children to master skills that foster independence. For instance, dressing up and dressing dolls help children to learn to dress themselves.

Confidence

Successfully trying new activities and becoming increasingly independent helps children to build confidence. Many play activities specifically foster confidence – games that involve talking in a group for instance, or the act of joining in with singing and dancing. Activities that involve appropriate risk taking can also boost a child's confidence – learning to ride a bike for instance, or putting their face in the water at a swimming pool.

Sharing

To behave in a socially acceptable way, children need to learn how to share. This is not an easy task, because it requires a child to put what is fair, or another person's feelings, above what they want themselves. In group settings, practitioners tend to spend quite a lot of time helping children to cope with sharing, and supporting them to resolve disagreements over objects desired by more than one child.

Self-esteem

When children have positive play experiences in which their contributions, ideas and feelings are respected, there is a positive effect on their self-esteem. When a child feels good about themselves, they are likely to approach play enthusiastically, and this will influence how much they benefit from activities. Playing with both friends and adults helps children to feel accepted, loved and valued.

Communication skills

Play promotes conversation and non-verbal communication between children, and between children and adults. Generally, children soon learn to put across their own ideas, and to understand other people's ideas – this is the basis for all shared play. Resources such as play phones and walkie-talkies can promote communication during play. (Also see Intellectual benefits, page 157).

Play also promotes social skills such as:

- taking turns
- learning to follow the rules – this includes rules that relate to socially acceptable behaviour (such as using good manners and respecting other people) and rules that relate to safety (such as no running up the slide or no jumping from the climbing frame)
- learning to get along with others.

Figure 11.6: Play promotes conversation between children.

Creativity benefits

Play has a wonderful way of promoting creativity. When children can play freely with access to a wide range of resources, creativity will naturally occur.

Imagination

Children use their imagination effectively when:

- they think and behave imaginatively – this includes problem solving, mark making, crafts or imaginary play
- their imaginative activity is purposeful – their play fulfils an objective. For example, making a tall tower that does not fall down, or getting from one side of the room to the other without touching the floor
- they express creativity in a unique way, creating something original – for example, a child may create a picture, a model, or their own song or dance.

Activity

Talk to the parent of a child aged around three or four years. Ask them to tell you about the development of their child's social skills. How does the child cope with sharing, taking turns, following the rules and getting along with others? How has the parent supported their child's development of social skills?

? Did you know?

Under the UN Convention on the Rights of the Child treaty, children have a right to play.

Activity

Benefits of play

1 Explain what the term 'benefits of play' means in practice.
2 Think of one type of play and explain some of the ways in which children benefit from it. The more detail you can include, the better.

Test your knowledge

1 If a child plays alone, what type of play are they engaged in?
2 Give two examples of play activities that promote co-operative play.
3 Discuss how play benefits children in terms of mental stimulation.
4 Name two pieces of playground equipment that promote physical play.
5 Name a social skill that is a benefit of play. Discuss the impact that this skill may have on a child's relationships with others.

Assessment preparation

The OCR model assignment will ask you to:

For Learning outcome 2, you will need to explain the types of play from birth to five years of age. You should also give examples of the benefits of learning through play.

1 Name the types of play for children from birth to five years of age.
2 Explain the types of things you might expect children up to two years of age to be doing when they are engaged in each of the types of play. Give as much detail as you can.
3 Explain the types of things you might expect children aged three to five years to be doing when they are engaged in each of the types of play. Give as much detail as you can.
4 Children benefit greatly by learning through play. How many benefits can you think of? Explain these, giving as much detail as possible.

Assessment guidance

Learning outcome 2: Understand the benefits of learning through play
Making Criteria for LO2

Explain or outline the types of play from birth to five years, and give examples of the benefits of learning through play.

Mark band 1	Mark band 2	Mark band 3
2.1 Uses a **few** specific examples of types of play.	**2.1** Uses a **range** of specific examples of types of play.	**2.1** Uses a **wide range** of specific examples of types of play.
2.2 Outlines some of the benefits of learning through play.	**2.2 Explains most** of the benefits of learning through play.	**2.2 Explains in detail** all of the benefits of learning through play.

Table 11.2: Grading explanation bands.

 Top tips

Command words:
- outline – set out the main characteristics
- explain – set out the purposes or reasons

The evidence you need to produce:
- stages and types of play
- benefits of play of children from birth to five years.

Examples of evidence format:
- presentation with notes.

When creating this evidence, it may help to:
- show images of children playing within your presentation, to help explain the stages and types of play
- practise your presentation aloud.

Learning outcome 3

Be able to plan different play activities for a chosen developmental area with a child from birth to five years

About this Learning outcome

It is important to provide fun, interesting activities that will give children the chance to learn new things and develop their skills. By providing a broad range of activities, you can promote children's learning and development in each of the developmental areas. To do this successfully, you need to be well prepared. This involves thinking things through carefully in advance, then making written plans. In this learning outcome, you will learn how to plan a range of different activities for a chosen developmental area.

Assessment criteria

In this learning outcome you will cover:

3.1 How to plan a range of different activities for a chosen developmental area:

- aims
- types of activities chosen
- reasons for choice
- safety considerations
- timescale
- resources
- methods of observation
- methods of recording.

Getting started

Think back to when you were a young child. Write down your earliest memory of taking part in an organised activity, such as making a Christmas card at nursery, or playing a circle game at school. Now thought-storm the things you were likely to be learning during the activity. For example:

- learning to use scissors more effectively
- learning to write your name
- learning how to take turns
- learning how to cope emotionally with being out of a game.

Share your list with a partner. Together, decide which areas of development were promoted by the activity. For example:

- learning to use scissors more effectively = physical development
- learning to write your name = physical development and intellectual development
- learning how to take turns = social development
- learning how to cope emotionally with being out of a game = social development.

Did you know?

Play activities often promote more than one area of development. For example, when a child learns to write their name, they are developing the physical fine motor skills needed to control a pencil well enough to form letters. They are also developing their intellectual skills by learning to recognise and remember the letters that make up their name. This includes remembering the sequence of the letters.

3.1 How to plan a range of different play activities for a chosen developmental area with a child from birth to five years

There are numerous different play activities you can provide for children. There are well-loved traditional activities, for example sharing nursery rhymes, as well as all the imaginative new things you might consider in a moment of inspiration – an imaginary game where children pretend they are a crayon being used by a giant perhaps! It is exciting to have so many activity options. But for all round learning and development, children need a balanced programme of activities.

A really good way of making sure that children receive this is to plan a number of activities to promote each developmental area in turn. This way, no important aspect of learning and development is left out.

Good practice

Planning play activities well helps promote each area of development thoroughly. It also allows you to ensure that you provide activities that are well organised, safe and relevant for the children you look after. Happily, this will also increase the activities' fun factor.

In this section, you will learn about the things to consider and write down when you are planning a range of play activities for a chosen developmental area. This includes:

- aims
- types of activity chosen
- the reason for choice
- safety considerations
- timescale
- resources needed
- methods of observation
- methods of recording the activity.

Case study

Charlotte works in a pre-school. She has been asked to plan several different play activities for three-year-old Amina, that should all promote Amina's creative development. Charlotte starts by thinking about what she already knows about Amina's creative development – she looks at Amina's development records, and observes Amina playing, paying attention to the play choices she makes. Over time, she notices that Amina rarely chooses a mark making activity such as painting or drawing. Charlotte knows that mark making is an important part of creative development.

Questions

1 Do you think Charlotte is taking a good approach? Support your answers with reasons.

2 Why is it helpful for Charlotte to know that Amina is not attracted to the current mark making activities on offer? Explain this in detail.

Activity

Plan different play activities for a chosen developmental area.

An example activity plan written by practitioner Charlotte (from the case study) is provided below, to show how you can plan different play activities for a chosen developmental area.

1 Read Charlotte's activity plan. Do not worry if all of the sections do not make sense to you just yet.

2 Write down your first impression of the activity, supporting your answer with reasons.

ACTIVITY PLAN	Name of child: Amina
Completed by: Charlotte Preston	Date: 6/3/17
Aims: To promote creative development through mark making	
Type of activity: Outdoor painting with rollers on a large sheet of paper placed on the floor.	Reason for choice: Amina often chooses physically active play outside and rarely paints at the indoor easels. A different, more physically active outdoor painting opportunity may appeal to her and spark her creativity in a new way.
Safety considerations: Clean up spilt paint quickly as it will be a slip hazard. Position activity away from busy spots such as the ride-on toys and the entrance, as Amina will be on the floor. Make sure hands are washed thoroughly after the activity for hygiene.	
Timescale: Allow 10 mins to set up the activity, 20 mins for the activity to take place, 15 mins to clean up afterwards.	
Resources: Four paint trays, four different colours of paint, four rollers, messy play mat to cover the ground, large roll of paper, apron.	
Methods of observation: Naturalistic observation, three minutes.	Methods of recording: Take a photo during the activity and a photo of the finished painting. Print these out and put on the 'Our Activities' pin board.
Outline of activity:	

Table 11.1: Planning an activity. Have You observed children playing in any of these ways? *(Note that this is just one example of how to undertake this aspect of the learning outcome. You do not have to use this as a format/template for your work.)*

Figure 12.1: Sample activity plan for three-year-old Amina. Have you come across a plan like this before?

Now look at the points to consider when planning play activities to promote a chosen developmental area. You will find it helpful to refer to corresponding sections of the example activity plan as you go.

Aims

This is the section of a written plan that shows the purpose of the activity, or in other words, how a child or group of children are expected to benefit from taking part. Plans should include one or more clearly stated aim per activity.

It is important to think carefully about your aims. Later, when an activity is finished, it will be evaluated. The evaluation process involves considering how well the activity actually met the aims in practice. You will learn how to evaluate activities in Learning outcome 4. You will see that in the example, Charlotte's aim is written simply and clearly.

Types of activity chosen

This section of the plan is a brief description of the activity. It may help you to think of it as a clear, specific title for the activity. From this line alone, other practitioners reading the plan should have a good impression of the activity to come. This is important, because in a busy group setting such as a nursery, staff need to be able to see what's happening that day at a glance.

Reasons for choice

This section of the plan gives you a place to record the relevance of your activity in promoting the developmental area you have chosen. In other words, it is your chance to explain the link between your activity and the developmental area that it promotes. You will often find that you can also use this section to explain why the activity is relevant to a particular child.

In the example, practitioner Charlotte has made very good use of this section. In just two sentences, she has told us:

- how the activity is relevant to promoting creative development through mark making (the developmental area chosen). We learn that

this is a different mark making activity to the ones usually offered, and that it could spark Amina's creativity in a new way
- how the activity is relevant to Amina – we learn that Amina will benefit from a mark making activity that appeals to her preference for playing outside and being physically active.

Safety considerations

In Unit R018 Learning outcome 5, you learnt about child safety, including how to keep play areas safe by carrying out risk assessment. Using those skills, you should think carefully about any possible safety issues you will need to address before carrying out each activity that you plan.

Once you have identified safety issues, you will need to plan the measures you will take to limit the risk to an acceptable level. This information must be recorded clearly on the plan.

Activity

Reread page 61 of this book. Make notes on the key points to remember when assessing the risks of a play activity.

Timescale

This is basic information about how long it will take to prepare an activity, carry it out and clear away afterwards.

In a busy early years setting, a smooth-running routine is needed to ensure that everything happens when it should, including meal times, sleep times and outdoor play times. Events need to unfold like clockwork, without children feeling rushed or under pressure. Therefore, practitioners need to be mindful of the time it takes to carry out certain tasks. This comes with experience, but double checking that you are being realistic about timing at the planning stage is a very good start, as is asking someone appropriate to look over your timings if you are unsure about them.

✔ Good practice

Generally, new workers are most likely to underestimate the time it takes to complete tasks such as setting up an activity or clearing away. So take time to break down each task. For instance, you might initially think that you will be able to set out paint and brushes in a minute or so. But if in reality you have to mix the paint from powder first, it is going to take much longer. Likewise, if paint is going to be used again later in the day, it will not take long to put the pots and brushes to one side. But, if they need to be washed up, dried and stored away, it will take much longer.

Figure 12.2: Allow plenty of time to set up activities.

Resources

This is the place to list all of the resources needed for an activity. Do remember to check that these will be available for use at the right time. If a setting has particularly expensive or large resources, such as a tablet or set of drums, these might be shared by several different classes or groups. Also, be sure to agree arrangements with the person supervising you, especially if your activity requires:

- less common resources that they may not have (e.g. readymade *papier-mâché*)
- a large quantity of the same item that might need collecting over time (e.g. several empty washing-up liquid bottles)

? Did you know?

There are several different ways of recording activity plans. Many early years settings such as nurseries and pre-schools design their own activity planning forms. These are charts for staff to fill in. They are often displayed so that staff can refer to them during the play session. They also allow parents to see what their child will be doing.

- fresh ingredients (e.g. for cooking activities or messy play)
- expensive resources (e.g. craft items such as decorative beads).

Methods of observation

Observation is the term used to describe the process of a practitioner watching and recording a child's behaviour (the things that they do and say). Over time, these observations help you to build up a picture of a child's individual development. This picture helps you to track a child's progress, and to plan activities that will support and extend their learning and development in each area. Methods of observation include:

- naturalistic
- event sampling
- snapshot
- participant
- non-participant.

You will learn how different methods of observation are used below.

At the planning stage, practitioners will often think about how they could best observe a child taking part in the activity they are planning. They will then make a note of this on their plan. On the example plan, Charlotte has chosen to include a short naturalistic observation in the relevant section of her planning form.

🔑 Key term

Observation the process of watching and recording a child's behaviour to assess and track their learning and development.

Did you know?

Early years settings are required to keep development records for every child. Generally, each child will have their own file. During their time at the setting, it will be filled with observation records, and records of their activities. This will include some of the child's own work.

This section looks at a range of different observation methods. It is up to you to choose the method of observation that best suits your activity. This means thinking about the type of information you need to collect and the purpose for which the information will be used.

Naturalistic observation

Naturalistic observation is when a child's natural spontaneous behaviour is observed for a set period of time. During this time, other adults in the room will not lead or prompt the child, but they will respond if the child approaches them. This means that the child will most likely be engaged in a child-led activity, such as any type of freely chosen play. They might change activities and move around the environment during the observation.

The practitioner carefully watches the activity of the child, and writes down everything they see and hear the child do and say for the duration of the observation. This includes facial expressions and gestures. They also record how other children and adults interact with the child, including their speech.

This way of recording is often called a 'narrative observation'. Writing everything down is difficult to keep up, so this type of observation is only done for a short length of time – often less than five minutes.

Alternatively, a practitioner may record everything they see, but at timed intervals. For example, they may observe the child for three minutes every hour throughout a half-day play session. This variation on the narrative observation is often called a 'running record'.

NATURALISTIC OBSERVATION	**Name of child:** Amina
Completed by: Charlotte Preston	**Date:** 18/3/17 **Time:** 11.05 **Duration:** 3 mins **Location**: Outside play area

Amina sees the paint rolling activity set up. She walks towards it, stands still and looks. She takes an apron from the coat peg. Puts it on, fiddles with Velcro fastening, then leaves it undone.

She crouches down, takes a roller and dabs it in the yellow paint tray. She blobs it onto the paper. She laughs and points to the yellow splodge it makes. She rolls the roller up and back a few times, then across, smiling. Stands and holds the roller up, calls to nearby adult, "Look, look, Claire. It's yellow." Claire approaches smiling. "It's like sunshine, isn't it? Shall I help you with that apron?" Amina turns around and backs towards Claire and she fastens it at the back.

Figure 12.3: Naturalistic observation example.

Event sampling

This method of observation is generally selected when a practitioner wants to record when and how often a particular aspect of a child's behaviour or development occurs. For example, they may want to record information about when a child starts to cry, or when they show aggression towards adults.

Event sampling can take place throughout a single play session, a day, a week or perhaps even longer, depending on the individual circumstances and the frequency at which the behaviour occurs.

The practitioner prepares a form to complete in advance. Each time the behaviour or aspect of development in question is observed, the practitioner writes in a record of the time and circumstances.

Snapshot observation

This type of observation is when a practitioner notices a child doing something of interest and spontaneously observes them very briefly, often just for a minute or two.

A practitioner may begin to observe a child on seeing them show a new skill, or playing in a particular way that they have been hoping to capture. Snapshot notes are often made on sticky notes. On many occasions, these can be added to a child's file just as they are, making this method quick and efficient. Practitioners often say that snapshot observations build over time to document 'the learner's journey'.

Participative observation

This occurs when the observer deliberately interacts with the child during the observation.

Event no.	Time	Event	Circumstances
4	3.45pm	Arthur threw toy bricks at his key-worker	Tidy up time. Arthur continued to build with interlocking bricks at the table when everyone was asked to tidy up. His key worker asked if he'd like to put his construction on the shelf so he could continue building it tomorrow. Arthur shouted, "I want to take it home, but you won't let me!" He picked up a handful of bricks and threw them towards the key worker.

Figure 12.4: Event sampling example.

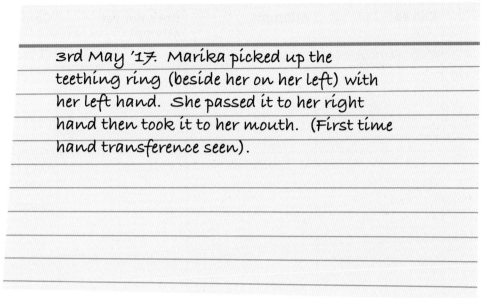

3rd May '17. Marika picked up the teething ring (beside her on her left) with her left hand. She passed it to her right hand then took it to her mouth. (First time hand transference seen).

Figure 12.5: Snapshot observation example.

The practitioner might ask the child to do certain things to see if they can manage particular milestone tasks, such as building a tower of blocks, or completing a puzzle. This information might then be recorded on a checklist form (see the example in figure 12.6 on page 170). Alternatively, a practitioner might ask a child questions to check their understanding (e.g. 'What happened then?') or for insight into their actions ('Why did you do that?').

Non-participative observation

This occurs when the observer is unobtrusive and does not interact with the child at all. This gives an authentic picture of the child's natural behaviour.

The practitioner will settle in a spot where they can see the child well without alerting the child to the fact that an observation is taking place. This makes recording an observation easier, as there is no need for the practitioner to write down their own speech or actions. But it can be tricky to find a spot that is close enough to allow you to hear everything without giving yourself away. There is a chance that the child will wander off to another part of the setting, and they may not play in a way that demonstrates the skills or behaviour you want to record. The narrative observation method is a popular recording choice for the non-participative observer.

? Did you know?

Practitioners regularly meet with a child's parents or carers to share their observations and development records. This helps everyone to work in partnership together, which is the best way to support and care for the child.

Activity	Can do	Attempts	Does not yet attempt	Comments
Pulls self to standing position by holding a support (e.g. furniture)	✓ 30/8/17			Does frequently. Strong stance.
Stands alone		✓ 30/8/17		Very recent – only seen on a couple of occasions.

Figure 12.6: Participative observation example.

Initial observation

When a practitioner first meets a child, observation will help them to get to know him or her. Learning about a child's preferences and character will not only help them to establish a good rapport with the child, it will further help the practitioner in planning appropriate activities. The better a practitioner knows a child, the more effective their planning.

Activity

Carry out an initial observation to meet the child you will study and to inform the choice and planning of activities. Try to arrange to spend time with a child under the age of five, for whom you can plan some activities to promote your chosen developmental area. This can be:

- a child in your family
- a child you meet as the result of arranging a visit to a group or organisation (e.g. a toddler group, pre-school or nursery).
- a child that comes into lessons for observation purposes
- a child that is known to you and their parents have agreed you can observe.

During your time with the child, carry out a naturalistic observation. Think carefully about how this can inform the choice of activities that you will plan for them.

Methods of recording

Once a method of observation has been chosen, a practitioner will plan how to record the observation.

Charts

Filling in a chart can be a very user-friendly way of recording a lot of information quickly and effectively during a period of observation.

Photographs

Photographs are an excellent way of recording a snapshot of a child engaged in an activity. For example, a photo of a child smiling with friends at the top of a climbing frame could capture confidence (social development) and the level of their large motor skills (physical development). Photos are also a good way to keep a record of an end product created by a child that cannot be kept, e.g. a house a child has built with blocks or even a snowman. Video recordings can also be used in a similar way.

Written methods

Some observations will be written out in full, with the practitioner noting as much detail as possible. See 'naturalistic observations' below for an example.

Examples of a child's work

Some of the work children produce – such as art and craft items, their drawings and their early writing – can be kept as an excellent, accurate record of what they did during an activity. These work samples can be kept in a child's development files. Some items may be displayed within the setting for a little while first. Students must support the child's work with written explanations sharing an understanding of what the child has achieved/met the developmental norms.

 Good practice

Photos, video recordings and any sort of observation must never be made without the written permission of a child's parents or carers. When made, these must only be used for the purpose intended, and must not be passed on to others. Full-face photos of the child must not be submitted – they should be taken from the side or blanked out. And personal information, for example full names and addresses, should not be used. Students working in an organisational setting (such as a nursery) must also have the additional written permission of that setting before taking photos or video. For this qualification, large numbers of photos are not expected or required.

Stretch activity

Produce a plan for an activity that promotes your chosen developmental area

Decide which developmental area you would like to focus on. Choose from:

- physical development
- intellectual development
- social development.

Thought-storm four activities that promote your chosen area. Write them down.

Now, select your favourite activity of the six. Write up your own activity plan for your favourite activity.

Test your knowledge

1. Why is it important to plan play activities?
2. Why is it important to have an initial meeting with the child before planning any activities?
3. Give three examples of headings you would expect to see on an activity planning form (e.g. aims).
4. If you identify an activity safety consideration at the planning stage, what should you do?
5. Name a common mistake made when planning activity timescales.
6. Explain why some of the work children produce can be an effective method of recording.

Assessment preparation

The OCR model assignment will ask you to produce plans for different activities on a chosen developmental area.

You will also need to do an initial observation, in order to meet the child you will be studying and to inform the choice and planning of activities.

1 What do you need to get in writing before carrying out an observation?

2 Explain as many different methods of observation as you can. Give as much detail as possible.

3 Explain how meeting a child and carrying out an observation can inform your choice and planning of play activities for them.

4 What are the benefits of planning a number of activities to promote a single area of development?

Assessment guidance

Learning outcome 3: Be able to plan different play activities for a chosen developmental area with a child from birth to five years

Making criteria for LO3

Explain the types of play from birth to five years and give examples of the benefits of learning through play.

Mark band 1	Mark band 2	Mark band 3
3.1 Produces plans for activities for a chosen development area, most of which are **outlined**: aims, types of activities chosen, safety considerations, timescales, resources. **Some** reference to initial observation. Produces an **outline** of the different methods of observation and recording used. Draws upon **limited** skills/ knowledge/ understanding of unit R018.	3.1 Produces plans for activities for a chosen development area, most of which are **described**: aims, types of activities chosen, safety considerations, timescales, resources. **Some** reference to initial observation that **informs planning**. Produces a **description** of the different methods of observation and recording to be used. Draws upon **some relevant** skills/knowledge/ understanding of unit R018.	3.1 Produces plans for activities for a chosen development area, most of which are **explained**: aims, types of activities chosen, safety considerations, timescales, resources. **Clear** use of initial observation to **inform planning**. Produces an **explanation** of the different methods of observation and recording to be used. **Clearly** draws upon **relevant** skills/knowledge/ understanding of unit R018.

 Top tips

Command words:

● explain – set out the purposes or reasons

● plan – consider, set out and communicate what is to be done.

The evidence you need to produce:

● plan different play opportunities

● explain different observations

● methods of recording different play activities.

Examples of evidence format:

● written activity plan

● chart.

When creating this evidence, it may help to:

● think about the things the child already knows and can do in relation to the chosen developmental area

● think about the things the child is likely to learn next in relation to the chosen developmental area.

Learning outcome 4

Be able to carry out and evaluate different play activities for a chosen developmental area with a child from birth to five years

About this Learning outcome

Activity planning and preparation is the first stage of providing good play activities for children. The next step is to introduce the activity to children effectively and to support them as they participate. When done well, this makes a big impact on children's levels of enjoyment and how much they benefit from taking part, so it is a key skill for you to learn. Recording and evaluating the activities you provide will help you to perfect the skill. The play activities you carry out will also provide opportunities for child observation. In this learning outcome, you will learn how to carry out a range of different activities for a chosen developmental area.

Assessment criteria

In this learning outcome you will cover:

4.1 How to carry out a range of different activities for a chosen developmental area:
- introduce the activities
- methods of observing the activities
- methods of recording the activities
- compare the child with the expected developmental norms for the area chosen.

4.2 How to evaluate the activities:
- strengths and weaknesses
- recommend improvements
- draw conclusions.

Getting started

Imagine that you work in a pre-school. Three-year-old Dayne will be attending for the first time today. During their initial visit to the pre-school, Dayne's dad remarked that it will be good for him to try messy art and craft activities, because he has only experienced drawing at home.

Make a list of all the experiences and skills involved in messy art and craft activities that will be new to Dayne. For example, putting on an apron and using a glue stick.

4.1 How to carry out a range of different activities for a chosen developmental area

In Learning outcome 3, you learnt how to plan a range of different activities to promote your chosen area of development. A good written plan gives you the best possible start. But how you carry out a plan in practice is just as crucial to the success of an activity. In fact, it usually has the most impact on:

- how much children enjoy an activity
- how long children spend engaged in an activity
- how effectively children learn during an activity
- how effectively children develop their skills during an activity.

To carry out any activity, and for this Learning outcome, you will need to:

- introduce the activity to the child and support them as they play
- observe the child participating in the activity
- record the activity
- compare the child with the expected developmental norms for the area you have chosen to promote.

Let's look at each of these in turn.

Introducing activities

Children need to know what to do in order to engage with your activities. So often, you will need to provide them with an outline or explanation when you first introduce the activity to them.

? Did you know?

How long a child spends on an activity partly depends on how much they enjoy it. But it also depends on the length of their **attention span**, or in other words, how long they are able to concentrate on a task. This varies greatly between individual children. But generally, the younger a child is, the shorter their attention span will be.

When it comes to planning the introduction, it helps to think about the individual child's experiences. You can do this by asking yourself a few key questions. If you know the child well already (perhaps they are a family member), you may know many of the answers. But there is no need to worry if you do not – you can simply ask the child's parents or carers. If you are visiting an early years setting (such as a creche) to carry out your activities, you can ask a member of staff instead.

Has the child taken part in this type of activity before?

This information helps you to judge how much detail is needed when introducing your activity. This is important as a child may not feel confident to engage in a new type of activity if it is not fully explained to them. However, if a child has undertaken a similar activity before, over explaining yours can be off-putting. For example, making a collage with pasta will not need much explanation if the child has made collages with bottle tops and buttons in the recent past.

Is the child familiar with the resources you will be using?

Imagine that you plan to play a simple game of Snakes and ladders with a child. If the child has previously played another board game involving a dice, they will be familiar with throwing a dice and will understand that the result of the dice throw is related to action on the board. But if their experience of board games is limited to Lotto, in which a dice is not used, they will need an introduction to the purpose of a dice and how to use it.

Does the child have the skills needed to carry out any tasks required independently?

This question helps you to plan the support a child is likely to need during an activity. For example, many pre-school children will need help with the task of cutting with scissors, even if they have taken part in lots of arts and craft activities. This is because the skill of using scissors is often not perfected until the end of the pre-school years.

✔ Good practice

Generally speaking, it is absolutely fine for children to need some support with a task during your activity. But, if a child will need a lot of support all the way through in order to be able to do the activity, have a careful think about whether it is appropriate for the child's age and stage of development by asking yourself the following questions:

- Have I selected an activity that is currently too advanced for the child?
- Could there be a way to simplify the activity?
- Can I plan something similar that is more appropriate? (For example, instead of making a model from clay, perhaps a child can make one from salt playdough, which will also set hard if left to dry out, but is easier to manipulate.)

? Did you know?

When you are planning activities for a group of children, think carefully about whether the activity is suitable for everyone. Some children may have an individual need that will make it difficult or impossible for them to participate. In this case, you should adapt the activity so that it is an **inclusive activity** (meaning that everyone can join in). If this is not possible, plan a different activity that is suitable for everyone instead. This ensures equal opportunities for all.

Figure 13.1: Children will need support for some activities.

Case study

Sanjeev works at a creche. He has been planning activities for Friday's play session, and has included a parachute game. His supervisor tells him that five-year-old Barney has just been booked in for the session. Barney is a wheelchair user, and will not be able to stand up to play parachute games alongside the others. This means that he will be too low to grasp the parachute when everyone else takes hold of it. Sanjeev decides to adapt the game to make it inclusive. Instead of having the other players stand up for the game, he decides to have them kneel down. This way, they will be around the same height as Barney when he is sitting in his wheelchair, so they will all be able to hold the parachute and play the game together.

Questions

1 Do you think the solution is a good one? Support your answer with reasons.

2 What would Barney have thought about the activity if it had not been adapted?

3 How might the other children have felt if the activity had not been adapted?

 Key term

Inclusive activity an activity in which everyone can join in, including disabled children or children with additional needs.

Setting out activities

Always give some thought to how you will present your activity, because this is a key part in its introduction to a child. An activity that is well set out will be more appealing, and this will affect how keen a child is to participate from the start. Activities will be most successful when a child feels drawn to them and cannot wait to get started.

Let's say that the planned activity is imaginary play in a home corner, for example. You could lay the kitchen table with a dinner set, and perhaps sit some teddies up to the table, seemingly ready to eat a meal. You could also put pots and pans on the play cooker, with play food inside. This is likely to entice children to play. It also gives them a play idea to follow up – making dinner for the waiting teddy family.

Alternatively, if your activity is to play with a train set, you might piece part of the track together on the floor and position some trains on it, before introducing the activity to a child. You might also place some spare pieces of track alongside. This is more attractive than just showing them a box

Figure 13.2: Set out activities attractively.

containing pieces of track and trains. Children are likely to want to continue making the track so that they can push the trains around on a journey.

Study a child of an appropriate age in order to get the best out of the activities

Studying a child of the appropriate age will help you to get the best out of the activities you are planning to carry out. The more you get to know how children of a similar age tend to behave, play and interact with others, the better. While watching and/or playing alongside a child, you will be able to gain insight into what a child of their age tends to:

● understand

● know

● enjoy doing.

Activity

What age child will you provide activities for?

Try to arrange to spend time with a child around the same age. This can be:

- a child in your family
- a child you meet as the result of arranging a visit to a group or organisation (e.g. a toddler group, pre-school, nursery or creche).

Allow the child to play freely and naturally. Play alongside them, and take notice of the play choices they make and the things they do and say. Think carefully about how this can inform the way you will carry out your own activities for a child of the same age.

It will also give you insight into when they need support or help.

All of this will help you to make your own activities more effective because:

- you can tweak your plans in light of what you learn (e.g. you may decide to make your activity more challenging or to simplify it)
- you can choose activities that the child is likely to enjoy
- you can anticipate where help might be needed and think through how best to provide it.

Supporting activities

When carrying out activities, it is important to provide children with the level of supervision and support that they need. This is essential for keeping children safe and happy. Generally, the younger the children are or the more challenging an activity is, the closer the supervision required.

In a group setting, children can play safely and independently during some activities as long as adults in the room are keeping a general eye on things, and are ready to step in if needed. The children can approach an adult if they need assistance or if they would like an adult to participate in their play. But some activities would not be safe for children without close

Activity

Imagine that you are undertaking work experience in a crèche.

1. In the playroom, a small group of children aged three to five years are independently playing shops. A girl approaches you and asks if you need to buy anything. What do you think she wants you to do?

2. In the toddler room (for children aged one to two years), the staff have set up a paddling pool with shallow water. What level of child supervision do you think will be required? Give reasons for your answer.

? Did you know?

You can use praise and encouragement to motivate young children to persevere with tasks that they find challenging during activities. It is important to show that you value them having a try by praising their efforts as well as their achievements. Phrases like 'Good try!' and 'You are almost there!' can be very helpful.

one-to-one supervision from an adult. See Unit R018 Learning outcome 5 for further safety information.

Methods of observing activities

If you are planning to observe a child while they carry out your activity, you will need to consider carefully which observation method to use.

You will find it helpful to refer to Learning outcome 3 when making these decisions. It is a good idea to review pages 166–169 now.

Methods of recording activities

In addition to formal, written child observations, there are a few other methods that practitioners can use to record their activities.

Written report

Keep a record of the time and date on which an activity was carried out. You may also record the names of the children who participated (first name only), and perhaps a brief summary of what happened, for example, how the children played. You should also record anything particularly noticeable – perhaps the children were engaged for an extended period of time. This type of written record is often recorded, perhaps in a designated place on the planning document itself.

Feedback sheets and written evaluations

You will learn more about these below. They can be used to record evidence from children (e.g. a child's work, including drawings, and arts and craft products).

Comparing a child with expected developmental norms for the area chosen

As a practitioner, you will use the information you have gathered during observations to track a child's progress. You can undertake this by drawing conclusions from what you have seen.

For example, if you observe a child using a knife and fork well, you may conclude that they are able to use some tools independently.

You would then compare the development you have seen with the expected developmental norms for a child of that age, within the developmental area in question.

This enables a practitioner to spot when development is not consistent with the expected norms. This is important, because the child may need extra support, such as more opportunities to participate in activities that will help them to develop a particular skill.

Sometimes, practitioners will notice that the difference between a child's development and the expected developmental norms presents cause for concern. In this case, they will follow their setting's procedures for discussing the matter with parents or carers. They are likely to recommend that the parents access outside support from a professional such as a doctor or health visitor.

Figure 13.3: Feedback from parents and carers can be very helpful.

Did you know?

Early years practitioners are often the first to spot when a child has a specific individual need, such as a communication difficulty.

Good practice

Child observations and any information about them should always be kept confidential.

Stretch activity

How to carry out a range of different activities for the chosen developmental area

Take the child observations you have made during your planned activities. Recap which area of development you chose to promote. Now:

1 read through the observations carefully

2 read through the expected developmental norms for the chosen area, for a child around the same age. (You can use the information provided in Learning outcome 1, or another development milestone chart if you prefer.)

3 compare the two sets of information. Do the observations reveal evidence of the child having achieved any of the expected development milestones? Make notes of your findings

4 does the observation reveal evidence of the child not having achieved any of the expected development milestones? (For example, did they have difficulty doing a task you might expect them to be able to do?) Make notes of your findings

5 draw a conclusion about the child's current developmental progress. Do they appear to be on track?

4.2 How to evaluate activities

Evaluating activities is the process of thinking about how effective your activities have been. It enables you to identify what works well and what can be improved. This leads to the provision of higher quality activities. It also helps you to be as effective as possible in your role.

Throughout the evaluation process, you will be working towards answering this key question, 'How well did my activity meet my aims?'.

An important part of evaluation is recalling the activity in your head. But before you start the evaluation process, it pays to gather together some physical evidence to consider.

Observations you made at the time

This can include written child observations and any activity reports you may have written. It can also include entries made in a reflective work diary or notebook.

Feedback you were given by parents or carers

This may have been given verbally, or a written feedback sheet on your activity may have been completed. (Perhaps you were required to get written feedback as evidence of your activity.)

Evidence from children

For example, children might have given you verbal feedback on the activity, which you wrote down. Or perhaps their work products show evidence of how well the activity met their needs.

Once you have gathered your evidence together, start by looking through it all carefully to refresh your memory. Then you will be ready to start the first part of the evaluation process – identifying the strengths and weaknesses of the activity.

Strengths and weaknesses

To identify the strengths and weaknesses of an activity, it helps to ask yourself a series of questions about:

- how well you planned the activity
- how well you introduced the activity
- how well you supported the child during the activity
- how much the child enjoyed and benefited from the activity.

This requires some critical thinking, so it is important to take the time to really reflect on events.

Recommend improvements

The next stage in the process requires some creative problem solving, as it is time to:

- review the answers you have given so far, picking out any weaknesses
- then suggest what could be done to overcome each weakness, should the activity be repeated.

This is a very positive part of the process, as you will start to see what you can do differently next time to really make your activity the best that it can be. The improvements you recommend may be suggestions from others (such as parents or carers) and/or your own ideas.

Templates and writing frames cannot be used for the creation of assessment evidence. For future assessments please refer to 'Administering internal assessment' – a notice sent to all centres in December 2014 from OCR. This provides clarification about the rules surrounding the production of evidence for internally assessed units for Cambridge Nationals.

 Good practice

When evaluating, it is important to be honest about how the activity went, particularly if things did not go as well as you would have liked. Only then can you learn from your experiences.

Draw conclusions

The final task in the evaluation process is to sum up by drawing conclusions. One of the most effective ways of doing this is to answer this all-important summary question:

Taking into consideration all of the strengths and weaknesses you identified, how effectively overall were the aims of the activity met?

Again, you will see that there is a place on the sample evaluation form to record this information.

You might also like to consider whether it is worth repeating the activity with the improvements suggested incorporated, or taking everything into consideration, it would be better to come up with a new activity to meet the same aims.

Lastly, think about how you can apply the things you have learnt as a result of this activity when you plan other, different activities. The case study below gives an example.

 Case study

Kyle is a student on an early years course. He completes his work experience in a crèche twice a week. He recently evaluated an activity he undertook at music time. On reflection, he realises that it would be better next time to introduce the activity to children (explaining what they are going to do) before he gives out the musical instruments. This time around, children tended to be quite distracted during the introduction. Most of them were looking at or fiddling with the musical instruments he had handed out. Some of them began playing their instruments right away and did not want to stop and listen. Kyle thinks about this a bit more, and realises that he can apply his learning to other activities too. For example, when he leads a gardening activity tomorrow, he can explain what to do before giving out the cuttings each child will plant.

Questions

1 Do you think this tactic will help Kyle to make his gardening activity more successful? Explain the reasons for your answer.

2 Could this tactic be helpful to you in any of your planned activities?

Stretch activity

How to carry out a range of different activities for the chosen developmental area

1 Choose one of the activities you have carried out.

2 Gather together all evaluation evidence you have from the activity.

3 Carry out each step in the evaluation process, including drawing conclusions.

Test your knowledge

1 Explain why it is important to introduce activities to children clearly.

2 Name two methods of observation and the advantages of using these methods.

3 What is the purpose of evaluating activities?

4 What is the purpose of recording activities?

Assessment preparation

The OCR model assignment will ask you to carry out, record and evaluate the planned activities for the chosen development area. It is also advised that you study a child of an appropriate age in order to get the best out of the activities.

1 Describe how studying a child of an appropriate age help you to get the best out of the activities?

2 Explain the sort of things you might expect to cover when you give a child an outline of an activity at the introduction stage.

3 Describe how to carry out and record as many different types of observations as you can.

4 Outline the purpose of comparing a child with the expected developmental norms for the area chosen.

5 Explain the process of carrying out an activity evaluation.

6 Describe why is it important to identify the weaknesses of an activity.

Assessment guidance

Learning outcome 4: Be able to carry out and evaluate different play activities for a chosen developmental area with a child from birth to five years

Making ctiteria LO4

Carry out, record and evaluate the planned activities for the chosen development area. It is advised that you study a child of an appropriate age in order to get the best out of the activities.

Mark band 1	Mark band 2	Mark band 3
4.1 Carries out activities for the chosen developmental area and **produces brief records** for the observations. Provides a **basic explanation** of some comparisons to the expected developmental norm chosen. A **limited range** of examples will be given for **some** of the comparisons.	**4.1** Carries out activities for the chosen developmental area and **produces detailed records** for the observations. Provides a **sound explanation of some** comparisons to the expected developmental norm chosen. A **range** of examples will be given for some of the comparisons.	**4.1** Carries out activities for the chosen developmental area and **produces comprehensive records** for the observations. Provides a **detailed explanation, with reasoning** of some comparisons to the expected developmental norm chosen. A **wide range** of examples will be given for some of the comparisons. ⇒

Mark band 1	Mark band 2	Mark band 3
4.2 With reference to both the plan and activities: A **basic evaluation** is produced, which may give **limited** suggestions for improvements. A conclusion that **outlines** whether aims were met. There may be **some** errors in spelling, punctuation and grammar.	**4.2** With reference to both the plan and activities: A **sound evaluation** is produced with **some relevant** suggestions for improvements. A conclusion that **explains** whether the aims were met. There may be **minor** errors in spelling, punctuation and grammar.	**4.2** With reference to both the plan and activities: A **thorough evaluation** is produced with **detailed** and **relevant** suggestions for improvements, with **justification** for those changed. A conclusion that **explains** whether aims were met with **some** relevant **justification**. There may be **few, if any,** errors in spelling, punctuation and grammar.

 Top tips

Command words:

- evaluate – make a qualitative judgement, taking into account different factors and using available knowledge/experience.

The evidence you need to produce:

- carry out the different play opportunities
- evaluate the different play opportunities
- suggestions for improvements
- compare the child with the development norms.

Examples of evidence format:

- written report
- feedback sheets from parents/guardians/carers
- evidence from children (drawings)
- written comparison
- written evaluation.

When creating this evidence, it may help to:

- complete the evaluations soon after the play opportunities have been carried out, while they are fresh in your mind
- consult parents/guardians/carers about possible improvements to the play opportunities.

Read about it

Carolyn Meggitt, Tina Bruce, Julia Manning-Morton, *Childcare and Education* 6th ed., (Hodder Education, 2016)

Tina Bruce, *Cultivating Creativity* 2nd ed., (Hodder Education, 2011)

Jean Marshall, Sue Stuart, Lindsey Robins, *OCR Home Economics for GCSE: Child Development* 2nd ed., (Hodder Education, 2009)

Understanding Child Development 0-8 years 4th ed., Jennie Lindon, Kathy Brodie (Hodder Education, 2016)

The Development Matters guidance. Look through the development tables from page 8 onwards. Visit: www.foundationyears.org.uk/files/2012/03/Development-Matters-FINAL-PRINT-AMENDED.pdf.

Glossary

Anaphylactic shock: a severe allergic reaction, and a life-threatening situation.

Antibodies: proteins made by the body that can latch on to foreign viruses and bacteria, making them ineffective.

Apgar score: a score given to evaluate the physical condition of a newborn on assessment of their vital signs.

Attention span: the amount of time for which a child can concentrate on a particular activity.

Barrier method: a method of contraception in which a device or preparation prevents sperm from reaching an egg.

Centile charts: charts showing the expected pattern of growth of a healthy baby, against which comparisons can be made.

Child grooming: occurs when someone establishes an online 'friendship' with a child, intending to entice them to meet up when trust has developed.

Co-operative play: when a child plays alongside one or more other children.

CPR: cardiopulmonary resuscitation.

Creative play: when children express themselves by creatively responding to something that sparks their imagination.

Cyberbullying: occurs when a child is bullied online, for example in a chat room or via social media.

Durability: the ability to withstand wear and tear.

Durable: made to last.

Ergonomics: the science of design applied to make products efficient, safe and comfortable for use.

Feeding solution: the process of deciding what to feed a child, preparing and storing food and feeding a child.

Fine motor skills: the small, delicate manipulative movements children make with their fingers.

Flammability: the ability of a substance to ignite or to burn.

Gross motor skills: the large movements children make with their whole bodies.

Hand–eye co-ordination: using the vision system to control, guide and direct the hands to carry out a manipulative task.

Hazard: an item or situation that may cause harm.

Hormonal method: a method of contraception in which hormones prevent eggs from being released from the ovaries, thicken cervical mucus to prevent sperm from entering the uterus, and thin the lining of the uterus to prevent implantation.

Immunity: when an organism has the ability to resist disease.

Inclusive activity: an activity in which everyone can join in, including disabled children or children with additional needs.

Intellectual development: the development of the way the child's brain processes information received from the surroundings and other people.

Literacy: the ability to read and write (young children will be developing this ability).

Macronutrients: the structural and energy-giving calorie components of food.

Manipulative play: physical play involving delicate, operational movements made with the fingers.

Micronutrients: micronutrients enable necessary chemical reactions to occur in the body.

Numeracy: the ability to recognise, understand and work with numbers (young children will be developing this ability).

Nutrients: the nourishment that comes from the food we eat.

Nutritional analysis: the process of researching and understanding the nutritional value of specific foods and meals.

Observation: the process of watching and recording a child's behaviour to assess and track their learning and development.

Onlooker play: when a child happily watches other children at play.

Parallel play: when children play alongside one another but do not play together.

Physical development: the development of gross motor skills (large movements) and fine motor skills (small, delicate movements).

Physical play: this happens during activities in which children use their manipulative or large motor skills, develop balance or co-ordination, develop the senses or exercise the body and limbs (promoting fitness).

Pre-term: a baby born before week 37 of pregnancy.

Recovery position: a safe position in which to position an unconscious, breathing child.

Reflexes: the physical movements or reactions newborn babies make with their bodies without consciously meaning to do so.

Risk: the likelihood of a hazard actually causing harm.

Self-confidence: this is when a child has a feeling of belief and trust in their own ability.

Self-esteem: this is when a child has a sense of self-worth or personal value.

Senses: sight, smell, hearing, taste and touch.

Social development: development in the ways in which children experience and learn to handle their own emotions and relationships with others.

Solitary play: when a child plays alone.

Transition: a process or a period of change from one state or condition to another, through which young children usually need support, e.g. moving from a bed to a cot, starting to eat solid foods, starting pre-school, sleeping in their own bedroom.

Transition stage: this links the end of the first stage of labour and the beginning of the second stage of labour.

Vaccine: a biological preparation that provides or improves immunity to a specific disease, commonly given via an injection.

Weaning: the process by which babies are introduced to solid foods.

Index

Index